THE CHAOS STRATEGY

The Plan To Take Over America

2nd Edition

CURT DAVIS

Curt Davis is a well-known Kentucky attorney – and a concerned American
citizen. He is a widely traveled missionary evangelist, who along with his wife
Alma, has conducted citywide crusades in many parts of Central and South
America. Learn more about the author by going tot he book website:
chaosstrategy.us

Book cover by: Marvellous Works

Library of Congress Catalog Number: 2016957829

First Printing: November 2016
16 17 18 19 20 21 22   10 9 8 7 6 5 4 3 2 1
Printed in the United States of America

BIBLIOGRAPHY

I have chosen not to use a bibliography in *The Chaos Strategy*. Reasons for this decision are twofold: (1) For the most part, the book is fiction. The plot and narrative did not actually take place. I made it up. (2) The rest is factual content which came from my own research. I have alleged many historic and present day facts in this book which the more inquisitive reader may want to verify independently.

Modern technology and the internet have revolutionized research. What once required a visit to a public library lasting several hours can now be found on a smart phone, iPad or your laptop in a few minutes.

In order to verify the facts or statements I make in The Chaos Strategy, I suggest the use of a key word search of the internet using three or four words that are as unique as possible to the facts alleged. It works almost every time.

For example, if the fact stated is that Senator John Doe made the statement before Congress on April 15, 2006, "all Cretans are slow bellies," you need only google the three words "cretans slow bellies." You will find hundreds of references that will tell you that the statement was not made by John Doe at all, but by the Apostle Paul, quoting another person. He made the statement almost 2,000 years ago. The reference is found in the King James Bible in the book of Titus, chapter 1, verse 12.

If in doubt about the reliability of a source, I start with Wikipedia to get an overall view and then go from there. It is widely accepted as a reliable source although the contributors are unpaid volunteers. The research method is a matter of personal preference, of course.

ACKNOWLEDGEMENTS

I want to acknowledge and thank my dear wife Alma, whom our pastor has nicknamed "The Latino Fire." Her patient and undying support in the arduous journey of researching and writing this book was the push that kept me going. She endured months of solitude in the same house with me while I worked. She suffered many nights of interrupted sleep when I would get out of bed to record the thoughts that the Holy Spirit was giving me.

My heartfelt thanks goes out to Sue, Caity, Greg, Linda and last, but not least, my able assistant of eleven years, Sue Ann. They were each a rich source of advice and help in the preparation of the manuscript.

FOREWORD

Don't ask me how I knew, but when the President removed the bust of Winston Churchill from the White House his first week in office, I felt that it was a symbolic gesture that could have paradigm implications for Western Civilization.

I began a study of the historical clash of Christianity, Islam and Socialism/Communism that still rocks our world today, and I found that it was all prophesied in the Bible 2500 years ago. I discovered that there would be a worldwide attempt to mix the ideologies and the attempt would fail. I discovered that each of these ideologies envisions world conquest and that in the end one will prevail.

The Chaos Strategy is a novel about David and Maria, a Christian couple, planning their wedding and someday having a house full of children. They are caught up in the maelstrom of the present day clash of these ideas and a secret plan to take over America. It is a story of hope – and faith in God – when the world seems to be falling apart.

TABLE OF CONTENTS

THE ASSIGNMENT

"**D**avid, this is John. Where are you?"

I recognized the voice of the Secretary immediately and fumbled for my glasses on the end table. I remember thinking at the time how unusual it was to be awakened by my boss at three o'clock in the morning. I instinctively reacted with the same sense of urgency.

"What's up?" I shouted back, sitting straight up in bed.

"There will be an emergency meeting of the Committee Sunday morning," he blurted. "I will not be there. The President thinks it best that someone else go. We have agreed that you will represent us..."

There was a long pause and then he continued, "Your plane leaves at 8:30 tonight from Anacostia-Bolling and you will fly directly to Tel Aviv. My secretary will email the contact information for the courier. He will have the anticipated agenda, although not much is known at this time. Biographies of its members and the latest briefings on national security are summarized. All of it is classified, of course. I don't have to remind you of the sensitive nature of these materials."

"Of course not," I replied, trying to hide my aggravation at being reminded, like a schoolboy, of the danger of my breaching security after twenty years of what my superiors and peers had described as distinguished service in the State Department. I wanted to tell him that he was a recent appointee and that I had been with the Department much longer than he.

"Will anyone be going with me?" I asked.

"You will be alone." The Secretary took a deep breath. "Congratulations, David. You will soon see how important this assignment is to your career, and for that matter, to the future of the world."

The tones on my cell phone told me that the conversation was over. I lay back on the bed trying to gather my emotions in a sea of swirling thoughts that made little sense.

After smashing the piñata at last year's office Christmas party, it was unofficially announced that I had been elevated to Assistant Secretary. "Not bad for a 41-year-old bureaucrat," I mused, poking fun at myself for being a career government employee.

The Committee was made up of prominent religious, political and financial leaders in the Middle East. It had been brought together by Tony Blair in his role as Special Envoy chosen by the Quartet — United States, United Nations, European Union and Russia — to attempt peace between Israel and the Palestinians. It was a loosely knit assembly with no formal membership. I had always looked at the group as an effort by Prime Minister Blair to widen the range of his mission to benefit the entire region, as well as tapping into a rich source of information and advice.

The primary qualifications the members seemed to possess were political power, religious influence, and a whole lot of money. Some of them were among the richest and most powerful people on the planet. And I was to represent the United States.

The Secretary hinted that the meeting could possibly have far reaching consequences for the world. I had no idea what that meant — and the meeting was less than 72 hours away. My thoughts came racing like live rounds from the muzzle of a machine gun. "I have to get with it. Oh, I have to call Maria. I hope she understands."

Maria and I had been engaged for six months. I first met her at Macy's, where she modeled as a live mannequin, when I was on assignment in New York City three years ago. I was dating another lady, whom I knew was expecting something under the Christmas tree, and there were only two more days left to shop. Approaching a mannequin, I stopped to look at this fancy blouse and jeans combination that I hoped might fit my budget. Maria told me later that I backed off and then walked around her, cocking my head this way and that whistling some crazy tune, and she began to feel uncomfortable. I don't remember any of that, but I do remember standing in front of a mannequin and screaming when it came to life. We both saw the startled look on each other's face and burst out laughing.

I went back the next night and there she was. After convincing her that I was single and had a job, she agreed to meet me at a nearby street café for tea after work — for fifteen minutes — no more. We both lost track of time and two hours later I learned that she had resigned her job two years before as a paralegal for a large law firm in New York and was pursuing a law degree. She had found a night job at Macy's to support herself as a full-time law student during the day. Fall was her favorite season of the year because of major league football. Yellow was her favorite color. Her cat was named Baxter. There was a small tattoo on her left wrist and she was an avid student of Bible prophecy. She was thirty-five years old. I fell in love that night.

I detected a light accent on our first meeting and was not surprised that she had come to America from Panama twelve years earlier.

"No! No! No! You are not going," she came back. "That's final. We had plans for the weekend. Don't you remember?"

"But Maria, this is the opportunity of a lifetime."

"What's it about?"

"I don't know what it means, honey," I said as calmly as I could. "All I know is that I have to be in Tel Aviv Sunday morning. I can't give you the details. It's classified stuff. Trust me, it's over the top and security will be as tight as it gets. Safety concerns will not be an issue."

There was a noticeable change in her voice. I felt the switch from disappointment to grave concern. "I have an odd feeling about this whole thing, David. I'm going to be praying real hard for you."

Her mood changed again as she tried to lighten the conversation with her sweet imploring voice, which could not hide the pout behind it. "I want you to bring me something from Tel Aviv. I have a right to be mad, you know."

"I promise, Maria. I have to go by the nursing home and see Mom. Jonathan said that her mind is better, but that she is failing fast. She asked for me yesterday. You will be able to reach me on my cell until five o'clock today. I have to go, Hon. I love you."

"I love you, too."

Mom had been a quiet little Pentecostal girl from the coalfields of West Virginia who, because of her poverty and academic excellence, had won a scholarship to Harvard. There she met dad at the birthday party of a friend. He was a bombastic mixture of Russian Jew and Italian descent who gave up the security of a teaching career to make a good living for his family selling wholesale groceries after a tour of duty in Vietnam. Dad had passed away unexpectedly in 1984 after fathering my brother and me. We were the only children and identical twins. Mom's quiet demeanor and frail one hundred pounds could not disguise the inner strength that guided us through the hard times that followed.

I bolted into the lobby of the nursing home. It was past two o'clock in the afternoon. Time was getting away. The receptionist was on the phone and seemed unaffected by my pacing back and forth in front of her desk. Finally, she pointed to the guest register and waved me on back.

Mom was sitting up in bed. I was stunned at how well she looked. She was alert and well oriented, and greeted me with a big smile as she held out both arms for a big bear hug.

"Mom, you are looking great! How do you...?" Before I could finish the sentence she took both my hands in hers, grasping them firmly and looking straight into my eyes.

"David, I have a message for you. You have run from God all your life, but the Father wants you to know how much He loves you. It is time that you answer the call of God that He placed on your life when you were a child. He has an important assignment for you. This is your appointed time."

There was a long silence. Then she sighed deeply and lay back on the bed and closed her eyes. "I must rest, but I want you to have something," she said, pointing to her old, worn out Bible. "It's on the end table, here," she continued, opening her eyes in that direction, "Do you see it?"

"Yes, Mom."

"I want you to have it."

I could tell she was getting weak, so I thought it good to excuse myself, "Mom, I have to go now. I have an important meeting in Israel this week. Do you need anything before I go?"

"No, son .., thank you, anyway .., I ..," she strained as she lay back in a more comfortable position on her pillow. "You must remember to pray for Israel...They are God's people you know."

I chuckled. Israel had always been her pet prayer project and the theme of much of her conversation.

"I know, Mom."

She didn't react. Thinking she was falling asleep, I turned softly toward the door.

"David," she called.

"Yes, Mother."

In a calm monotone voice, she spoke without opening her eyes, "I will see you soon...very soon...look for me...on the shores of the Great Sea." Then she fell asleep.

"It is beginning to look more like January in Washington," I thought minutes later as I approached my car. It was snowing and I knew I had to beat the five o'clock traffic.

"Oh, my Lord," I said out loud, "Mom's Bible." Turning as if on a dime, I made a mad dash across the parking lot. Forcing the automated doors, darting past the startled receptionist, I hurried down the hallway and then to mom's room. I tip-toed as I entered.

There is no way I could have been prepared for what awaited me.

The bed was empty; the white sheets folded at the corners, and tucked neatly beneath the mattress as if awaiting barracks inspection. The pillow-slips were fresh, and there was no sign of any personal effects in the room. Thinking I was in the wrong room, I turned to leave when I noticed the Bible on the end table. It was exactly where I had last seen it just two minutes before. I picked it up and headed up the hall.

"Nurse! Nurse! Nurse!" I heard myself screaming as I approached the nurses' station. "Where is my mother? Where is my mother?"

"Calm down...sir...please, calm down! Now...now...please get hold of yourself." Realizing the commotion I was making, I consciously tried to regain control of my senses and attempted to explain as calmly as possible,

"I am not crazy. I know I am not crazy. I visited with my mother today. She was in room six. I left her not five minutes ago. I just went back to her room and she is not there! There is no sign of her!

"Except...except...this!" I held out the Bible, realizing then that I had been frantically waving it at her while I talked.

"What is your mother's name and date of birth, sir?" She quizzed, as she thumbed through a desk type organizer and then went to a computer screen.

"Marietta...Marietta Flink. Uh...her date of birth would have been... October 8, 1945."

It seemed like a long time passed and then she turned and looked at me, asking bluntly, "Sir, who are you?"

"My name is David Flink."

"Who is Jonathan Flink?"

"My brother."

"Do you know how to reach him?"

"Well, I don't know right now…but…"

"Mr. Flink, we have been trying to reach him all day. He is listed as the next of kin to contact in case of emergency. Please excuse me. I'll be right back."

In a couple of minutes she returned with uniformed security standing a few steps behind her. Then she continued, "Sir, I hate to inform you, but your mother passed away this morning."

"This morning?"

"Yes, I am so sorry."

"But I just talked to her. I know I just talked to her…what time…what time did she pass?"

"Mr. Flink. Your mother died…at 9:11 this morning."

MOM'S BIBLE

The Secretary was extremely nervous. He was discussing details ordinarily of interest to those under him, explaining over and over the importance of the mission.

"Call me when you can. I will make myself available."

"Yes, Mr. Secretary."

"Where is the Packet?"

"It's in my carry-on, sir. I just got on the plane. It's right here beside me."

"Have you been able to read it?"

"No. But I will soon. I did check the contents against the list inside. Everything is there."

"Did you see the envelope?"

"The one addressed to the Prime Minister?"

"Yeah…the Ambassador will meet you at the airport in Tel Aviv. There will be no fanfare. You will be taken to the office of the Prime Minister in Jerusalem. You will personally deliver the envelope to him. No one else. Do you understand?"

"Yes, sir."

He paused and sighed deeply. It unmasked a deep concern about something that was bothering him. "I am not sure what this is about," he said. "I am sure that the President will explain later. I just know that these are hazardous times and I keep thinking about my grandchildren." I could tell that he was stressed. I couldn't help but feel sorry for him.

He went on. "We have to fly under the radar screen. That is not easy to do these days, you know. But no one can know. Absolutely no one. This thing is completely compartmentalized. The left hand will not know what the right hand is doing. Only you and the members of the Committee will know the reason you are in the region."

"Yes, sir."

"You will spend two days in Tel Aviv. Then the following day you will fly to Dubai for the meeting with the Committee. Do you understand?"

"Yes."

"David," he sounded personable for the first time, "I'm sorry about your mother."

"Thank you, John. She was quite a lady. I talked to my brother, Jonathan. We are postponing arrangements until I return. She's in a better place, you know."

He paused, and I could almost see his features harden, as if he shook off anything personal and went straight back to the matter at hand.

"David, this whole matter is so far outside normal channels that only a handful of people know about it." The sober tone had returned. "The President is counting on you, David. In fact, we all are. Good luck." He hung up.

"What a day! There is so much...," I said out loud to myself as I literally fell into a big leather recliner, which had been installed in the turbo jet. Alongside was other plush furniture, including a sofa. A flat high definition TV, a work desk, and a wet bar nearby.

"Ahhhh, this feels good..." I thought, forgetting for a moment that I was on a Boeing 737 headed for the Middle East. Exhausted, I closed my eyes.

The President had assigned two Secret Service agents to my flight going to Tel Aviv. John said they were veterans and then added off the record that the older one had once been with the CIA and served as a sniper in Cambodia during the last days of the Vietnam War. "His name is Frank," I was told, "He doesn't miss."

I knew Emery personally. He was the younger of the two. We had attended many of the same DC parties and I had worked out with him at the gym. We were evenly matched in one-on-one basketball. Both agents, I was assured, were regarded by the White House to be among their best and most loyal.

"How odd," I said to myself, "that Emery would be assigned to me on this trip. I didn't dwell on the improbability long — just glad that he was along. A familiar face gave me comfort, I guess, in unfamiliar surroundings.

Emery introduced his associate, Agent Frank Adkins. We chatted a few minutes and they excused themselves through a door to quarters toward the rear of the plane. I hadn't expected the Secret Service on the trip. I was surprised, since the Department had its own security forces. "I guess the President wants this mission to be directly under his thumb," I mused. "They will have a direct line to the White House — not a bad idea." I will admit that it added to the mystique of the whole scenario.

The Secret Service, although marred by the recent conduct of some of its members, was always highly regarded by the American people for its proud service. I was glad that they were with me.

I drew in a deep sigh, pausing a moment to take in my emotions. They seemed to be a blend of relief and anxiety. Relief, in that the strangest day of my life was about to end. Anxiety, in that a heavy foreboding of some sort of imminent unknown danger was setting in.

"Mr. Chandler, this is Captain Hardesty, your flight commander," came a crisp voice over the intercom. "Our flight time is approximately nine hours to Tel Aviv. Weather conditions should make for a smooth flight. The flight attendants are here to serve you. Let them know if you need anything." I shut my eyes and fell asleep.

When I awoke, I glanced at my watch. It was 10:34 p.m. EST. Then, in an instant of time, I relived the entire day. Catapulting out of the recliner with both arms upraised, I heard myself shouting, "God, what does all this mean? I lost my mother today and then I talked with her five hours after she died? It's insane. Am I crazy, God? Or is this some sort of cruel joke?"

"Mr. Chandler, are you alright?" interrupted a flight attendant.

"Yes, oh, yes, thank you, I'm fine. Sorry, must have been a…must have been a bad dream."

It took a second for her words to sink in. "My name is not Chan…" I stopped mid-sentence, realizing that I was on a covert operation and that the mission had been totally compartmentalized and my name would be Wilbur Chandler to those on the flight. I sank slowly back into the big recliner.

After a minute or two I began quietly weeping. I heard myself whisper, "At 9:11 this morning a poor little Pentecostal girl from the coal fields of West Virginia went to heaven. She was our rock — our family fortress. She is gone. Things will never be the same again."

The sobs came and I tried to suppress them. I couldn't hold it back. After a few minutes, I settled down and continued my prayer, "And to top it off, Lord, you have sent me on some mysterious secret mission that might change the world. Please help me. What is going on?"

"It was an angel, David. I am telling you, it was an angel," came the reassuring words of Maria I had heard earlier in the afternoon when I called her from the airport. "You have been chosen of God for this hour. Something big is coming down and you will affect the outcome. Listen to Him, David. He will show you what to do. I know you will do what He says."

I looked at the Packet next to me, and felt my lower jaw jut slightly outward as it responded to some inner determination. "I will study you tomorrow and the next day," I thought. "But there is something I must do first. I have some unfinished business."

I stared out the window. In the darkness, the full moon dominated and an eerie stillness filled the night.

"Lord, it's been a long time…" I began, not sure that I knew how to finish the sentence. Like the proverbial flash, my life passed before me and I had to admit that God had not been in the picture.

"Please forgive me, Lord. I have sinned against you. Have mercy on me. Take me back."

Don't ask me how, but I immediately knew that God had heard me. It was simple and it was real. A load lifted from me and a peace quietly filled its place. Jesus had moved in. I was confident that if I were to die before I got to Tel Aviv — I was ready to meet God.

I reached for Mom's Bible, which I had placed in my carry-on in Washington. It was still there. I felt that God was going to use it to speak to me. Then, releasing a deep breath, I turned the cover. On the flyleaf was the robust handwriting of a younger woman. I paused a minute and took in the emotion of her loss before turning the page. There, mom had printed with the precision of an ancient scribe on sacred manuscripts:

FOUR WINDS STRIVE ON THE GREAT SEA

Dan 7:1 In the first year of Belshazzar king of Babylon Daniel had a dream and visions of his head upon his bed: then he wrote the dream, and told the sum of the matters. 2 Daniel spake and said, I saw in my vision by night, and, behold, the four winds of the heaven strove upon the great sea. KJV

THE HOLY BIBLE
THE KORAN
THE COMMUNIST MANIFESTO
THE EVOLUTION OF THE SPECIES

12

Dan 2:41 Whereas you saw the feet and toes, partly of potter's clay and partly of iron, the kingdom will be divided; yet the strength of the iron shall be in it, just as you saw the iron mixed with the ceramic clay… 43 As you saw iron mixed with ceramic clay, they will mingle with the seed of men; but they will not adhere to one another, just as iron does not mix with clay. NKJV

I chuckled. She was always one for drama and suspense. Leaving your jaw ajar until the next shoe dropped.

Under these words she had written in bold cursive — apparently at a later date:

No Resolution - they won't mix

I closed my eyes for a few minutes, pondering the writing. I don't know if it was a vision or my mind playing tricks on me. But, like bright lights on a Broadway marquee, I saw the words spoken earlier by the person I thought was my dying mother:

"I WILL SEE YOU SOON ON THE SHORES OF THE GREAT SEA."

THE FLASHPOINT

"**M**r. Chandler, this is Captain Hardesty. I hope you are enjoying your flight," came the voice over the intercom again. "We are approximately five hours from Tel Aviv. The temperature is 64 degrees. The skies are clear. There is a gentle breeze off the Mediterranean. For January, it's a beautiful day in Israel. Meanwhile, if you need anything, let us know."

For a second or two, I forgot again that Chandler was my name for the mission, and thought that the Captain was speaking to someone else. I glanced at my watch and decided to reset it. We would touchdown approximately at two o'clock in the afternoon Tel Aviv time. For the last two hours before landing, my mind went back to the times I had been in Israel before — three times on official duties and once as a tourist.

NINE MONTHS BEFORE

"Nine months ago," I said to myself. "Seems like it was just the other day that I was on the Sea of Galilee."

Shortly after Maria and I had announced our engagement, Mom congratulated us with an expense-paid vacation to Israel with her church group. She had already signed up beforehand, but insisted, cocking her head slightly with pursed lips and a smile as only she could do, "The only reason I am going is to be your chaperone."

"It was wonderful," I mused, recalling the details of the trip. I learned a lot. Most of it went as one might expect until the day we took a boat ride on the Sea of Galilee. The three of us were stragglers, getting to the boat dock five minutes late and to our chagrin, discovered that our group had sailed without us.

Totally devastated, we stood on the dock yelling at the top of our lungs as four boats carrying our group moved beyond earshot. Maria kept screaming, "You are leaving us behind." But to no avail.

A young man with a Middle-Eastern look and a slight accent saw our plight and graciously invited us aboard a nearby boat. "Climb on. You can go with us. We'll have a great time," he exclaimed with a big smile as he reached out, gesturing for the ladies to come aboard.

"My name is Omar Al-Kazaz. I am from Saudi Arabia and this is my friend from college days, Elliott Tipton."

Both men looked to be in their mid to late thirties and were dressed in jeans, as you might expect vacationers to be. Omar wore a light tan straw hat that defied conventional dress, in that it appeared far too expensive for faded jeans and a tee shirt.

"Elliott, where are you from?" I asked.

"New Hampshire."

"Elliott and I studied at Columbia University together," Omar stated, as the operator started the boat. Responding to the noise, he spoke much louder, "And excuse me. These are our friends, Eddie and Jill, the best videographers on the planet."

"I'm David. This is my mother, Marietta, and Maria, my fiancée. We're here on vacation."

Elliott was already seated and gestured, pointing to empty seats, "We are the only ones on the boat. Please sit anyplace you like."

"Isn't this nice? Thank you so much," exclaimed Mom.

"It's much too big for us. It was the only one available. It is good that we can share it with you," Omar continued.

I would have guessed the boat to be about forty feet long and eight to nine feet wide, with room for fifteen to twenty people. It was an inboard and it was beautiful, in a rustic and yet classy sort of way. The inside and outside of the hull and the deck, as well as the seating, were unpainted. Rich tones of a varnished wood surrounded the passengers. The seats were straight back wooden benches, which lined the inside of the hull so that the passengers faced one another. A white canvas canopy, with wavy edges, gold stitching, and tassels, protected the people from the elements. The Star of David, mounted on a mast, waved proudly in the wind.

"It must be seventy-five degrees and the sun is out," Omar stated. "This is perfect weather for a winter cruise."

We sat down on the benches under the canopy. The three of us faced Omar and Elliott. The two young videographers, preferring the sunlight, sat on a small elevated, triangular platform at the bow, crowned with a carved figurehead of a teen King David.

"This is a Cadillac," I whispered to Maria. "I wonder how much it cost?"

The young people were laughing and cutting up, enjoying the sun with their faces to the wind.

"Do you think they're married?" Maria asked.

"I don't know," I answered, leaning back, taking a deep breath while savoring the cool clean air through my nose, "But this breeze is fantastic."

In a few minutes, we learned that Omar and Elliott had come to Israel on business and had a couple of days before their assignment began. When I told them that I worked for the U. S. State Department, Omar was eager to talk. His English was very good, so I was not surprised when I learned that he had lived much of life in New York and studied journalism in America.

Mom nudged Maria. I heard her whisper, "The Holy Spirit just told me that this meeting is no accident."

"I understand that many Americans come here. Are you with the group on the other boats?" Omar asked.

"Yes, we are. It's a Christian group from Arlington, Virginia. They do a pilgrimage here every year — to the Holy Land."

"Holy Land! Unfortunately, over half of the world considers it holy," he replied.

By the look on his face, I realized then that my unguarded statement had pulled an emotional trigger. He continued, "And therein lies one of the big obstacles to the future peace of the world."

I hadn't expected such a sweeping philosophical statement so early in the conversation and I thought, "Uh oh! I hope this trip doesn't turn into a religious debate." My guard went up, but it was quickly overpowered by my wish to be friendly to our gracious hosts. "What do you mean?" I asked.

"The Israeli-Palestinian struggle over control of this land is just the tip of the iceberg. The issue involves the world. Can't the Jewish people see that there will be no peace in the world as long as they insist on occupying territory they don't own?"

"Uh..."

He continued, "I'm sorry. I didn't mean to say all that, but it has been on my mind all day. I don't know. You may be Jewish. Excuse me."

"My father was Jewish."

Mom didn't miss a beat. She spoke out immediately, "Please go ahead. We want to hear what you have to say."

"Jerusalem is the most explosive spot on earth. It ignites the passions of the world. It is the flashpoint of world tensions. It is as holy for Islam as well as it is for Christians and Jews. It is our third holiest site — behind only Mecca and Medina. Mohammed ascended into Heaven from Jerusalem."

Omar continued, "I'm sure you understand the issues, David. Your father was Jewish, your mother is Christian and you are employed by the US State Department. I am sure that you understand the possible ramifications."

I consciously tried to appear dispassionate and objective about the issue and yet get to the heart of the problem. "From childhood I was taught that God gave this land to Abraham, the father of the Jewish people. When Israel became a nation in May, 1948, I was told that it was a fulfillment of the Scriptures. That the Jews were dispersed among the nations for disobedience to God and that He re-gathered them to welcome the Messiah when He returns."

"You are talking about Jesus, right?"

A diplomat by experience and training, I quickly added, "I'm not saying that I believe that or that I don't. Just that it was what I was taught."

Both Mom and Maria gave me that, "you ought to be smacked" look. They knew I believed that Jesus was the Messiah. Their obvious disappointment did not help my guilty conscience. No one heard my silent prayer, "Jesus, please forgive me."

Elliott joined the conversation and was even more passionate than Omar. "Israel must retreat to the 1967 boundaries that were in place before the Six Day War! And this includes relinquishing control of the West Bank, East Jerusalem, and the site which Christians and Jews call the Temple Mount. And if they don't, the conflict could soon explode into a full-blown regional war that will probably pull in the nations of the world. We are looking at World War III, and it's a safe bet that it will be nuclear — that's how serious this whole thing is."

I had expected Maria's reaction sooner. "Christians have a stake in the future of Jerusalem, too. It is where our Lord was crucified and arose from the dead, Sir. He ascended into heaven from Jerusalem and will rule the world from there, when He comes back in the clouds of heaven as King of Kings and Lord of Lords. He will sit on the throne of David."

She didn't stop. "Sir, have you ever considered why the Jews mourn and pray at the Western Wall?"

"No, I've always wondered why."

"Well, I can tell you why. For fear of starting World War III. That's why! It is as close as their own government will let them get to where Jewish scholarship believes the Holy of Holies and the Ark of the Covenant were located. It was where God resided among His people. The Temple Mount defines who they are as a people."

"Honey, you sound like an old-fashioned gospel preacher." I turned to Omar. "And, Omar, let me say something to you, please, if I may. I fully share with you the concern over the danger posed to the region and the world if this conflict is not resolved. Something has to be done or we are in big trouble."

It was as if the operator knew that he needed to intervene. He cut the engine back and we quickly came to a stop. He spent about five minutes describing the squalls that frequently arose on the Sea of Galilee. "The winds come primarily from the west off the Mediterranean. They cross the hills of northern Israel and plummet down the east-west ravines on the east side, some 1800 feet to the Sea of Galilee. The ravines become like tunnels and the winds increase dramatically. The Sea becomes a churning mass."

"Oh, great!" Mom exclaimed. "I love the story of Jesus when He was with His disciples in a boat and commanded the storm to cease, and it obeyed Him. Don't you guys just love it? No matter how great the storm gets in the days ahead, Jesus will be in control."

The operator slowly pushed the throttle forward.

No one said a word for a minute or two. Then Maria raised her hand and asked, "May I say something else, please? Sir, you spoke a few minutes ago of the possibility of war. According to the Bible, that is exactly what is going to happen. There will be a final war. It will end, Sir, in what the Bible calls the Battle of Armageddon. It will take place only a few miles from where we are sitting. The armies of the world will gather to fight against the Lord from Heaven," Maria added, "if you can imagine that."

"Oh, we believe in the final conflict just as you do."

"And you will admit, will you not, that jihad, or holy warfare, is an integral part of Islam?"

"Absolutely!"

"And that not all jihadists are suicide bombers?"

"I'm a Wahhabi Sunni. We are commanded to work hard to bring in the worldwide Caliphate."

"And that means the worldwide implementation of Sharia Law."

"Yes, in the end Allah will prevail."

"Do you believe in the prophets of the Old Testament?"

"Yes, we do. And we believe that Jesus was a great prophet. And we believe that he will return to the earth."

"Sir, did you realize that the prophet Zechariah saw that there will come a time when Jerusalem will become a heavy load for all nations and that they will unite against this tiny country?"

"No."

Maria reached for her Bible like an ole west gunslinger. "Let me show you something. You won't believe this. It's incredible."

After a moment of searching, she cleared her throat and stated, "Okay, here it is. I'm reading from the King James Version, Zechariah chapter 12, verses 2 and 3. This is what he prophesied. Get this:

Behold, I will make Jerusalem a cup of trembling unto all the people around about…3 And in that day will I make Jerusalem a burdensome stone for all people: all that burden themselves with it shall be cut in pieces, though all the people of the earth be gathered together against it.

"Is that reminiscent of anything you've heard lately? How about the talking points on the No Spin Zone?" she added.

"That's not all. Wait just a minute…until…okay." She stood and exclaimed, "This is Zechariah again. I'm in chapter 14, verse 2 - 3. She began to read:

For I will gather all nations against Jerusalem to battle...3 then shall the Lord go forth, and fight against those nations, as when he fought in the day of battle."

Elliot was quick to intervene. "You guys aren't too swift, fighting over an ancient city which has no significance other than it is a battle ground of two antiquated world views. Science has long ago proven both to be myths."

Maria continued, "Jerusalem is the City of God the Great King. He put His Name there. The Bible says His Son Jesus will rule the world from there when He comes back. Jesus will save the world."

Mom spoke out, "Satan knows the Bible and he is against God and Jesus. He tries to copy what God does. He has a counterfeit plan. His plan is to rule the world, as well, through the Anti-Christ. He plans to rule it from Jerusalem. The battle for Israel is a spiritual battle between the forces of good and evil. Battle lines are forming as we speak. The world doesn't realize it, but pre-Armageddon events are being reported daily by the media."

Omar seemed to be enjoying the discussion. "We Muslims believe in the Hebrew prophets, too, and I find it pretty amazing that events are shaping up like the Bible says they would."

Omar had a puzzled look. "There is something very strange here!"

"What's that, Omar?" I asked.

"You Christians believe Jesus will rule the world from Jerusalem when He comes; and Muslims believe the same about the Mahdi. That he will oversee jihad from Jerusalem and take over the world. How can this be?"

Maria jumped back in. "Maybe one of them is a counterfeit?"

Thoroughly convinced that the inference made by Maria was the end of the conversation for the rest of the trip, I turned my head and gazed at the misty Golan Heights only a few miles away.

I remembered how it had been acquired in the Six Day War and was still at the heart of the Israel-Palestinian conflict. Suddenly, an impression came over me that I was not only geographically near the site of the final conflict, but close in time, as well.

Maria did not let up. "Omar, the Bible says that Israel will be without friends in the last days. She will stand alone and all her enemies will be cut in pieces."

I was not surprised at Maria's boldness, but gestured to her to lighten up. Omar picked up on my body language and said, "Oh, it's okay! Our Messiah, the Mahdi, is coming back and Jesus is, too. Jesus will bow to him. And they will…"

Maria finished his sentence. "… Jesus will kill all the infidels who do not adopt Islam and impose Sharia law upon the world." She hesitated and then said, "That includes Christians and Jews."

"Maria, be nice!" I snapped.

"I'm sorry. I didn't mean to be rude, Omar," she apologized.

I knew I had to be careful. The last thing I needed to do as a high level official of the US State Department was to make a statement that would be construed as critical of Islam. In fact, I probably had said more than I should have already. I scoped the boat instinctively, making sure that no cell phone cameras were in use.

"What brings you guys here, Omar?" I asked, trying to change the subject.

"It's a special assignment. I'm with Al Jazeera and Elliott is an independent correspondent who has been retained by the New York Times. We are covering the same subject matter. I will be doing my first documentary. It truly is a great honor for me — especially such an important event."

"You've got my attention. Are you free to tell us what is it?"

"It's okay. We are here to cover what has been named The Kerry Peace Accord."

"Say nothing further. You may be covering the biggest story of the century. This is huge!"

Elliott was expressionless, except for a slight affirmative nod of the head.

"We know. I am greatly humbled. But a few of us realize that a covenant between Israel and her neighbors is the best hope for peace in the region…and maybe world peace, for that matter."

Maria's response was immediate. "You know, gentlemen, what you are describing sounds very scary. The Peace Plan sounds too much like the seven year Covenant that Israel will make with the Anti-Christ during the period the Bible calls the Great Tribulation. Jesus spoke of it and quoted the prophet Daniel, who said that it would be a time of worldwide devastation like no other time before it and like no time after it."

The operator cut the engines to idle to point out the site where it is believed Jesus fed the five thousand. It was quiet for a minute except for the hum of the engines and waves splashing against the hull of the boat.

Maria continued, "The Anti-Christ is coming and he will probably be awarded the Nobel Peace Prize for negotiating the Covenant. He will be charming and intelligent. He will be acclaimed the Savior of the world. But he will be an imposter, a liar and a deceiver — full of the Devil. After three and one half years, he will break the Covenant and announce that he is God. Read the Book of Revelation. It's all there. It's as plain as day."

"I don't know about all that, but I stand by my original statement. Allah will prevail!"

"Well, since we all feel free to express our minds today," Elliott exclaimed, "let me say what I think. We all agree on one thing. Israel is a flashpoint that could end in nuclear war. Don't quote me on this, but I think her extinction would be a small price to pay for the survival of the race.

"And, if I may, let me add something more. I don't care who is god or what his name is. I don't even care if there is a god. My only concern is that we learn to live at peace with each other as humans. I believe that global government is the only answer to the problems we face. And that the Marxist Model of world government is the only way possible that we can bring all people together to meet the challenges of the future."

Mom shot back like a bullet. "You sound like Karl Marx."

"I know, maybe that's where I got it."

"He was an atheist."

"I know!"

"He was also a Satanist."

"I don't believe in Satan."

"He said the revolution would be violent and that it would eventually take over the world."

"I know."

Somehow, I knew that Mom would not let the conversation end there. I was waiting for her response, and then…

"What are you and Omar going to do?"

"What do you mean?"

"Each of you subscribe to one of two intellectually incompatible and opposing world views. Each believes he is right. Each believes his view will take over the world someday — by force, if necessary. Both Islam and Marxism, or as most euphemistically like to call it, Socialism, are aggressively pursuing their visions of world domination and are growing by leaps and bounds in the world today."

"I think I get your drift."

"Incompatible world views. Incompatible objectives. You represent over half of the world's population. You are best friends, now. In the end you will clash. What will you do?"

"Well, I don't know. I never thought about that. I guess we …."

Mom didn't let up. "And what about Christianity? How will we fit in? Jesus, too, had a vision of world conquest. He commanded His followers to 'go into all the world and make disciples of all nations,' not by the sword, but by proclaiming the good news of the Kingdom of God.

"He said that He was coming back in the clouds of heaven, with the holy angels, in power and great glory. That He would forcefully take over the reins of world government. The Bible says it will be the last battle of history, which we talked about a few minutes ago. It is known, today, throughout the world as the Battle of Armageddon."

Elliott stood up, holding on to one of the canopy struts, squinting as water droplets from the wake of the boat hit him in the face. He was obviously trying to shake off the whole conversation. He joked, with a look on his face halfway between a snarl and a grin, "I guess we will all have to get in a big blender, turn it on, and see what comes out."

Mom failed to see the humor. "What's wrong with this picture? Look at this! We have three totally incompatible world views, all of which have the same objective of world conquest and rule. Each envisions a New World Order that is totally different from that of the others."

Maria joined in, "And, sir, you don't even believe in God? How are you going to mix that with Christianity and Islam?"

Mom paused a bit and concluded, "The scary part is that the commitment of each has already been measured."

"How's that?"

"In actual rivers of blood."

Their jaws were set. Their eyes locked like two eighth graders in a staring contest. Elliott lost. Mom won. I knew she would. He cleared his throat and looked away in resignation. "At some point, to have peace, we'll have to blend, won't we?"

The rest of the trip was spent listening to a tour guide pointing out the points of interest where Jesus and the apostles had taught and healed the people some 2,000 years before.

"David, can I ask a favor of you?" Came a voice from behind as I stepped down from the boat onto the dock. It was Omar. "Would it be possible for the group and me to join your party tomorrow on the way to Jerusalem?"

It caught me by surprise, but I managed to reply, "Well, I don't see why not."

"I want to better understand the Christian commitment to Israel. We Muslims can't comprehend why you support them so faithfully."

"I will ask the Pastor and we'll see what he says."

I had a feeling that the Pastor would not mind. Maria and I had accompanied Mom to her church a number of times and we liked him. His name was Thomas Fitzgerald. He had served as senior Pastor of Hosanna Temple in Arlington for twenty years. I enjoyed his stories about growing up in Detroit's inner city and how it prepared him for ministry that could speak to the needs of people at all levels of the social spectrum. He preached one sermon I will never forget. He spoke about being real. That it was the greatest virtue — real with others — real with ourselves — real with God. He said, "It'll get you to heaven every time."

His wife, Delores, had passed away five years before in a tragic automobile accident while they were on a mission tour in Brazil. His teenage children, Ruth and Thomas Jr., were in school in Virginia with his parents until he returned home from the trip.

Omar was persistent. "Tell him that I am from Saudi Arabia and that my father has given tens of millions of dollars to American universities. We are investing heavily in the education of American youth."

Maria did not say a word until we were safely out of earshot. "Yes, and they want us to believe that they are spending all these millions to promote American patriotism and the Constitution. Jihad is not reserved just for the battlefield, David. Their agenda is a worldwide Sharia using any means they can. They are infiltrating every facet of our society. You name it — banking, business, education, and the media. They are in top levels of our government, formulating government policy. You should know that, David."

"Are we fighting?"

"No, of course not. I just get exasperated when people can't see what is going on."

"Its okay, Maria. You don't have to get so fired up." I continued to plead.

"They what?" questioned the Pastor when he was told of Omar's request.

"Yes, it's true. Omar has requested that he, Elliott, and his photographers travel with us tomorrow to Jerusalem. They will follow in their minivan."

We were all suspicious, but after praying about it the Pastor and the rest of the group consented — after some resistance from our tour guide.

"This may be groundbreaking," commented the Pastor. "I believe it must be from God. Let's trust Him and see where it goes."

Maria poked me in the ribs and said, "Yeah, maybe they'll get saved. Wouldn't that be something?"

Our group meandered back toward the tour buses. After a head count and a short prayer, someone asked,

"Pastor, where do we go from here?"

"Megiddo."

"What's that?"

"Armageddon!"

WHY ARMAGEDDON?

The whine of the big jet engines brought me back to the present. I checked my surroundings. I was on a 737 somewhere over the Mediterranean, escorted by two Secret Service agents on my way to Tel Aviv. In my briefcase was a personal letter from the President of the United States to be personally delivered to the Prime Minister of Israel. I had been commissioned by the President to meet with some of the wealthiest and most powerful people in that part of the world.

I had no idea what the subject matter of the meeting would be. I turned the light off near my recliner and stared blankly into the darkness outside. I saw a cluster of lights somewhere far below and wondered if it was an island off the coast of North Africa.

Then I began to drift off.

NINE MONTHS BEFORE

It was mid-morning when our group arrived from Galilee to the ruins of Megiddo. The big tour bus pulled into the Welcome Center. After a rest room break, instructions from the tour guide, and an admonition by Pastor

Tom to stick together, we made the trek up the narrow stone steps to the top of the hill.

Omar and Elliott were only a few steps behind when we reached the summit. "You guys make it okay?" I asked.

"I glanced at the brochure down at the Center and it said that the city had 30 layers representing one generation after another, and that it took 5,000 years to reach its present height," exclaimed Omar as he took a deep breath. "I wish Megiddo had had a shorter history. The hill wouldn't have been so high. I'm definitely out of shape."

The atmosphere was clear that day. Visibility was at least ten miles. The vast expanse known as the Valley of Jezreel — commonly called Armageddon — lay below us.

"It's breathtaking," someone exclaimed.

"Is this where Armageddon will be fought?" someone questioned.

"Yep, sure enough, and they tell me that you will be able to swim a horse in the blood that will be shed here."

"Hubert! That's awful! Stop it," scolded his wife, Ethel.

Hubert looked to be in his mid-sixties. He was jovial, balding and overweight. He had fussed the entire time about his inability to order sausage, eggs, and gravy in Israel.

He came from southeastern Ohio and claimed to have fished with Bob Evans many times. He had retired early, having sold a world of heavy construction equipment to the Japanese. He and Ethel bought a Winnebago and were now sharing Jesus in RV parks across America.

Ethel was a pretty lady with a poofy hairstyle, who had greatly influenced her husband in the right direction since their high school sweetheart days. His favorite description of their relationship was, "I do what she says. Being hen-pecked is not as bad as I thought it would be."

Hubert continued his exposition of the Bible's description of Armageddon. "I think it's going to be a nuclear battle, too. The Bible says that their flesh shall be consumed while they stand on their feet... along with their eyeballs in their sockets and tongues in their mouths. Ain't a pretty sight, I'll tell you that."

In a few minutes, a hush slowly settled over the crowd. The mood seemed to grow more somber as the group took in the grandeur of the view and the reputation of the sight before them. I found myself trying to imagine the armies of the world gathered in the plain below for the last battle of history.

My trance was interrupted by the familiar voice of Pastor Tom. "Okay. We are ready to begin our tour of Tel Megiddo. Are you ready to take over, Benjamin?"

Benjamin was our tour guide and had been with us since our arrival in Israel two days before. He had been born in Israel some twenty-five years before and was extremely articulate in the English language. He knew his subject matter well, and had a knack for colorful descriptions of names and places that made ancient Israel come to life. He was a big hit with the group. He accompanied our worship songs on the bus with a mean acoustic guitar.

"Sure, let's go gang."

For the next hour, we took in the marvels of Megiddo. Benjamin was quick to point out that it had been designated by UNESCO as a World Heritage Site. He showed us the granary and the stables that had housed horses for the armies of Solomon, as well as the deep shaft that led to springs outside the city walls.

"Are we having a good time?" the Pastor asked as we assembled in a broad, level place overlooking the Jezreel Valley. Only a stout metal fence separated us from the valley below.

"We will take a little longer than usual, today. It will be a time of prophetic teaching and reflection from this historic vantage point overlooking the valley," the Pastor announced. "It's a little chilly, but a beautiful day."

We all looked at each other and began to look for ways to be comfortable. Some took off their jackets and sweaters, lay them on the ground, and sat down on them. Some had little tripod portable stools, while others had inflatable cushions. There were rocks nearby. Many were standing. Maria and I sat on the ground on our jackets. Mom sat on a lawn chair that some-one had retrieved from the tour bus.

Pastor Tom stood with his back to the fence facing the group, with the Jezreel Valley behind him.

"You guys remind me of what the crowds must have looked like when Jesus preached to them in the wilderness," he commented.

"I want to begin today by recognizing two very distinguished guests who joined our group yesterday, and say on behalf of Hosanna Temple, 'Welcome gentlemen. We are glad you are here today.'"

"Thank you."

"Elliott, tell us who you are and why you are here."

"There isn't much to say except that I'm an independent news corre-spondent hired by the New York Times and I'm here to cover the initiative by our President to bring peace to the Middle East."

"We are talking about the Kerry Peace Accord, right?"

"Yes, that's it."

"And Omar?"

"Thank you. I work for Al Jazeera, an international satellite news net-work. We are based in Qatar and are viewed worldwide. Starting out in Arabic, we recently purchased a network from a former vice president of the United States and now can be seen twenty-four hours a day in America in English. We are a young organization, less than twenty years old, and are aspiring to soon become the most trusted and most objective news source in the world."

Maria cupped both hands and whispered into my ear, "I watch it some-times on Direct TV, and in my opinion, it is the world's leading advocate for the blend of globalism, Socialism and Islam. It is seen around the world."

"It may be, honey, but I understand it has not gone over as well as expected in America."

"Thank God!" she added.

I looked around and Elliott had stood up and was smiling. "It isn't fair," Elliott joked, "Omar got more time than I did."

There was some laughter and I could sense that the group was beginning to feel more comfortable with its guests.

Pastor Tom then introduced a special speaker. He was an old friend from college by the name of Bob Morgan who had gone on to acquire a doctorate from Dallas Theological Seminary. He had gained prominence on the prophetic lecture circuit as a speaker on the subject of *the last days*. Slender and tall, with silver gray hair, he spoke with a soft voice. We had come to affectionately call him, The Professor.

He began, "Let me start by giving you a little history of this great valley. We are approximately 60 miles north of Jerusalem. Below us here is what is known in Hebrew as the Valley of Jezreel. From west to east — from the Mediterranean to the Jordan River — it cuts across the nation.

"Its historic significance cannot be overstated. Trade routes from the three continents — Europe, Asia and Africa — passed through this valley. And many say that it is the site of more wars than any other piece of real estate on earth. It was here that some of the bloodiest sagas of Israel's history took place — to name a few:

Here Deborah, the prophetess, and Barak, her commander, routed the Canaanites who had 900 chariots of iron.

Here Gideon, with 300 men, defeated the Midianites.

Here King Saul, and his son, Jonathon, were killed in battle by the Philistines.

Here bloody Jezebel had Naboth put to death and then seized his vineyard for her husband, King Ahab.

Here Jezebel was later eaten by dogs at the wall of Jezreel.

Here Jehu, aspiring to be King of Israel, killed both the King of Israel and the King of Judah on the same day.

Here the beloved good King Josiah died in a battle against the Egyptians.

Napoleon and his armies fought the Turks here in 1799. He is quoted as making this prophetic statement:

"There is no place in the whole world more suited for war than this… all the armies of the world could maneuver for battle here.. (It is) the most natural battleground on the face of the earth."

"As we talk about this, today, if you have any questions as we go along, feel free to ask and I will try my best to answer them for you. We are going to be very informal today," the Professor concluded.

I am sure that everybody was as surprised as I was when Elliott immediately raised his hand. "Sir, I guess I'll be the first responder. There is something I don't understand. Why does there have to be a Battle of Armageddon at all? If God is in charge of history as you Christians claim, it would seem to me that He could come up with a better ending."

"That's a good point, Elliott. The problem with your question, however, is that it assumes that God is the only actor in the drama. It doesn't recognize that all the evil in the world comes from the devil. God originally delegated authority over the earth to Adam and Eve. They handed the devil the reins of government when they submitted to his lies and fell into sin. He temporarily rules the world and he will not go down easily. It is here… right here in this great valley, that his rule will end."

"You aren't asking me to believe that malarkey about the apple and the serpent are you?"

The Professor looked startled. It was obvious that he was caught off guard by the outburst.

"So, all the bad stuff in the world comes from the devil. Is that what you are saying?"

"Exactly." He stated, quickly recovering from the ambush.

"I don't mean to be rude, but this whole Bible thing is nothing but fairy tales."

The Professor continued as if he hadn't heard. "The problem is that the master of deception rules the world. And people listen to his lies. They become enslaved to the deception and cannot escape. At times, entire nations are bewitched and fall under the spell of his delusions."

"I wouldn't suggest," Elliott replied, "that you give this speech to the General Assembly of the United Nations. I don't think it will go over well."

The Professor laughed awkwardly, "I haven't been invited lately."

"I doubt that you will be."

The Pastor stepped forward and lifted his fist in victory. "The good news is that Jesus came to destroy the works of the devil — which He did in magnificent fashion — when He prayed for the people and healed them spirit, soul and body."

Mom was sitting in front of Maria. She turned around and whispered, "Look at Omar! He is totally absorbed in the discussion."

Elliott calmly intruded, "I had a question and then I was interrupted by this senseless prattle about sin, the devil and Jesus."

There was an audible gasp from the crowd. It was obvious that not everyone agreed with the idea of an open forum. An older man stood up. "I didn't pay good money and come half way around the world to hear my Lord blasphemed." The Professor pleaded, "Please, just a minute, sir, please!"

It was an awkward moment of silence followed by mingled comments from the group, some more audible than others. The Professor scanned his audience with the stern look of a teacher when his students are misbehaving. Finally, things calmed down and there was silence.

He continued, "We all agreed that we would conduct the teaching today in an informal manner, allowing anyone to express himself. Let's all be kind to each other and make an effort to respect one another's opinions, even if we disagree with them."

The old man reluctantly sat back down, but remained positioned on the edge of his seat.

"Thank you."

Omar jumped to his feet. "I am sorry if you are offended. I am sure that Elliott meant no harm. Personally, I am intrigued by this whole discussion. I want to hear more." He turned and stared at Elliott then exhorted, "Lighten up! Okay?"

Elliott appeared to be genuinely surprised by the whole episode. "Oh, I'm sorry… please excuse me. No offense intended. It won't happen again."

Maria poked me in the ribs and said, "He doesn't mean a word of it."

The Professor was unfazed. "We are entering a brand new age. The day when God takes over. When He takes over the reins of world government and brings in the Kingdom of God when Jesus returns.

"Preceding His coming there will be a period of great trouble in the world. It is the main topic of the Book of Revelation, called the Great Tribulation. It will be a time of God's wrath and judgment upon the nations because of their sins. Jesus described it like this in Matthew 24:21-22. Who can look it up for us?"

"I can," volunteered Ethel as she quickly thumbed through an old tattered and torn King James copy. "Here it is." She adjusted her glasses and began to read:

For then there will be great tribulation, such as has not been since the beginning of the world until this time, nor ever shall be. And except those days should be shortened, no flesh be saved; but for the elect's sake those days shall be shortened."

The Professor picked up. "The days will be mercifully shortened by the glorious appearing of the Lord Jesus in the clouds of heaven, with the holy angels, when He comes to rule. Before that day the evil in the world will get worse and worse. In fact, Jesus said that the world would become more hostile for Christians in the last days. If the statements of Elliott offend us, then we may need to get used to it."

Elliott resumed, "Nice rally of the troops, preacher. But to get back to my original question. We were talking about this place here — which you call Armageddon. My question was, 'Why does there have to be a Battle of Armageddon?'"

"We belong to God. He created us. He owns us. We were made for His good pleasure. We have rebelled and have chosen to go our own way by breaking His law. All of us have sinned against Him. But He still loves us."

"A God who loves?" enquired Omar, "That has to be a good thing. I have never heard of that before."

"Yes, Omar. He sent His only Son to save us and the world from the penalty of sin which is to be forever separated from Him in a hell prepared for the devil and his angels. He said that all we had to do was believe and we would be forgiven of our sins and receive eternal life. We have rejected Him."

Omar didn't respond. But Elliott asked, "Is this the place you take up the offering?"

"Armageddon, Elliott, is the final battle of history between good and evil. Man in his sin has rejected the rule of God. Armageddon is the day that God forcefully takes over the rule of man and of planet earth. Those who have rejected Him will be destroyed. It is not too late to repent. There is still time before the coming of the dreadful Day of the Lord."

There was a moment of silence as the group waited for Elliott's response. He didn't say anything. He just turned his head and looked across the valley.

"May I ask a question?"

"Certainly, Omar."

"I'm a Muslim. We believe in the Last Days. What are the signs of Jesus' coming and Armageddon? And how will it take place?" Omar asked.

"Omar, Jesus gave us many signs of His coming. In Matthew, chapter 24, He states that there will be false Christs, earthquakes, wars and rumors of war, famine, and epidemics. And He said that as we approached the time of the end, that these catastrophic events would grow more frequent and intense. Like birth pangs in a terminally pregnant woman.

"How will it happen? Jesus will lead the armies of heaven against the armies of the world who will be gathered here. Let me read from the New King James Version beginning with Revelation 19:11:

Now I saw heaven opened, and behold a white horse; and he who sat on him was called Faithful and True, and in righteousness he judges and makes war... 13 He was clothed with a robe dipped in blood; and His name is called The Word of God. 14 And the armies in heaven, clothed in fine linen, white and clean, followed Him on white horses. 15 Now out of his mouth goes a sharp sword, that with it He should strike the nations. And He Himself will rule them with a rod of iron. He himself treads the winepress of the fierceness and wrath of Almighty God."

Omar didn't comment. He seemed to be someplace else. Deep in thought.

The Professor turned and stated, "Elliott, I hope this explains it to your satisfaction."

"Your answer is plain enough. I just can't accept it."

"Having defeated all his enemies, Elliott, Jesus will then rule the world from Jerusalem for a thousand years and it will be the summation of all the dreams of humanity for the perfect world of love, peace, and prosperity. The words of the prophets describe it best. Ethel would you read: Micah 4:3-4, please?"

She quickly found the place and began to read:

And he shall judge among many people, and rebuke strong nations afar off; and they shall beat their swords into plowshares, and their spears into pruninghooks; nation shall not lift up a sword against nation: neither shall they learn war anymore. But they shall sit every man under his vine and under his fig tree; and none shall make them afraid.

The professor nodded his thanks to her and continued, "At the end of the thousand years, there will be the awesome and fearful event the Bible calls the Great White Throne Judgment. The Books will be opened and all who have rejected Christ will be judged out of the Books. If their names are not found written in the Book of Life, they will be cast into the Lake of Fire."

Elliott was having a hard time controlling his cynicism. "I think I'll call in sick that day."

"I don't think so Elliott. The Bible says, 'It is appointed unto man once to die and after that the Judgment.' You have an appointment you cannot break. Everything that is hidden will be brought to light."

Pastor Tom shouted, "The good news is that there will be a New Heaven and a New Earth for the people of God. We will be with Him in paradise forever and ever. Let's stand and praise Him!"

The discussion was getting to me personally. I had grown up in a Christian home and attended church all my life. At the time all of this was happening, I served as a deacon in my church, but I had some stuff in my life that I knew wasn't right. I knew I wasn't ready should Jesus return that morning. I tried to shake it off.

THE ASSYRIAN

"**D**avid, I hope you are enjoying our discussions today," commented the Pastor. "I'll bet you could add some interesting comments if we gave you the chance."

"Oh, I don't know about that. I think the group would rather hear what God says about the times in which we live. The Professor is doing a great job."

"I agree. But if you feel like it, just jump in and say whatever you like. I am sure that the people would like to hear what you have to say. You know, we don't often have high-level government officials on our trips."

"Thank you."

"By the way, I think you are in for a pleasant surprise. Your mother is going to teach on a revelation she says God gave her. It's intriguing. I believe God has spoken to her."

"If she says God spoke to her, watch out!"

Elliott was very anxious to get things underway after the break. "I have one more question."

"Go ahead," the Professor replied.

"Omar and I joined your group because we wanted to understand why you Christians are such avid supporters of Israel. There is no rational explanation that I can see why people who claim to be moral stand behind a nation of imperialistic thugs."

It was obvious that the group was fed up with him. A chorus of boos swept through the crowd.

"Excuse me, Elliott. Not rational?" the Professor responded. "It is very rational if you believe that there is one God, that His name is Jehovah, that He has revealed Himself to man, and that the revelation is contained in the Holy Bible."

"What does that have to do with it?"

"Because the Bible states plainly that the Jewish people were chosen of God to bring a Messiah into the world. It also states that God gave this tiny little piece of real estate to Israel. He promised it to Abraham and to his seed forever."

"Of course your position would be rational then, if you believe the Bible and that is what it says," he admitted.

The Professor had abandoned all notes and was walking back and forth gesturing forcefully. "The issue is not logic or reasoning. Logic begins with a basic premise, which develops to a conclusion. The problem lies in the basic premise that forms the basis for your belief system, Elliott. The basic premise is always an assumption that we make about reality. Do you believe that the Bible is the Word of God?"

"No, of course not."

"Okay, then. That is an assumption, or faith judgment. We make the opposite faith judgment that it is. Both of us, then, applying perfect logic, will come to different conclusions about Israel or God or any other matter of faith. Do you see that?"

Elliott didn't answer.

"The problem is that your assumption is wrong, but your logic is perfect. You believe that there are no absolutes — that it all happened by accident. There is no God. There is no plan. There is nothing. I will grant you this. That you are very logical. You begin with nothing and you end up with nothing. You are very logical."

"I don't think he meant that as a compliment, Elliott!" Omar joked, smiling at his friend.

Elliott appeared angry. "The Jews came here after World War II and illegally occupied land that was not theirs. They took it away from the Palestinians. It is a moral outrage."

"That's what I mean, Elliott. This so-called 'illegal occupation' is your basic premise — the assumption upon which your logic is built. It is the rose-colored glasses through which you perceive the facts. As a result, you can never escape the bias. You are trapped in your own logic."

"I suppose you Christians have no bias, right?"

"Of course we have a bias. Our faith is our bias. We believe that there is a God, and that He has revealed Himself to man, and that revelation has been codified in a Book — the Bible. It is the Word of God and it is very plain. It is our objective authority. It says one thing and one thing only. God gave this land to the Jewish people! Period!"

The Professor kept on going, "Elliott, what is the basis of your position that Israel should give up this land to the Palestinians?"

"On the basis of common decency. The Israelis should restore to the rightful owner that which they have taken at gunpoint."

"Do you own your home, Elliott?"

"Yes."

"Is it in the United States?"

"Yes."

"Then, it seems to me that you should deed your home back to the Native Americans."

Elliott didn't respond, but Omar laughed out loud, "Touché. He got you on that one, Elliott."

"And furthermore, Elliott, a Jewish remnant has remained continuously in this land since the days of Joshua, some thirty-five hundred years ago. And they have been the only people to have ever formed a nation state on this soil.

"You and Omar have come to Israel to cover the Kerry Peace Accord, which is based on obtaining a mutually acceptable partition of this land between Israel and the Palestinians. I can tell you one thing from reading the Scriptures; even if both sides agree, God doesn't. He does not want His land divided."

Elliott was trying to change the subject, "We are here to report the news, that's all."

"Do you know what the real news is, Elliott?"

"That's why I'm here. To find out."

"The real news is that twenty-five hundred years ago the prophet Daniel, speaking by the Holy Spirt, stated that there would be an agreement between Israel and surrounding nations in the last days. It would resolve issues, not only between them, but would also affect the peace of the world. And that it would be presided over by a worldwide political figure, whom the Bible calls the Anti-Christ."

"This is the real news here today," Pastor Tom joined the conversation. "Two young men are here by the names of Omar and Elliott who represent worldwide news organizations. They are here to cover an agreement that exactly fits the description of the one prophesied by Daniel."

Pastor Tom arose to his feet, and looking at the group, enquired, "I want to ask you a question. Please give me your sincere opinion. Do you believe the Kerry Peace Plan could be the very covenant prophesied by Daniel?"

Most of the people raised their hands or spoke affirmatively that it could be.

"See, Elliott. This is but a random sample of millions of us who believe the Bible and what it says about the last days."

"Does the Bible say what the subject matter of the covenant will be?" Omar asked.

"The Bible is plain. It is the partition of the land," replied the Professor. "And I can tell you that God will not be pleased with the outcome of the negotiations. God spoke through the prophet Isaiah about the division of the land. Isaiah chapter 28 and verse 15 calls it a covenant with death, and with hell."

"You have to be kidding!" exclaimed Elliott. "I'm sorry. But this idea that Omar and I are fulfilling some ancient prophecy is a little bit too far-fetched for me."

"Don't be such a cynic, Elliott." Omar pleaded.

"The land is the issue," the Professor softly restated his position. After congratulating the group for its participation, he resumed his typical quiet teaching.

"Where is my Bible?" he asked, "Hmmm. It was here a few minutes ago. I don't see it."

A young lady volunteered her iPhone. "Oh, thank you! Please find Isaiah the tenth chapter for us." She quickly reacted and handed the phone to him.

"Thank you. Now, before I read these Scriptures to you, let me say that more and more serious Bible scholars are teaching that the words 'King of Assyria' or the 'Assyrian' are names for the Anti-Christ, and that they apply to the days in which we live."

"Uh oh, Omar," Elliott quickly reacted, half smiling and half smirking, "That means he's a Muslim."

Omar simply looked his way for a second and then became engrossed once again in the teaching.

The Professor continued, "Omar asked a few minutes ago, 'What are the issues covered in the covenant of the Anti-Christ?'

"First, let me say that many times in the Bible, God has promised the land of Israel to Abraham and his seed after him. One example of this is recorded in the Book of Psalms, in which God states that His covenant with Israel is forever."

Turning the phone this way and that, and squinting to read the text in the bright sunlight, the Professor finally made it out. "Okay, this is what it says in Psalms chapter 105, verses 8 through 11. Can everybody hear me?"

Many responded enthusiastically while leafing through their Bibles.

Pastor Tom shouted holding up his forefinger, "What is the number one authority for all matters of our faith and conduct?"

"The Bible!" the people shouted back as they laughed and remarked about the question.

Pastor Tom smiled and added, "Go ahead, Professor."

"You have them trained well, Pastor. Let me commend you."

"If the foundation is destroyed, what will we do?"

The Professor resumed, "Okay. Psalms 105 is only one of many Scriptures found in the Bible that grants this land to Israel. This is what it says:

He hath remembered his covenant forever, the word which he commanded to a thousand generations. Which covenant he made with Abraham, and his oath unto Isaac; and confirmed the same unto Jacob for a law, and to Israel for an everlasting covenant: saying, *Unto thee will I give the land of Canaan, the lot of your inheritance.*"

The Professor continued, "Should we not be amazed that 3500 years after the promise of the land to Abraham, that the division of the tiny land of Israel is a prime concern for the peace of the world?

"The Bible also teaches that there will be another covenant formed in the last days between Israel and other nations. It will remove the boundaries of the land set by the covenant between God and Abraham. The role of the Assyrian, or the Anti-Christ, in the formation of this covenant is prophesied in the book of Daniel, chapter 9, verse 27. It establishes the length of the covenant:

And *he (the Anti-Christ) shall confirm the covenant with many (nations) for one week (7 years)*, and in the midst of the week (3 ½ years) he shall cause the sacrifice and oblation (the Temple worship and services) to cease.

"Again, Daniel foretold the part played by the Anti-Christ, and that it would be a covenant that divides the land. The reference is found in Daniel, chapter 11, verses 36 through 39. I encourage you to read the entire passage, but for today, I will read selected portions. It says:

He shall exalt himself, and magnify himself above every god, and shall speak marvelous things against the God of gods, and shall prosper till the indignation be accomplished...he shall...increase with glory...and *shall divide the land for gain.*"

"Professor, if you will give me the Scripture quotations, I will look them up and mark them for you in my Bible," Ethel volunteered.

"That will be better, I think. I am having difficulty seeing them on the iPhone screen in this sunlight. Thank you."

He handed the iPhone back to the young lady, thanked her, and handed the citation list to Ethel.

He then went on, "Isaiah, who lived 150 years before Daniel, prophesied that God would judge the Assyrian for his arrogance and for removing the boundaries of the land of Israel. This is found in Isaiah, chapter 10, verses 12 and 13:

It shall come to pass, that when the Lord hath performed his whole work upon Mount Zion and on Jerusalem, I will punish...the king of Assyria, and the glory of his high looks. For he saith, by the strength of my hand I have... *removed the bounds (boundaries) of the people,* and have robbed their treasures.

"The Apostle Paul foretold the time when the Assyrian will become the most powerful man in the world. He will announce that he is God and force the world to worship him. This is found in II Thessalonians, chapter 2 and verse 4. It reads:

> Who opposeth and exalteth himself above all that is called God, or that is worshipped; so that he as God sitteth in the Temple of God, shewing himself that he is God.

"The world will become convinced that Israel is supernaturally sustained, and the Anti-Christ will deceive all nations into thinking they can defeat God in battle. They will gather here for the last battle of history. This account is provided by the Apostle John, and it is recorded in the book of Revelation, chapter 16, verses 13 and 14. He stated:

> And I saw three unclean spirits like frogs come out of the mouth of the dragon (Satan), and out of the mouth of the beast (Anti-Christ), and out of the mouth of the false prophet. For they are the spirits of devils, working miracles, which go forth unto the kings of the earth and of the whole world, to gather them to the battle of that great day of God Almighty."

Pastor Tom had moved from the front to the rear of the group. I heard his voice behind me, "I would like to comment here, Bob." His confident baritone voice was reassuring before you knew what he was going to say. "Some folks are deeply distressed about what the future holds." He paused, and then said, "We don't have to know everything about the future to be confident in the promise that everything is going to turn out great. Like our Lord Jesus, we will look past the cross to the awesome joy that lies before us. He has a word for us today. 'Look up — great days lie ahead for the people of God.'"

The Professor resumed, "Joel was one of the earliest of the writing prophets. He prophesied of the Day of the Lord during the ninth century BC. His prophecy is recorded in the book of Joel, chapter 3, verse 2. He saw the armies of the world gather in this valley we overlook here, today. This is the place where God will settle the score with those who have scattered Israel and parted His land:

> I will also gather all nations, and will bring them down into the valley of Jehoshaphat (judgment), and will plead with them there for my people and *for my heritage Israel, whom they have scattered among the nations, and parted my land."*

Omar had been sitting on the ground with his elbows resting on his knees and his chin in his hands. He seemed genuinely amazed at what he was hearing. He seemed eager to contribute, "Everybody knows that the recognition of Israel as a state, and the partition of the land, are the tough issues in the peace accord attempt. That this is prophesied in the Bible is astounding."

"As you can see, Omar, God himself laid out the central issue of the covenant of the Anti-Christ over twenty-five centuries ago. It is the division of the land of Israel. Those who agree to divide the land of Israel will suffer the judgment of God."

I turned my head to look at Tel Megiddo. A random splattering of date palms stood erect like sentinels against the white clouds and blue sky. Beneath them were the dry, lifeless ruins of the ancient city. It was as if they were standing guard over the valley until their watch was over. I could hear a gentle breeze blowing through the branches.

"Can you tell us more about the Anti-Christ?" Omar enquired.

"Certainly," the professor continued, "he is mentioned many times in the Bible under different names. He is called the Man of Sin, the Son of Perdition, the Lawless One, the Wicked One, the Seed of the Serpent, the Beast, and the Assyrian.

"He will come from the Mediterranean part of the world. The word Mediterranean is formed from two Latin words meaning the middle of the land, referring to the three continents, Africa, Asia and Europe. In the Bible, the term for the Mediterranean is the Great Sea.

"John the Apostle was imprisoned on the Isle of Patmos, when he saw the visions recorded in the Book of Revelation. Patmos, which was an island prison then, is a tourist attraction, today. It is located on the Aegean Sea, which is part of the bigger Mediterranean. John saw the Book of Revelation unfold while standing on the shores of what was then known as the Great Sea. He records what he saw in Revelation, chapter 13, verse 1:

> And I stood upon the sand of the sea, and saw a beast rise up out of the sea, having seven heads and ten horns, and upon his horns ten crowns, and upon his heads the name of blasphemy."

"Seven heads and ten horns. What does that signify?" Omar asked.

"It means you don't want to mess with that guy," joked Elliott.

The Professor continued, "The seven heads represent seven Gentile empires that have ruled over the nations. They were in order of their appearance, Assyria, Egypt, Babylon, Medo-Persia, Greece, and Rome. One is yet to come. It will be the last — the revived Roman Empire.

"They all will have come from the Great Sea Basin. The one which ruled the world at the time John had the vision was the great Roman Empire. It stretched from the British Isles to the Persian Gulf and beyond. It included North Africa from Egypt to Gibraltar.

"The ten horns speak to the times in which we live, today. They represent ten political subdivisions that will lend their strength to the Anti-Christ for a short time when he arrives. This is a future event that will take place, from all indications, very soon."

"Am I going too fast?" asked the Professor. He paused and stated, "I will assume from your silence that you are still with me.

"Okay. If so, let us tie these Great Sea world powers into a dream that Nebuchadnezzar, the great Babylonian Emperor, had 600 years before Christ. He had the dream after successfully conquering the world. The dream is recorded in Daniel, chapter 2.

"In the dream Nebuchadnezzar saw a great metal image which had a head of gold; a breast and arms of silver; belly and thighs of brass; and it had two legs of iron; and feet with a mixture of iron and clay. Then a stone cut out without hands struck the great image in the feet shattering it into pieces 'making them like the chaff of the summer threshing floors and the wind carried them away.'

"Does anybody know what the Stone cut out without hands stands for?"

There immediately followed a hearty response from the group, "Jesus!"

"Who?"

"Jesus!"

The Professor cupped his hand behind his ear, "I can't hear you! Who?"

"Jesus!" the people replied again.

"Jesus is the Stone who will destroy once and for all the kingdoms of this world, and replace them with the Kingdom of God when He comes back," one lady shouted with her Bible poised above her head.

A round of chatter and laughter followed giving us a short break and then the Professor stated "We need to move on.

"Back to Nebuchadnezzar's dream. There was a young Jewish slave in the Emperor's Court whom God used to interpret the dream. His name was Daniel.

"If you remember, I said that we needed to connect the seven heads of Revelation 13 with Nebuchadnezzar's dream of the Great Image. That is not hard to do historically. They are one and the same thing. They depict the same world empires that dominated the Great Sea.

"The difference is that John lived hundreds of years after Daniel and looked into the past. He saw 'seven heads' representing seven world empires.

Two of them existed before Nebuchadnezzar. Daniel looked into the future and saw the remaining five of the seven heads.

"Daniel interpreted the dream, 'You are the Emperor of Babylon and you are the head of gold.' Daniel's interpretation included the succeeding Medio-Persian, Greek and Roman Empires, each corresponding to body parts of the image. The two iron legs represent the two eastern and western divisions of the last world kingdom, the Roman Empire.

"First. The iron represented the great military strength of the Roman Empire. In the New King James Version of Daniel, chapter 2, verse 40, we learn it will be the mightiest of the kingdoms:

And the fourth kingdom shall be as strong as iron, inasmuch as iron breaks in pieces and shatters everything; and like iron that crushes, that kingdom will break in pieces and crush all the others.

"Second, we see that it would be split and have a two-fold nature, signified by the two iron legs of the Great Image.

"History confirms the Biblical record, which predicted the great Roman Empire would be divided into two legs. The transition from one empire to two was gradual, beginning in the third century AD. In 325 AD, Constantine moved the capital from Rome to Byzantine in Asia Minor, and renamed it Constantinople, and called it the New Rome. So complete was the division of the empire that historians later dubbed the two halves as the Western Roman Empire and the Eastern Roman Empire.

"In the fifth century AD, the Western Roman Empire collapsed and disappeared from history, although there would be repeated efforts to restore it later. Rulers like Charlemagne, Charles V, and believe it or not, Hitler, who called his regime the Third Reich, attempted and failed to revive the ancient Imperial Rome.

"The eastern half continued to exist for another thousand years until the fall of Constantinople to the Muslims in 1453. The longevity of the eastern leg, I believe, is significant and has been overlooked for the most part by prophecy scholars. Most of us are westerners who have assumed that Western Civilization would produce the Anti-Christ and the revived Roman Empire. There are more and more reasons to doubt this assumption.

"The legs of iron, thus, represent the once greatest of all military and political powers — the unmatched Roman Empire. It will rise again in the last days as the mightiest military and political power in the history of the world."

"I've always enjoyed the study of mythology," Elliott scoffed.

"Come on, Elliott. You wouldn't believe it if it ran over top of you," Hubert jabbed him.

"Yeah, Elliott," someone chimed in.'

The people laughed and a guy next to him punched him lightly on the shoulder in jest. Elliott smiled politely but folded his arms in defiance. The atmosphere was getting more relaxed, but I could tell that the folks were not happy with his comments.

The Professor resumed, "In today's world, secular, atheistic, Christian, Socialistic Europe and the Islamic Middle East, stand poised to assume their prophetic destinies. This geophysical combination not only will fit the boundaries of the old Roman Empire, but will embody the two legs of the Great Image. The Bible teaches that the coming world ruler will bring about the One World from this base.

"Third. Besides being divided into two parts, his kingdom will have another odd peculiarity. It will be comprised of elements that do not mix. This can be readily seen in the anatomy of the Great Image, which had feet made of iron and clay. Let's read Daniel's description of the kingdom found in chapter 2, verse 42, from the New King James Version:

And as the toes of the feet were partly of iron and partly of clay, so the kingdom shall be partly strong and partly fragile. 43 As you saw iron mixed with ceramic clay, they will mingle with the seed of men; but they will not adhere to one another just as iron does not mix with clay.

"Another thing I should mention is that the metal image represents the Gentile kingdoms of the world, which have occupied Jerusalem since Nebuchadnezzar conquered it in 606 BC. Jesus called this period the 'times of the gentiles' and predicted that Jerusalem would be trampled by gentiles until the appointed time for their end. This will take place when Christ returns.

"Now we fast forward to the present day. And we prophesy from Scripture that the Roman Empire will come to life again. And we further prophesy from Scripture that it will eventually come under the rule of one man. From there he will extend his rule over all the earth. The Bible calls him the Anti-Christ or the Lawless One. I will get to him in a minute.

"Now, who sees the present day significance of the two-legged division of the Great Image into East and West?"

"I think I do!" replied Omar.

"What is it?"

"One leg is Muslim. The other leg is Christian and Socialistic."

"Thank you, Omar. Who knows what won't mix?"

"I know," replied Hubert. "Iron and clay won't mix."

"What else?"

Hubert stated, "Christianity and Islam won't mix."

"Precisely. Dr. Flink will be speaking later and she will get into that in-depth. Now, let's get back to the Lawless One, or the Anti-Christ. Is everybody with me?"

"Yeah, we're with you."

"In the beginning, the Lawless One will need to convince world leaders that he is the man that can bring peace and save the world from nuclear annihilation. Let me ask you a question. What better way to prove it than to bring about a peaceful solution to the Israeli-Palestinian question?"

"That would remove the greatest obstacle to peace in the world," concluded Omar.

"You got it, Omar. The Anti-Christ will have the charisma to pull the whole deal off. The Bible says that he will get his power from the dragon, or the devil. Jesus said he was the Father of Lies."

"You haven't expressly stated, but I get the idea from what you have said that you believe he will be Muslim?"

Looking at Omar, the Professor bit his lower lip and attempted a faint smile at the same time.

Hubert responded, "A Muslim peacemaker in world politics. That doesn't sound like any Muslim I know."

The Professor continued, "That's because he won't be like any Muslim you know, Hubert. The Bible says that, 'by peace he will destroy many.' He will conquer by promising a bridge of peace between the competing forces that are clashing in the Middle East and the world. The big three are Christianity, Islam and godless Marxism. The union will be heralded by all peoples as the salvation of the world and the beginning of the new era of peace for mankind."

Elliott raised a fist as if in triumph. "Sounds good to me. I'm beginning to like this guy."

The Pastor hadn't said anything for a while. He added, "The Bible says that when they shall say 'Peace and safety, then sudden destruction shall come upon them as travail upon a woman with child.' In other words, when the world thinks that man has finally succeeded in bringing universal peace via the New World Order — then all you-know-what will break loose. Instead of peace, the Anti-Christ will preside over the period called in the Bible the Great Tribulation, which is also called The Day of the Lord. It will be a time of trouble like no time before it and no time after it. There will chaos, bloodshed, famines, epidemics and earthquakes on an unprecedented scale. The demons in hell will be unleashed upon those who take the Mark of the Beast. And upon those who practice sin and rebel against God. Men will pray to die and death will escape them."

Omar had been very quiet with his hand cupped over his mouth as if in deep thought. "That's what we believe, too. This is incredible. That worldwide devastation will take place just before the Last Day. There will be universal chaos that will end only when the Mahdi returns. We're together on that. We believe that he will govern and bring peace to the world."

"In fact, part of the jihad strategy is to add to the chaos in order to hasten the Mahdi's coming. Isn't that true, Omar?"

"Some are more aggressive than others, but to be honest with you, many of us will do what it takes to bring him back."

"But the point is that it is a major tenet in Islamic eschatology to do all that is possible to create instability in the world in order to bring him back."

"Yes!"

The Professor asked for water and turned back toward the group, "Whether the Anti-Christ is alive I cannot say. But I can say this, the Bible description of the last days is like watching CNN or Fox News. It is a good bet that he is alive.'"

"Where do you believe he will come from?" Omar asked.

"Are you asking for my personal opinion?"

"Yes."

"There are several reasons, which I don't have time to go into today, that I believe, he will come from the region of present day Turkey, Iraq and Syria."

"Well, that blows my theory," interrupted Hubert, with a look of surprise and resignation.

"And what is that, Hubert?" asked the Professor.

"I thought all along that the President might be the Anti-Christ…"

"Hubert, I can't believe you said that!" Ethel exclaimed, turning red and looking the other way shaking her head.

"But I guess not. I have heard a lot of talk about where he came from, but I haven't heard anyone claim that he came from the Middle East."

There was a stillness that settled over the crowd. I wondered if it were from the shock of the suggestion. Or the shock of someone stating it publicly...or because the people were pondering the possibility.

"Isn't all this talk about the ancients irrelevant for the problems we face today, Professor?" asked Elliott. "What does all this stuff mean if I live in Haiti and I don't know if I will eat tomorrow?"

"Excellent point, Elliott. But the Bible tells us that Satan is the author of all the poverty, disease and sin in the world today. Bible prophecy tells us that there is a better day coming when Christ will end the rule of Satan over mankind and he will be cast into the Lake of Fire, never to torment man again. Until that day comes, we must all work together to make the world a better place. Good will triumph over evil in the end."

"So, that's what the fuss is all about, huh? The war between good and evil?"

"Exactly. And the showdown will take place here...at Armageddon."

THE FOUR WINDS

After a short break of stretching our legs and chatting with each other, we found our places. Pastor Tom opened the session with a prayer for revelation and understanding. He then introduced the next speaker.

"I promised earlier that I had a surprise for you. I think you are really going to enjoy our next speaker. She has received an intriguing revelation that she is convinced is from God. I was skeptical at first, but the more I looked at it, the more convinced I became that it has special meaning for the times in which we live.

"She did her undergraduate studies in history and political science, and went on to get her doctorate in philosophy — all of them at Harvard. In years past, she has served as an attorney, pastor and conference speaker. She has authored three books on Bible prophecy, one of which was a New York Times best seller. You may remember it, *The Jeremiah Papers*. At the present time, she teaches one of our adult Bible classes at the church. Here she is; our very own Mom Flink. Doctor, it's all yours."

Mom was never one for formalities. She thanked the Pastor for his kind remarks and launched into the subject matter of her talk.

"Well, here we are!" she began, "At Armageddon! The site of the last battle of man. The end of the world. Not really. Just the end of the world as we know it. Jesus of Nazareth will return to gather his followers and set up the Kingdom of God on planet Earth. Not much of a battle really. The Bible says, 'His enemies will be destroyed by the brightness of His coming.' The kings and rulers will cry for the rocks and mountains to fall on them and hide them from the face of the Lamb. May this place be a warning for all of us — to have our robes washed white in the blood of the Lamb and to meet Him with confidence in that day."

Maria jabbed me in the side, "She is very confident."

"This discussion, today, is not about the future, but about the present. How prophecy is being fulfilled today, not how the Bible describes tomorrow, but how it describes today.

"What I have to say to you today may be a little different from what you are used to hearing in a Bible study in your neighbor's living room. Take that worried look off your faces. It will not challenge any of your cherished beliefs. It is simply a different perspective about end-time events that are taking place before us every day."

"Well, that's encouraging," commented Pastor Tom, feigning a sigh of relief. "We were afraid that we might have a heretic in our midst."

"No, nothing like that. I'm harmless."

"Except when she gets behind the wheel," I interjected.

"Ladies and gentlemen, the man who just interrupted me is my son. He thinks he is Horatio Alger because he came from humble beginnings and by hard work he is now a big shot in Washington. He has a twin brother who also works in our national capitol. They both have done well. Now, if you will forgive a proud mother for bragging on her children, I will proceed."

"David, you know that you were Mama's favorite," she continued.

"I know, Mom. But you always told Jonathan the same thing."

"I know."

I whispered to Maria, "I wish she wouldn't do that!"

"You asked for it. Just keep a low profile from now on."

She continued, "In Daniel 12:1, an angel tells the Prophet Daniel that there is coming a time of trouble on earth that would be so devastating; that there had never been a time like it before and there would never be a time like it afterward.

"And then the angel added a very interesting observation about the time of the end. This is the way The New King James Version describes it in verse 4:

> But you, Daniel, shut up the words, and seal the book until the time of the end; many shall run to and fro, and knowledge shall increase.

"What does this verse tell us?"

Mom answered her own question. "It tells us that the revelation of the Word of God through Daniel would be sealed until the end time. And then it would be unveiled. We are the generation that will see it come to pass. The angel goes on to characterize the time of the end when these things will be revealed. It will be a time of great strides in technology and world travel.

"What could more accurately describe the times in which we live? Congested highways, crowded airports and the exponential increase in knowledge. We are living in the times described in the Bible."

"Yeah, I can see that!" replied Billy, one of our teenagers. "My teacher says that there is more technology in my iPhone than it took to land man on the moon. And that technology and stuff is doubling every eighteen months. Do you mean to say that all this is in the Bible?"

Billy was a seventeen-year-old high school junior who had come on the Holy Land tour with his parents. He had been saved in a Walmart about six months before, as the result of youth witnessing teams that had gone out from the church on a Friday night. His progress in the faith since his conversion had been quite remarkable, according to Pastor Tom.

"Yes, Billy, it is. And the cool part is that the book will be unsealed and there will be a time of great revelation in the things of the supernatural, just as there will be in the natural. God is opening the secrets of His Word so that we may survive the trying days ahead. There is great revelation coming to your generation."

"Wow, I can't wait to see what He is going to do."

"Billy, let me tell you a story. A few months ago, I was praying and reading my Bible. The Book of Daniel, actually. Now, what we need to understand about the Book of Daniel is that it is the superstructure on which Biblical prophecy hangs. Jesus quoted it more than any other book in the Bible. It is impossible to understand what is going on in the world today without a working knowledge of the Book of Daniel. I want to call your attention to another Daniel Scripture, also referencing the New King James. It is chapter 7, verse 2:

I saw in my vision by night, and behold, the four winds of heaven were stirring upon the Great Sea.

"The word *stirring* used in this verse can also mean to *strive* or *whip up*. The idea conveyed is one of ferocity. The winds *whipped* up the great sea. Anytime there is a reference in the Bible to the Great Sea, it always means the Mediterranean. If I'm not mistaken, it is found thirteen times in the Bible and in each case the context refers to the Mediterranean.

"When I came across this verse, the question arose in my mind, what are the Four Winds?

"I then looked up the word *winds* and found that it was the Hebrew word *ruach*. It is found thousands of times in the Old Testament and is the same word translated *wind, breath,* or *spirit* in the King James Version of the Bible. Or, believe it or not, it can be translated as *mindset* or *ideology*.

"I then asked myself the question, have there been four ideologies that have come out of the Great Sea Basin? If so, what are they?"

"You have my attention!" Mr. Ike responded.

I didn't know his last name. He was known, simply, as Mr. Ike. He was a stately looking, retired professor of biology from Alabama. He always dressed in a coat and tie. Easy to like and extremely well read, he was popular with the group. His widower status did not hurt him with some of the single ladies.

"Billy, the answer came to me immediately. I knew what the Four Winds were. They are the four major ideologies that compete against each other and strive for mastery in the world today. They drive our politics, religion, and economics. They clash and there is much bloodshed. Their interaction fills our history books and the daily news. We see the bloodshed on TV and the internet daily.

"Twenty-seven nations have nuclear warheads now. The Four Winds are stirring up old and new hatreds and are blowing stronger every day. They beg the question whether Civilization itself can survive."

I was intrigued. "Mom, what are the Four Winds?"

"Okay, here is what, I believe, the Lord has shown me. The four ideologies come from four books, all of which stem from the Great Sea Basin. Four books that have changed the world. They are the most influential writings of history.

"In chronological order from first to last, they are the following:

"*The Bible* — a compilation of sixty-six books, written over a period of 1600 years by forty different authors. Christianity and Judaism came from the Bible. Christianity is the largest religion in the world with approximately 2.2 billion adherents. There are 13 million Jews in the world.

"*The Koran* — written by Mohammad between 609 and 632 AD. Islam is the second largest religion in the world, with a world population of some 1.5 billion followers.

"The Communist Manifesto — written by Karl Marx, a German political philosopher, was published in 1848 AD. Estimates of those under Socialism/Marxist rule have been estimated as high as one-third of the world's population.

"And, then, you have the *Origin of the Species* by Charles Darwin. It was published in 1859 AD"

"Why can't everybody be cool? Why do these books stir up hatred? Why do we have to kill each other?" asked Billy.

"That's a good question, Billy. The Bible says that there are demonic principalities and powers that rule the world. The Bible says that the devil comes to steal, kill and destroy. And that he is coming in the last days with great wrath because he knows his time is short. He is wreaking havoc, anarchy and destruction. He is inspiring hate in the world."

"I tried to tell my class that and the teacher rebuked me and sent me to the principal's office."

"Another big reason is that the people who embrace these ideologies all have the same goal, which if reached, mutually excludes the others. They are fighting for the same prize."

The statement peaked my interest. "What is the prize?" I asked.

"The issue, pure and simple, David, is who will rule the world?"

"Well, the chips are high enough," Hubert responded.

"Christians believe that Jesus will rule the world."

"Islam believes that the Mahdi will rule the world," Omar said.

"Karl Marx taught that Communism would seize control of the world through violent revolution. Lenin launched a program called *Comintern,* which united all Marxist groups throughout the world. Joseph Stalin had a nine-point plan for world conquest and took over the nations of Eastern Europe after World War II. NATO was formed to stonewall Communist aggression in Europe. After a prolonged civil war, China became a Communist nation in 1949. Since then, tens of thousands of young Americans fought and died fighting Communist aggression in Korea and in the rice patties of Vietnam.

"From this point in my presentation today, I will try to refer to Communism, Socialism and Fascism using the word Socialism. I can find no real difference among the ideologies. They are all Marxist.

"The only distinction seems to be the Communist's state ownership of property, which supposedly makes it different from Socialism. However, when contrasted with Socialism's illusion of ownership, with its heavy taxation and regulation, there is no real difference. Adolph Hitler's Fascism was a socialist movement. So I will simply use the term Socialism in reference to these ideas."

"I can understand the clash between Christianity, Socialism and Islam, but how did evolution of the species make the list?" asked the Professor.

"Darwinism, well, that's something different. Its ardent advocates believe that a highly evolved, genetically engineered super human will rule. It does not have its own separate agenda for world domination. It divides the world, however, on the issue of intelligent design by a Creator versus the idea that the universe happened by accident. The Wind of Darwinism is a definite force in the world, playing a support role adding strength to the humanistic and secular Socialist mode. Except for the people who believe in a theistic evolution, it provides another excuse for removing God from the picture. It finds its best expression in godless humanistic Secularism."

"I've never heard this Four Winds idea before," added Mr. Ike. "This is intriguing."

"I've given it a lot of thought. There are other winds that are blowing across the world landscape, such as New Age and militant Atheism, for example.

"The Origin of the Species hit Europe and America like a bombshell and became an instant runaway bestseller. Strictly from the point of world impact and influence today, it definitely makes the most influential list."

"Darwin's bottom line is that man is an animal," volunteered Pastor Tom. "It doesn't take a genius to understand how the theory has affected the morality of the world. I can see why it's on the list."

Mom hesitated and Mr. Ike continued, "You know, the sheer numbers of those involved in this conflict make its implications staggering."

Elliott rejoined the conversation, "I take it that you are saying that old-fashioned greed and lust for power are not the motives that drive modern warfare — but they are ideological in nature."

"No. No. I'm not saying that at all. Violence, lust, greed and power are still the culprits. They are now ideologically justified. It's easier to behead innocent men, women and children if Allah rewards you for doing it.

"Let me add that it's easier for the Socialist politician to repress his lust for power, and the oppression and misery it finally brings, if he can convince himself that the deception he is selling is good for the people."

"Elliott, I believe the point is this. The Bible is saying that there are four major winds that are blowing and their interaction will soon determine the future of the world."

"Assuming that your premise is correct, that God is behind all this, what is the significance of The Great Sea? Why not the Gulf of Mexico?"

"Because God has spoken and what He speaks comes to pass. Every event recorded in the Bible took place here. We know that the final conflict will take place here. God was manifest in the flesh here. Jesus will rule the world from here. God is in control, and apparently it is God's place of choice for unfolding His purposes."

"Four Winds! So what?"

"I don't have to tell you what the issue is, Elliott. These winds represent three quarters of the world's population. And all of them are proactive. Some of them are armed with weapons of mass destruction and are spending billions on delivery systems that can deliver death and destruction to your front door.

"And there is a new spirit in the world today. Expansionism is the spirit of the age. Islam is expanding. Young Christian missionaries are going into places that they cannot disclose, even to family members. The black flags of Islam are waving across the Middle East. Violent jihad is now beheading people in America. Russia is expanding to restore the former Soviet Union. China is expanding its military budget and building military installations in the Pacific. And the rhetoric between the major players is getting more hostile every day. If there ever was a time the Four Winds stirred, it is the day in which we live. It is only a matter of time until there is a full-scaled clash.

"Let me read for you the Amplified Bible translation of Daniel, chapter 7, verse 2:

> I saw in my vision by night, and behold, the four winds of the heavens [political and social agitations] were stirring up the great sea [the nations of the world]."

The Professor exclaimed, "I will have to admit that your interpretation of the Four Winds describes the ideological war going on in the world today."

"And it's going to get worse, Professor. Listen to Jeremiah when he describes a whirlwind that is God's judgment on the nations for their sins in the last days. That will result from the clash of the Winds. This time I'm reading from the King James, chapter 23, verses 19 and 20:

> Behold, a whirlwind of the Lord is gone forth in fury, even a grievous whirlwind: it shall fall grievously upon the head of the wicked. The anger of the Lord shall not return, until he has executed, and till he has performed the thoughts of his heart: *in the latter days you shall consider it perfectly.*

"Also in the King James, chapter 25, verses 32 and 33, Jeremiah repeats the prophecy and emphasizes that the devastation from the whirlwind will be worldwide in scope:

> Thus saith the Lord of Hosts, "Behold, evil shall go forth from nation to nation, and a great whirlwind shall be raised up... And

the slain of the Lord shall be at that day from one end of the earth to the other end of the earth… they shall not be lamented, neither gathered, nor buried, they shall be dung upon the ground."

"And finally, the prophet completes his whirlwind prophecy in chapter 30, verses 23 and 24:

Behold, the whirlwind of the Lord goeth forth with fury, a continuing whirlwind: it shall fall with pain upon the head of the wicked. The fierce anger of the Lord shall not return, until we have done it, and until he have performed the intents of his heart: *in the latter days ye shall consider it."*

Mom paused before making her next statement. She closed her eyes and seemed to wait for the words. I think the audience sensed something special — something prophetic — a word from God, maybe.

It was a full fifteen seconds before Mom broke the spell of silence, "I just want to say from my heart that God has spoken to this generation in many ways to let us know that America is being judged for her sins.

"The prophet Daniel saw the four winds striving upon the Great Sea. Jeremiah, his contemporary, saw the winds reach a whirlwind fury in the last days. I personally believe the fury began on 9/11. Since that day I think we all knew that our world would never be the same.

"Two weeks ago, a friend and I visited the National September 11 Memorial Museum in New York City. One of the displays was a piece of steel that had fused with two pages from the Bible."

"I saw that on the news the other day," someone interjected.

"Yeah!" the Pastor commented, "the steel melted but the Word of God refused to burn."

Mom continued, "And just as amazing as that, is the content of the pages. It is passages from the Sermon on the Mount, chapters 5 and 7.

A small portion of chapter 7 is displayed where Jesus talked about two houses — one built upon a rock and the other built upon the sand. I could actually read the text.

"The lesson Jesus taught was that those who built their house upon a rock would survive the storm, while those who built upon the sand would be destroyed. I will read from the book of Matthew, New King James Version, chapter 7, verses 26 and 27 where Jesus explained the analogies:

> But everyone who hears these sayings of Mine, and does not do them, will be like a foolish man who built his house on the sand: and the rain descended, the floods came, and the winds blew and beat on that house; and it fell. And great was its fall."

"Sounds to me like God was talking to America loud and clear when the towers came down," Hubert exclaimed. "America has been building her house on the sand for a long time."

"That isn't all, Hubert. At the time I did not notice that there was a small fragment of this verse fused to the steel that appeared to be set apart from the other text. I discovered a photo of it on the internet a couple of days later. I can't wait to go back and check it out firsthand. Listen to this! There were five words on the small fragment. This is what it said, '(the) winds blew...and it fell.'"

"I don't get it," Elliott exclaimed.

"It's really very simple. Daniel saw the four winds striving... Jeremiah saw them turn into a whirlwind...you and I saw it all happen on TV on 9/11."

Omar jumped to his feet, loudly exclaiming, "I believe you are on target! Muslims believe in the chaos and devastation preceding the Last Day. It signals the soon coming of the Mahdi. The wind is blowing stronger every day. Attitudes are changing."

It was as if Omar suddenly came to himself. He looked around and added before he sat back down, "So what do you think the answer is?"

"There is lot we can do. For starters we can pray. Organize prayer gatherings to pray for our leaders and the nations. We can inform people, via the Internet and social media, of the dangers that confront us. We can be bold!"

"I pray five times a day. What else can be done?"

"Don't get mad at me, Omar. But we pray in the Name of Jesus. The Bible plainly states that He is the only way to God."

"Ma'am, this kind of thinking is the whole problem," interrupted Elliott. "I can tell you that intolerance of this sort will not be permitted in the New World Order. We will require that all of us give up the differences that divide us. There will be absolute tolerance of what others believe."

"Think about it, Elliott. Are you being tolerant of what I believe?"

"No, you aren't," Omar spoke out, defending Mom. "Elliott, your hypocrisy is showing."

Maria and I looked at each other. She added, "Looks like the coalition between Islam and Socialism may be crumbling here today."

Mom was not through. "Let me ask you another question. Will I be allowed to pray in the Name of Jesus?"

"No, of course not! It offends others. It is divisive. If we will work at it, we can resolve our differences by allowing religion to unite rather than divide us."

"It sounds wonderful, Elliott. I suppose the harmony you have in mind is the multiculturalism of Europe, attempting to blend Islam, Christianity and Socialism. I am sure that you are aware that the heads of state for Britain, France and Germany have all openly admitted that multiculturalism is not working in their countries."

"That's because people must be re-educated to have the same viewpoint."

"Will that be done in concentration camps?" questioned Mr. Ike. "That's how they do it in North Korea."

Mom resumed, "Yes, you are right, Elliott. Christianity is divisive. It will respect the authority of government. It will obey its laws. It will pray for its leaders. But in the final analysis, it will obey God rather than man. For this reason, the princes of this world are afraid of Christianity. They are afraid of Jesus. Afraid that He will infect the population. The devil is trembling."

Billy was excited. "By the grace of God, I'm going to infect as many as I can!"

There was a roar of approval from the group.

"That's the point, Billy. We have been commanded by our Lord to proclaim the good news of God's love to all the world. And Christ is soon returning to rule all nations. He commanded us to proclaim the gospel to every creature."

"I don't see how it can get any plainer than that." He responded.

Mom sighed and spoke quietly, "I don't have to tell you that, unfortunately, Muslims feel as strongly as you do about advancing Islam. They are committed to evangelizing unbelieving infidels wherever they may be found. They call it *dawa*. It actually means to 'proselytize,' but in the real world it translates into the use of violent or nonviolent means to spread the faith, whichever is necessary."

"What does that tell us?"

"That we are on a head-on collision course with Islam!" Pastor Tom inserted, adding, "We are engaged in spiritual warfare and our weapon is the sword of the Spirit — the Word of God. And the word says to love one another. Love will ultimately prevail over hate.

"We Americans are inclined to engage in the debate as to whether Islam is a religion of peace or violence. It really doesn't matter what we think it is. The only thing that counts is what they think. And by all surveys, approximately 25 percent believe that violence is a legitimate way to spread Islam. That means worldwide that hundreds of millions are potential terrorists who believe that the Koran is a war manual."

THE THIRD JIHAD

I was watching Omar out of the corner of my eye. He had a strained look on his face, but remained silent.

Mom began the session, "A few minutes ago, we discussed the spirit of expansion and conflict in the world today. I want to continue that theme.

"Since WWII, the United States has been dedicated to a policy of containment of global ideologies that seek to conquer the world.

"At first, it was Nazism. The Nazis believed that the Aryan race was superior and should rule. We fought Hitler and the Nazis, who had conquered Europe. We declared war on, and defeated them, before they took over the world.

"At the same time that we faced off with Germany, we fought the Japanese after the sneak attack on Pearl Harbor. Their extreme nationalism stems from the Shinto faith, which teaches that the Imperial family dynasty is older than Japan itself. They believe they will eventually rule the world.

"And then it was global Communism, the Soviets advanced into Eastern Europe and imprisoned millions behind the Iron Curtain. We contained them. And then we fought the Korean and Vietnam wars to restrain global Communism once again in Southeast Asia."

Hubert reacted, "I fought in Vietnam. Two of my buddies died in my arms. I think about them every day."

Mom stopped and thanked him, and asked for a show of hands by the veterans in the group. There were seven of us.

"Since then, we have been involved in the Middle East, where a new global threat has arisen — the threat of global Islam."

"Surely, you are not putting Islam in the same category as the imperialistic Socialists and Nazis, are you?" Omar enquired.

"Let's take an honest look at Islam, Omar. The Muslim faith began in what is now Saudi Arabia in 609 AD, when Muhammad believed he was visited by the angel Gabriel. Over the next 23 years he wrote the Koran. It is believed that this revelation continued until the time of his death in 632 AD. Shortly after the first visitation, he began to proclaim that there was only one God; that his name was Allah; and that he, Muhammad, was his messenger. His audience was the Arabs in and around his hometown of Mecca, who worshipped many tribal deities."

Omar sat up straight and appeared to be listening to every word that Mom said.

"After ten years of disappointing results, he and his followers migrated to Medina. His message in Mecca had been conciliatory in nature and had failed to persuade the Arabs, Christians and Jews who heard him. Recitations in the Koran during this period reflect a peaceful tone and buttress the claim that Islam is a peaceful religion.

"After he arrived in Medina, the revelations continued and began to take on a more hostile mood. They supported the notion that those who were critical of Islam, or defected from it, should be put to death. He preached that the Meccans had tried to kill him, and that Islam should be advanced by the sword. With 10,000 volunteers, he returned and attacked Mecca. He was victorious. In the next ten years before he died, Muhammad had conquered and united the entire Arabian Peninsula in the worship of Allah. This was the beginning of violent jihad."

"She's reading your mail, Omar," Elliott joked. "I have to fly back to the states with a terrorist."

"Stop it, Elliott!"

Mom ignored the little spat, "The discrepancy between the Mecca and the Medina verses in the Koran is the reason there is so much debate on the question as to whether Islam is a religion of peace or violence. Verses quoted showing Islam as a peaceful religion were written during the initial Mecca period."

"And it begs another question," stated Pastor Tom. "Is Islam in America any different than in countries where it has the upper hand? Or are we in the Mecca stage where accommodation with American culture is necessary for its survival? Is Islam patiently awaiting the Medina stage, when the sword of Islam will be pulled from the sheath?"

"You can argue the Koran and the Hadith all day long," admonished the Professor, "but the historical record is the solid proof of Islam's violence."

Mom continued, "After Mohammad's death, the movement split into two factions over the issue of succession. The same issue divides Islam, today. The Shi'ites believe that a Caliph must be a descendant of Muhammad. The Sunnis believe that a non-descendant can hold the position. Currently, Sunnis comprise 80 percent of the Islamic population of the world.

"From Muhammad's death in 632 AD, until its advance was stopped in France at the Battle of Tours in 732 AD, Islam had spread west across North Africa through Spain into southern Europe. It had spread eastward through Central Asia as far as China. In little over a century, the Islamic empire reached from the Atlantic to the Pacific — territorially, the largest land acquisition in the history of man. This was the first great expansion. This was the First Jihad."

There was a visible reaction from the crowd as a few expressed surprise at the rapid advance of Islam in the first century after Mohammad's death.

"The second expansion of Islam began in 1299 AD. History knows it as the Turkish or Ottoman Empire. At its height it included Southeast Europe, the Middle East, Western Asia, the Ukraine and North Africa. It continued for over six centuries until 1922, when it collapsed in the aftermath of World War I."

"Did they kill the people back then? Like they do now?" asked Billy.

"Excuse me, for interrupting," Mr. Ike spoke out, "as far as I'm concerned, a picture is worth a thousand words. Beheading Americans live on TV! Herding people like cattle to mass executions! That tells me more about the nature of Islam than a thousand history books."

"We don't know that their earlier advances were violent," protested Elliott.

"Do you actually believe that they weren't?" Mr. Ike came back. "Come on now. Do you believe that you could get a one hundred per cent conversion rate in a swath 500 miles wide from Spain to the Wall of China by asking for voluntary conversions? Or peaceful annexations? I don't think so!"

"It's just plain old common sense. They had to convert or get their heads chopped off," Hubert explained.

"But the President says that those who commit such atrocities are not Islamic," Elliott insisted.

"What were they, then?" Hubert asked. "Quakers?"

Mom continued, "Tell that to those who went through the first two advances of Islam, who had to convert or die. Tell that to a US Marine who fought against Muslim pirates on the Barbary Coast in the early eighteen hundreds — who had to wear a leather neckband for protection and acquired for his branch of military service the proud name of Leatherneck. Tell it to him!"

A ripple of different reactions swept through the crowd in response to the surprising statement. Mom let things slide for a minute or so as the people visited their pride in the US military. She then raised her hands gesturing for quiet so she could continue.

She resumed, "The reality is that the same spirit of expansion is back. Mohammad was a master at psychological warfare. He employed terror to scare non-Muslims into submission. It has always been the weapon of expansionist Islam, whether through violent jihad or infiltration into western governments, it's basic nature remains the same. There is every reason to believe that Islam is in a season of expansion. This is the Third Jihad."

Billy's hand went up. "I've heard that word, jihad, a lot...what does it mean?"

"Sure, Billy. Jihad is a word found frequently in the Koran, and in its classical Islamic meaning defines the struggle against those who do not believe that Allah is God, or that Mohammad is his prophet. It is the name for Holy War.

"Let's go on. The Muslims are colonizing Europe. The Muslim population has grown in past years ten times the rate of the rest of the European population. The Charlie Hebdo massacre in Paris and the Copenhagen attack may have awakened Europe from its stupor. There are 'no go' zones in France, Great Britain, Germany and even the United States where police do not go. They are becoming independent Muslim fiefdoms where Sharia rules.

"It is reported that these Islamic enclaves have been formed in the United States with government approval, and that they are increasing. Baltimore, Little Rock, Texas, Minnesota, and New York are just some of those alleged on the Internet. Web sites openly advocate the worldwide goal of Sharia law, which jihadists hope someday will replace the Constitution."

"And they now have all the oil money to do anything they want," Hubert maintained.

"It is true," explained Mr. Ike. "Oil revenues have not all been wasted on fancy cars. They have funded jihad for decades. Saudi Arabia has been fiercely dedicated to jihad, particularly in the United States, funding Islamic studies in some of our major universities. News reports have claimed that millions have gone to prestigious American schools like Harvard, George

Washington, Columbia, and many others. It is also reported that as many as 100 colleges and universities across the country have received contributions or grants from Islamic sources.

"This is Cultural Jihad in action. Not suicide bombers, public beheadings or mass executions; but sophisticated manipulation of our freedoms by people in power to bring about the demise of America and what it stands for. Many feel that it is a greater enemy than the militant Muslim who shouts, 'We will destroy you!' in your face.

"Islamic influence over our children's curriculum has been immense. It is just one more example of the cultural jihadist war in America.

"School books glorifying Islam and barely mentioning Christianity have passed both the federal and local standards. And are being used in American middle schools and high schools, as well.

"Billy, did you raise your hand?"

"Yes. My little sister had to dress like a Muslim one day in school. Her whole class had to. It was one of their holy days."

"That information supports my next point, Billy. The American Center for Law and Justice (ACLJ) is filing lawsuits in cases like the following: public school students in Wisconsin have been asked to pretend they are Muslims, in Florida they have been asked to recite the Five Pillars of Islam and to make prayer rugs. In Tennessee, parents are protesting that their children are being instructed to write declarations that Allah is supreme."

The Pastor lamented, "I want to know why our churches are not warning people of these dangers. We are asleep. Jesus said there would be many false prophets and teachers. We need to hear from our pulpits that war has been declared on America. And that it has been going on for decades. At the forefront is the jihadist organization known as the Muslim Brotherhood."

"Yes," added Mr. Ike. "The Administration is coddling them, subsidizing them with millions of taxpayer dollars, and officially branding them as moderates. They are able to carry on without detection.

"It has been rumored for years that hard core jihadists have been advising the Department of Homeland Security, and even the President, affecting national policy on Islamic affairs."

Omar challenged him, "I don't think so. Give me one example of this."

"What about Mohammed Elibiary? He was a senior fellow of DHS' Homeland Security Advisory Council. Homeland Security reportedly let him go in September 2014 amid allegations that he used his twitter account to declare the inevitable return of the Muslim Caliphate. His tweets were later praised by ISIS and raised concerns that they may have been used for recruitment purposes."

"But they fired him, didn't they?"

"Yes. But why? Was it because his atrocious actions were unacceptable to the Administration? Or was he thrown under the bus because he got caught? And how did he become a senior advisor to the DHS in the first place?"

Mr. Ike went on, "And he had security clearance with access to classified documents. How scary is that?

"Which poses another question? How many jihadists are there who have been discreet about their allegiances and are still working as government advisors advancing jihad?"

I could tell that the people were becoming quite restless about the alarming facts they were not used to hearing. There was an undercurrent of rumbling among some of them. As a seasoned veteran in the State Department I was used to the scandalous. I felt sorry for some of the others who were obviously taken aback by the facts they were hearing.

"We need to know the truth, Mr. Ike. Even if it isn't what we want to hear," added Hubert.

"Thank you, Hubert. Let's face it. We don't want to believe it. But the Muslim Brotherhood is leading the parade in Washington. They proudly brandish the White House label of moderate Islam."

"It's true," exclaimed the Pastor. "Every informed person in America knows that the Brotherhood supports violent jihad around the world."

"Now, Pastor," Mom joked. "Are you getting a little touch of Islamophobia?"

"Call it what you want. If the Church does not stand up, America will die."

Pointing to the crowd with a sweep of his hand, he exhorted, "The best way to stand up is to get on our knees. America has to confess her sins and forsake them if she is going to be saved."

I looked at Elliott, expecting some sort of reaction to what the Pastor said. Instead of speaking, he simply shook his head from side to side as if in disgust, stood up from a squatting position, and walked to the edge of the crowd near the iron fence where I was standing. He smirked and said, "David, you wouldn't happen to know where I could get a good cold beer, would you?"

Mom regained the mike. "The Pastor is warning us that we as a people must pray. We must also identify the enemy. We can't stand up to the enemy until we identify him. Isolate him. And then destroy him."

Mom was emphatic. "Some people say that I am an expert when it comes to the threat of Islam. But I don't have to be an expert to say that the way we look at Islam in the West is absolutely worthless in assessing the present danger."

I had been wondering how long it would be until Omar spoke up. "What do you mean by that?" he asked.

"I mean that the present analysis by the West divides Islam into two factions — the moderates and the radicals. The radicals are terrorists. They are ISIS, Al Qaeda, Boko Haram, Al Shabab and the Lord only knows what else. They dominate media reporting, but are small in number compared to the rest of the Muslim population. We have been at war with militant Islam since 9/11.

"On the other hand, there is the moderate classification. They are our doctors, merchants, and neighbors next door. Most of them are good people who want to provide for their families and raise their children in a free America."

"So, what is the problem with that?" Omar asked.

"I'll tell you what the problem is," Mom answered. "Securely hidden from public view within the moderate classification are hundreds of thousands of cultural jihadists and terrorists. And there is no way to tell them apart. They all hide behind the moderate label."

By this time, Omar had gotten up and was walking to the iron railing. "In all due respect, Mom, I believe your fears are much too exaggerated. Who are these phantom extremists? Do you know their names?"

"That's just the point. No, I do not. They are beneath the surface."

"I had a barn that collapsed one time," Hubert reminisced. "I didn't see the termites until it was too late."

Omar was visibly upset, walking back and forth behind the group. "I know a lot of my people who have climbed to the top of their fields in US government, business and the professions. I just can't believe they are less than anything but good citizens."

"Omar, keep an open mind until I am through today. Okay?" Mom gently admonished him as she continued, "If the mainstream media or the US government says anything, it is usually lavish in its praise of so-called moderate Islam. The problem is that we mistakenly lump all those whom we do not recognize as radicals into this moderate category. It is an illusion. And a fatal mistake.

"The radicals and terrorists are easy to spot. They are Islam in its purest form. They are ISIS and Al Qaeda. They are the literalists who closely adhere to the original writings of Islam. They employ violent jihad like Mohammad and their ancestors did, striving for the Islamic goal of world domination."

"Where do you get off making claims like this?" demanded Elliott.

Hubert got testy, "Leave her alone! She's telling it like it is."

Mom answered Elliott. "I've spent ten years studying this. No one admits to being a terrorist in America. Everybody is a moderate. In 2007,

Pew Research Center took a poll of young American Muslims between the ages of 18 and 30. They found that 25% of them believed that suicide bombing was justified in defending Islam. Similar studies in other countries have shown comparable results."

"We're not ganging up on you, Elliott," Pastor Tom jumped in. "But the application of a little high school arithmetic and some common sense result in some rather terrifying conclusions. Do the math on it. There are 2.7 million Muslims in the United States. When you extrapolate the 25%, you get 675,000 potential suicide bombers in America. It will be a death sentence if we think that a great number of them are not waiting for the chance to blow us up."

Mom resumed, "We talked earlier about the Second Jihad. The Ottoman Empire ended during World War I, when it was defeated by the British. After suffering their first losses in the war, the Muslim Turks senselessly exterminated 1.5 million Christian Armenians by massacring the males, and driving the women and children in a death march into the Syrian Desert without food and water — murdering and raping as they went. Pope Francis called it the 'first genocide of the twentieth century.' In fact, it was in memory of this event that the word genocide first appeared in English dictionaries."

The Pastor spoke in a subdued tone, as if pondering the facts rather than making a bold declaration. "That happened only one hundred years ago. Islam is still the same today. If I may quote Erdogan, 'Islam is Islam.' If we are to survive, the model must be changed. We must face the facts. Not as we wish they were. But as they really are."

"How do you plan to change the model?" Omar asked.

"I'm afraid my answer to that question will alienate a lot of people. But I'm going to tell you what I think. In the end, Islam will unite its various factions against all non-Muslims."

"What makes you think that?"

"Mom Flink has been talking about expansionist Islam. In the times that Islam has expanded, it has been by bloodshed. I agree with her. We are in a season of expansion. When the time is right, terror will become the weapon of choice."

"But there are many good people in my religion. You need to recognize that," Omar insisted.

"Of course, I don't know anyone who doesn't agree with that. But radical Islam has shown its willingness not only to behead the non-Muslims, but fellow Muslims who resist the radical agenda. This has been the history of Islam from the beginning."

Omar spoke softly, surrendering to the truth of the statement. "It has been a problem."

"When Islam advances, then the closet radicals and cultural jihadists emerge to fill the ranks of violent jihad. And then the good, peace loving Muslims fall in. They are afraid not to. Better to march than to be decapitated. To break ranks is to perish. Islam will then be united in its offensive."

"When the consolidation takes place it is overnight and of paradigm proportions," added Mr. Ike. "There is no better example than the worldwide appeal and spread of ISIS as it beheads people in Libya, Iraq and Syria. Where would ISIS be today if it was not being resisted?"

"I don't like where this is going," Omar lamented.

"I know. Neither do I," stated the Pastor. "I don't want to say this. It is a fact none of us want to face. But if we are going to survive we must admit that the battle is ideological. The enemy is Islam itself."

"Then Osama bin Laden was right!" replied Omar.

"Why do you say that?"

"He said it was a war between Christianity and Islam."

Omar paused and then asked, "Do you have any solutions other than declaring war on Islam?"

"Like all other human issues, the Bible has the answer, Omar."

"I can't imagine what that could be," remarked Elliott.

The Pastor continued, "That each human being must be accountable for his own actions."

"How do we hold each one accountable?"

"We must separate the sheep from the goats. It will not be pretty. Non-jihadist, peace-loving Islam must join with us in the battle against their jihadist brothers. We must organize as a single fighting unit. Investigate, identify, isolate and neutralize the enemy one by one. It will be necessary to call names."

"Do you actually think that peace loving Muslims will join us?" asked Mom.

"I think that tens of millions of them will join us around the world, if we will step out and convince them that we are irrevocably committed to the eradication of Islamic jihad."

"Where do we do this?"

"The mosques of America will be a good place to start. Many have been and are seedbeds for radicalized youth. But all must be brought before a board of inquiry. Then we clean house in government, education, business and the media."

"That is ridiculous! You make Joe McCarthy sound like a saint," Elliott exclaimed.

"None of our options are good. Hopefully, Islam will police its own and be accountable to the culture that embraced it. If not, it must suffer the consequences."

"A lot of people will think this isn't fair!" Elliott objected.

"No, it isn't fair. Neither was it fair that 20 million civilians — innocent men, women and children — died in World War II because of the demented visions of Adolph Hitler."

"But that was war."

"That's the point. We have been at war since 9/11."

There was a short, unplanned pause in the conversation, which allowed us all to reflect on the gravity of the Pastor's words.

Mom broke the silence in a somber tone. "We were talking about the advance of Islam. The jihadist believes that the worldwide Caliphate is now within his reach. It was Osama Bin Laden who himself said, 'This is the Third Jihad.'"

She looked out across the great valley. What came next was more like thinking out loud than making a statement. "It's the final jihad. It will end here."

She recovered quickly from her pensive mood. "In this age of instant communication, the Arab Spring began in Tunisia and spread like wildfire into Libya, Egypt and Syria and has left the Middle East in flames. This was seen by the West as a welcome sign of populist demand for democracy and freedom. Instead, it has turned once stable nations into anarchy and chaos. It is not hard to see that it creates an environment for a strong regional power to take over bringing order out of the chaos. This fits the Islamic prophecies of the Mahdi, who it is believed will bring peace out of chaos."

"Let me add something here, if I may, Ma'am," asked Mr. Ike. "Division, strife and unrest are being fostered in our own country as well. Political leaders in high places are throwing gasoline on the fires of racial hatred and disrespect for authority, encouraging lawless riots in the streets. It is part of the devil's plan to turn us against each other."

"What does that have to do with the Middle East?" asked Elliott.

"It has everything to do with it. The spirit of lawlessness and division cannot be confined inside national boundaries. The Middle East, America and Europe are in an acute stage of civil unrest promoted by those who are orchestrating division and anarchy wherever they can. They envision order of a new kind coming out of the mess. It's called the New World Order. The loss of individual freedoms will be the price paid by the people."

"I can't believe anyone would intentionally foster anarchy to bring about change. Why would anybody want to do that?"

"Come on, Elliott. You weren't born yesterday. The revolutionist cannot seize control until the established system breaks down."

"I'll tell you what I'm afraid of," Hubert stated. "I'm afraid that some-body will slip across the border with a plutonium bomb in his backpack. The day that happens, it's all over. The government will take over."

"I know where you are going with this. You think that the President is a part of this so-called community of interest and that he wants to bring in a Socialist-Islamic State by creating strife, division and pandemonium among the people."

"He's doing a pretty good job at it, right now."

"Boys! Boys!" Mom interrupted. "Let's get back on topic."

SIBLING RIVALRY

Mom called for a break to stretch and allow heightened emotions to settle. It was a welcome relief, and for a few minutes there was laughter and chatter as the people milled about. A few headed for restrooms at the Welcome Center and others looked out over the great valley. When Mom stepped up to the front with mike in hand, most of the people began moving back to their places.

Mom began, "I hope you felt the ten minute vacation refreshing."

The people were still not settled down enough for Mom to begin her lecture. She said, "Let's wait a couple of minutes for everyone to find a place."

She paused for a moment, and with a pouty look on her face, exclaimed, "I miss Jasper."

"Tell them about Jasper, Mom," Maria egged her on.

"Jasper is my cat. He's adorable and sleeps with me every night. He is very conversational and loves to meow when I talk to him. I know I'm an indulgent parent. I feed him breakfast in bed every morning. He is so spoiled. If there are any cat lovers here, I would love to share photos with you after the lecture."

Hubert replied, "I have a cat joke…"

"You are not going to tell that joke, Hubert. It isn't funny," Ethel replied, before he could finish the sentence.

Mom smiled slightly at Hubert and then stated, "I would like for us to take a quick look at the major players in the Middle East today. In order to understand what is going on, it is absolutely necessary that we grasp one fact, which is that each of them, regardless of the particular branch of Islam embraced, is fiercely committed to the same goals. The extinction of Israel and the world dominance of Islam. And each wants to lead the final charge for world conquest. As a result, there is intense competition between them for dominance in the Middle East in order to position for that goal.

"This competition is a major key in understanding the Middle East and the unfolding of Bible prophecy pertaining to the end time. I suppose you could call it a form of sibling rivalry among the Arab states. At times, however, it is anything but a spat between brothers.

"The first leader to be reckoned with is the Supreme Leader of Iran. The Ayatollah Ali Khamenei. He is a Shi'ite cleric with a lifetime position as the Supreme Leader. The presidents may come and go, but the office of the Supreme Leader is a permanent fixture. Forbes lists him as one of the most powerful people in the world. He believes that Shi'ite Iran is the rightful leader of the Islamic faith and will lead Islam into a glorious future. Due to his age and bad health, he will not always be around. Looking at the field of those most likely to succeed him, there is little hope that his radical polices will not survive him.

"What is he like? What makes him tick? This is the man quoted as saying, 'The purest joy in Islam is to kill and be killed for Allah.'"

"Do you think there is anyone left who honestly thinks that Iran will not soon have the bomb?" asked the Professor. "The President has spearheaded a controversial nuclear deal with them that could have unimaginable consequences for the world."

"That is certainly the feeling of many smart people, Professor. In Iran's determination to become a world power, she has developed strong trade ties with Russia and China. The Russian - Iranian cohesion is based on oil and a common enemy, the United States. Russia supports Iran's plan for dominance in the Middle East.

"Iran is the backbone of Assad's regime in Syria and Hezbollah in Lebanon. It also is backing Hamas, a Sunni group, in its fight with Israel. And more recently, Yemen has joined the fold. Iran and Russia are arming these groups. Russia now has troops on the ground in Syria fighting rebels armed by the United States. It is easy to see why Iran is a serious contender for hegemony in the region. In addition to the support of the super powers, it has an army of over 500,000 men."

"Netanyahu would have destroyed her capability a long time ago, had it not been for the President." Hubert commented.

"There is always a bright side," stated Pastor Tom. "I am in contact with a young pastor there. He says there is a great revival of Christianity among the young people. God is launching a counter offensive in Iran."

"And in Latin America, Africa and China. At the present rate it is estimated that China may soon have more Christians than any other country on earth, including the US," commented Maria. "I just thought I would throw that in. The end time move of the Spirit is just beginning. Exciting times ahead!"

Mom continued, "Along with Iran's vision of a place at the table, she is vocal about her hatred of the United States. The government of Iran has issued policy statements referring to America as the Great Satan and Israel as the Little Satan, openly vowing to destroy both. These are official designations, not just temper tantrums. These are the trumpet calls to annihilate what they perceive as the two greatest obstacles to the rise of the Islamic global empire: the United States and Israel.

"A high level Ayatollah has stated, 'Israel will disappear from the face of the world once Islamic unity is achieved in the Middle East.'"

"God help us when they get the bomb!" interjected Mr. Ike.

I had my own ideas about the Middle East. It was my present assignment in the State Department in Washington. But I was fascinated by what my mother was saying. I asked, "Who are the other leaders?"

"The second person we need to watch in the Middle East is the President of Turkey. Tayyip Erdogan became President of Turkey in August, 2014, and before that served as its Prime Minister.

"A little history first. The Islamic Ottoman Empire began in Turkey in 1299 AD. The Christian name of Constantinople was changed to Istanbul. It was the capital city. When the Ottoman Empire came to an end in 1924, the more secular elements of Turkish society prevailed and they welcomed western values. Ankara became the new capital. In time, Turkey became an associate member of the European Union, joined NATO, and formed warm ties with Israel.

"Erdogan has been an Islamic activist from the beginning. He went to prison in 1998 for reciting poetry that glorified Islam's militaristic nature, putting him at odds with western secularism in Ankara. He is a Muslim to the core. After prison, he formed his own AK political party and was elected Prime Minister in 2003.

"Since then, he has changed the face of Turkey. Under his leadership, Turkey has been leaning toward the Islamic East, forsaking its friendship with Israel since the 2009 Gaza War. The Gaza Flotilla raid of 2010 by Israel, that killed nine Turkish soldiers, was an event that greatly enhanced Turkey's effort to distance itself from Israel and endear Erdogan to Muslims. The goal being, as one might suspect, to unite the Muslim Middle East under Erdogan rule.

"He sided with Hamas against Israel in the 2014 summer conflict, harshly condemning the airstrikes against Gaza. He overlooked the fact that the Israeli response was in reaction to the thousands of rockets that were being launched against Israel every day. He was quoted, 'their (Israel's) barbarism has surpassed even Hitler's.'

"His goal is to restore the Ottoman Empire to its former glory, by recapturing the lands once under its control. He has been quoted from a 2012 speech, 'On the historic march of our holy nation, the AK Party signals the birth of a global power and the mission for a new world order.'

"He is looked upon as a sort of god by his ardent followers. They have bestowed upon him a brand new mansion that has 3,200,000 square feet and 1,150 rooms.

"Don't be fooled by his claims of democratic rule, friendship with the West, nor his membership in NATO. Early on in his political career he was quoted as saying, 'Democracy is like a train. We shall get out when we arrive at the station we want.'

"Bashar Assad, the Shi'ite President of Syria, in a 2012 interview accused Sunni Erdogan of imperialistic ambitions, and went on to say that he thinks that he's a Caliph, and the new Sultan of the Ottoman Empire.

"Turkey is a Sunni nation and is aligned with the Muslim Brotherhood. To millions of Arabs looking for unification of Islam and the restoration of the Caliphate, Turkey probably has the most appeal as the candidate most likely to lead the charge.

"Erdogan understands what it is going to take to unite the Shia and Sunni tribes in the Middle East. It is their mutual hatred of the Jews. In a 2015 speech that got almost no coverage in the Western Press, he told a crowd of fellow Turks that it was time to refocus on the goal of re-taking Jerusalem, and to unite the Shia and Sunni tribes for that purpose."

Elliott quickly responded, "If all that is true, then why is he still in NATO?"

"It could be providential. He certainly will be in a strategic position to someday help unite the Middle East and the European Union.

"The third factor in the Middle East is the Muslim Brotherhood, or Ikhwan. There can be no meaningful analysis of Islam's pursuit of world dominion without recognizing the role of the Muslim Brotherhood. Although it vehemently condemns terrorism, it is the mother of Al Qaeda and Hamas. These two organizations are officially condemned as terrorist groups by the US government, while their mother organization is considered a moderate and held in highest esteem.

"While the US government sings its praises, Saudi Arabia, Egypt and the United Arab Emirates classify the Muslim Brotherhood as a terrorist organization.

"The Brotherhood is a transnational social movement that was founded in Egypt in 1928 by a Muslim scholar, Hassan al-Banna.

"Its purpose was expressed in its first motto, 'Believers are But Brothers.' The motto expresses the vision — the vision of uniting all Muslim believers of all nations in the pursuit of Islamic world dominion.

"The original slogan was later expanded. It gives a more detailed picture of their true identity. Let me read for you their five-point slogan:

1. Allah is our objective.
2. The Koran is the Constitution.
3. The prophet Mohammad is our leader.
4. Jihad is our way.
5. Death for the sake of Allah is our wish.

"The backdrop for the creation of the Brotherhood was the traumatic loss felt by all Muslims at the fall of the Ottoman Empire at the hands of the British in 1924. This event ended the last official caliphate on earth. There has not been one since. ISIS claims to have formed one."

"What is a caliphate?" Billy asked.

"A caliphate, Billy, is a group of nations under the rule of a single spiritual leader, a caliph."

"In my opinion," added Pastor Tom, "the Muslim Brotherhood is, hands down, the most dangerous Islamic group in the world."

"That's an interesting perspective. Why do you say that?" asked Mom.

"I say that because they are foxes in the hen house. The jihad they practice flies under the radar."

"You got it. They practice cultural jihad. The blueprint is found in its bylaws:

Make every effort for the establishment of educational, social, economic and scientific institutions and the establishment of mosques, schools, clinics, shelters, clubs as well as the formation of committees to regulate zakat affairs and alms.

"Cultural jihad is in sharp contrast to radical terrorism imposed by the sword. But they go hand in hand toward the common goal. The Brotherhood has successfully employed its social and political agenda for seventy-five years. The ultimate goal, like the terrorist, is the global Muslim Caliphate.

"The Muslim Brotherhood has the support of Turkey, Qatar, Tunisia, Libya, Hamas and a sizable wing of the Syrian rebels. They are in position to greatly influence the formation of a unified Middle East for the Anti-Christ. Or for that matter, the Mahdi, whom many Christian scholars, yours truly included, believe are one and the same."

I had been waiting for Omar to say something. I knew that the discussion was hitting close to home. I wasn't surprised when he stepped away from the fence where he had been standing and commented, "Let me say that I am absolutely intrigued with this idea of a united Middle East.

"My own nation, Saudi Arabia, to which I pledge my allegiance, is showing signs of mending old fences with the Muslim Brotherhood. The threat of Iran's growing influence will more than likely bring the Sunni nations closer together. I can see much more unity among old antagonists in the days ahead."

"What about ISIS?" asked Hubert.

Omar replied, "ISIS is an effort to establish the Caliphate. They were recognized early on as being very savvy in the use of social media and technology, and in recruiting fighters from other countries, including the United States. Their ultimate success, however, will not depend on the American-led coalition to contain them in Iraq and Syria, but on their ability to convince the Muslim world that they are, in fact, the heirs of Islamic prophecies that foretell a people who will bring back the Mahdi. I frankly don't believe they will ever be able to do that."

"Can I say something?"

"Sure, Professor," Mom responded.

"I don't believe that ISIS or any other overtly terrorist group will unite the Middle East."

"Why do you say that?"

"Because the Bible says that the Anti-Christ will appear as a man of peace. It also says that he 'by peace will destroy many.' His true nature as Satan incarnate will not manifest immediately, but only after he lures the nations into his trap. Then, his savagery will startle an unsuspecting world."

"Is ISIS a part of the Muslim Brotherhood, Mom?" Billy asked.

"The Brotherhood denies any association with any radical group. But the point is that ISIS came from al-Qaeda and al-Qaeda came from the Muslim Brotherhood. They have the same global vision of a World Caliphate. "

"May I comment?" asked Pastor Tom.

"Of course, you're the Boss."

"If it had not been for the Muslim Brotherhood, there would have been no al-Qaeda. If there had been no al-Qaeda, there would have been no 9/11.

"They have infiltrated every level of government. Like termites, they destroy from within. They work quietly and without detection. Many believe they are advising our military and the present Administration at the highest levels."

Omar immediately responded, "Your termite analogy is offensive. But I will have to agree, however, that your country has been very generous to my people. Many of those educated in your great universities have found a permanent home in America."

"I'm sorry if I offended you, Omar. I should have been kinder with my words."

Mom intervened, "I would like to mention one more thing about the Brotherhood that illustrates the influence of the movement worldwide. And then we'll move on.

"Sheikh Yusuf al-Qaradawi is the Spiritual Guide and spokesperson for the Brotherhood. He is a world famous Sunni theologian and Islamic scholar. His daily telecast on Al Jazeera TV is seen by 60,000,000 viewers worldwide. He is probably the leading jihadist in the world. He reportedly stated, 'We will conquer Europe! We will conquer America! Not by our sword but by our dawa!'"

"What is dawa?" Billy asked.

"It's like our evangelism, but more like proselytizing, using non-military means to spread Islam. It includes cultural jihad."

Omar spoke up, "Yusuf al-Qaradawi is very controversial in my country, but I had the pleasure of interviewing him for a documentary on Al Jazeera last year. He is a remarkable intellect, and probably one of the most popular men in the world."

"Please don't be offended, Omar, when I say that the fourth factor we need to watch is your own nation, Saudi Arabia. For the benefit of the rest of us, Saudi Arabia is the birthplace of Islam. It is also the number one oil producer in the world and the custodian of Islam's holiest shrines at Mecca and Medina. It is a Sunni nation and the Wahhabis branch is the dominant Islamic persuasion in the country. They are the extreme right wing in Islam. Osama bin Laden was a Wahhabi Sunni from a billionaire family in Saudi Arabia and, as you know, the founder of al-Qaeda.

"You have heard this already and it is a fact. Practicing any other religion than Islam in Saudi Arabia is illegal and there is not a single Christian church in the entire country. It is reported that public beheadings are common in the country and are carried out in the capital city of Riyadh for those who insult Islam or depart from the faith. This practice has been characterized by some as the most watched public spectacle in the country, other than soccer. The beheadings are internationally condemned because of the wide range of crimes to which they are applied."

I was frankly surprised that Omar did not comment. He bit his upper lip and looked away.

"The Wahhabis are rigid fundamentalists whom, many believe, are a bomb waiting to explode. Presently, the Saudis call themselves friends of the United States and we officially celebrate the friendship of this so-called moderate nation."

"Well, you know why," Mr. Ike remarked. "They are too busy pushing the cultural agenda of Islam in America to come out in the open. They don't want to blow their cover. Wasn't it King Abdullah before whom the President made his deep reverential bow right after he was elected?" he added. "I think the King passed away recently."

"Probably from shock," Hubert said, "from having the President of the United States bow before him."

I glanced at Omar. He had his hand over his mouth. He was snickering.

Mom continued, "Last, but not least, of the contenders for supremacy in the Middle East, is Egypt. The motto for the armed forces of Egypt is 'Victory or Martyrdom.' Approximately 500,000 men are active in military service. The Supreme Commander, Abdel Fattah el-Sisi, is also the President of the country.

"Eighteen days of demonstrations resulting from the Arab Spring forced the ouster of President Mubarak in 2011. Elections in 2012 overwhelmingly brought the Muslim Brotherhood to power under the leadership of Mohammed Morsi. In the spirit of the Brotherhood, he quickly dissolved the House of Representatives, fired top military leaders, and granted himself dictatorial powers.

"Public sentiment against him grew rapidly, with millions of protestors taking to the streets forcing his resignation. The military took over and since then the Supreme Commander of the military, el-Sisi, has been in power. Egypt is a major regional power with the strongest military in the Middle East, except Israel."

"I have another question, Mom. How does all this fit into what the Bible says about the last days?" asked Hubert.

I could tell that Mom was tired. I wanted to ask her if she was okay. It was like she read my mind, "Whew! Could somebody please turn the thermostat down?"

Maria reacted immediately with a cool fruit drink, which she had in a small sandwich cooler bag she had brought from the bus.

"Thank you, Maria, you are so precious," she stated. "Don't I have a beautiful daughter-in-law? They haven't set the date, yet. I hope it's soon.

"Okay, Hubert, to answer your question, let me say this. The prophetic significance of this struggle for dominance by the middle-eastern powers, is that a political entity will soon emerge from the Middle Eastern leg of the ancient Roman Empire, which will unify Islam and form the World Caliphate. It will unite with the Western leg, the European Union, to form the revived Roman Empire prophesied in the Bible. This combination of Eastern Islam and Western Christian Socialism will produce the Anti-Christ."

"Hmmm," the Professor added, "you talked about Turkey a while ago — that it is an associate member of NATO. Should your theory be correct about the unification of the Middle East with a Christian Socialist Europe combining to form the old Roman Empire, Erdogan might be the man most likely to pull it off."

Mom answered, "The mixture of Socialism, Islam and, now, Christianity has been going on for decades. But in the end, according to the Bible, the mixture will fall apart."

I was surprised that neither Omar nor Elliott had commented on this part of the discussion. Al Jazeera, in my opinion, was the poster-child for a united Socialism and Islam.

"Why do you think this Anti-Christ will come from the Eastern Division of the Roman Empire?" asked Omar.

"I will have a book out soon on that very topic, but let me touch lightly on one of the reasons, today. The Book of Genesis is the first book of the Bible and is called the book of beginnings. Many of the great doctrines of the Bible have their origin in Genesis and are developed in later books. In chapters ten and eleven we find the story of Nimrod. He was the founder of Babylon and later Assyria.

"Nimrod is almost universally recognized by Bible students as a type of the Anti-Christ. He was the first who sought to unify the world under a godless global government. He built the Tower of Babel, which not incidentally means 'confusion' or 'chaos.' It would certainly be in line with the doctrine of beginnings if the real Anti-Christ came from the same region.

"Many Bible scholars believe that one of the names of the Anti-Christ found in the Bible is 'the Assyrian.' I don't have time to go into it today, but I would think the best candidate for the role of Anti-Christ is a Muslim from that part of the world."

"You Christians and Muslims just need to tone it down, that's all," interjected Elliott, "you just need to let reason prevail and learn to live with each other like we infidels do."

COMPASSIONATE SOCIALISM

"I know some of this teaching may be depressing," Mom stated. "Unfortunately, we live in a world that is far from perfect. I wish for all our sakes that the world was a better place.

"The good news is that Jesus is coming soon, we will be caught up to meet the Lord in the air, and we will be forever with the Lord."

"You know, Mom," Pastor Tom stated, "the teaching of the Second Coming, which we once casually embraced as a doctrinal statement, is fast becoming the very anchor that will sustain us in the days ahead. We are to pray for His Coming. The last promise of the Bible is, 'I come quickly.' The last prayer of the Bible is, 'Come, Lord Jesus.'"

"Thank you, Pastor, for that word of encouragement. To be honest with you, I don't really like to talk about what is happening to our world, today. But it just so happens, that we apparently are the generation that God has chosen to be His witnesses for the Day of the Lord."

Mom was exuberant. She said, "Turn to your neighbor and say, 'You are blessed to be chosen for this hour.'"

The people responded almost inaudibly.

"Come on, I can't hear you! Say it like you mean it! Shout it out!" she exhorted.

The people responded with more gusto as they shouted to each other, "You are blessed to be chosen for this hour."

"Again!"

"You are blessed to be chosen for this hour!" They shouted at each other.

Mom continued, "Now, give somebody a big hug."

All the people were standing now. They greeted each other again, and found their places on the ground, improvised seats or near the metal fence. They were laughing and talking.

Mom began, "We learned earlier that Islam began the twentieth century by murdering 1.5 million Christian Armenians.

"Elliott, let me pick on you. Socialism has the bloodiest record of all for the twentieth century. Have you thought about it? The wars of the twentieth century: World War I, World War II, the Korean War, and Vietnam, were all caused by the aggression of Socialist government."

"I've heard that argument…"

"All of us need to be reminded of its evil history. The 1917 triumph of the Bolsheviks in Russia was a violent revolution and the international Communist Party was formed the next year. The program was the uniting of all the workers of the world for the coming world revolution. World War II resulted in the USSR invasion and occupation of Eastern Europe and Germany. By the end of the War in 1945, Berlin was divided and the nations of Eastern Europe had become Communist satellite states.

"The Communist revolution came to China shortly afterward. By the early 1960s, Communism had aggressively claimed almost half of the world's population. Its advance into other countries has been contained almost solely by the United States military. It could reasonably be argued that, were it not for the United States, the dream of Karl Marx for a worldwide Communist utopia would have already been realized.

"Communism in China has evolved from its Lenin principles into what it is today. While not abandoning its roots, it is a mixture of Communism, nationalism and capitalism. Its world presence is second only to the United States.

"And the spirit of Soviet aggression is alive and well. Russia and China are growing militarily. Putin seems intent on re-inventing the Soviet Union and is now taking over Ukraine. The Baltic States could be next. China is making statements that signal a future challenge to U. S. military presence in the Pacific and has surpassed the United States as the world leading industrial power. The European Union has chosen secular humanistic Socialism over Christianity and is leading the march to global government.

"With the United States forfeiting its world leadership role, Russia, China and Islam are racing to fill the vacuum. I don't believe that it is farfetched to assume that Putin and Xi Jinping are each entering the race to become the new world superpower that will command the New World Order.

"Few people are aware, Elliott, that Socialist governments have killed more of their own people in the twentieth century than enemies they killed in wars with other nations."

"That's preposterous! The reason I'm a Socialist is because Socialism is the most compassionate of all political philosophies. It distributes the wealth equally and cares for the poor and disabled. Your statement is preposterous."

"Oh, is it, now? Let me call your attention to a book entitled Death by Government, written by the recently late Dr. R. J. Rummel, professor emeritus at the University of Hawaii. He extensively researched the question of governments killing their own people between the years 1900 and 1987. His estimates do not include those killed in warfare with other countries. He admits that the figures are rough estimates and are probably mid-range between the highest and lowest estimates. The following is his list of mega-murderers of the twentieth century by name, country, estimated countrymen murdered, and years in partial and absolute power:

Stalin	USSR	42,672,000	1929 – 1953
Mao Tse-tung	China	37,828,000	1923 – 1976
Adolph Hitler	Germany	20,946,000	1933 – 1945

"There are several more socialist mega-murderers whom he lists, but these are the top three. You can check him out on the internet sources if you like. Decide for yourself.

"But I want to ask you a question. Do you recognize a common denominator in this list?"

Elliott didn't answer.

Mr. Ike responded, "They were all Socialists. They were all Marxists."

"Correct. Once its power is firmly established, Socialism has little tolerance for dissent in any form, especially evangelical Christianity. And the way they look at it, why should they tolerate dissidents who believe in a God higher than themselves?"

"Have you all heard about the recent document published by the United Nations?" the Professor asked. "It's a plan to reorder the world along the lines of socialistic principles. Its goal is to wipe out poverty and bring in a world of peace and prosperity. I can't remember the name of the document."

"You must be talking about Transforming Our World: 2030 Agenda for Sustainable Development?"

"Yes, that's it."

"You're reading my mind, Professor. That was the next point I was going to make. The document you referenced appears to be pointing to Socialism as the world model to solve all our problems. The Vatican has endorsed it with certain exceptions relating to abortion and gender identity."

"When you consider the genocidal record of Socialism in the twentieth century, one can't help but wonder why would we want to go that way in the twenty-first?"

"I can tell you why, Professor," Hubert exclaimed. "Because the world is believing the lies of the devil. The blind are leading the blind."

Mom continued, "In China, Christians who don't belong to the officially registered churches worship illegally. They are the house churches where tens of millions meet secretly to worship God.

"Christians in North Korea dare not share their faith, even with their families, for fear of imprisonment, torture, or even public execution. It is estimated by World Watch that somewhere between 50,000 to 70,000 Christians are imprisoned in the North Korean slave labor camps.

"Christian persecution is the number one civil rights issue of our time. The media and the United Nations just look the other way."

Elliott spoke up, "Your theory of the clashing of the so-called four winds is based on old data. Sweeping changes are taking place in the nations that were branded Communistic yesterday. The President of Russia believes in Jesus Christ. China has adopted capitalism. Our very own President has stated that America is no longer a Christian nation. Everything is changing."

"He has a point there, Mom. That the times are changing!" Hubert blurted out. "The Pope is now saying that atheists can go to heaven. I personally don't think he thought that one through."

"Yes, times are changing. And your trichotomy of Socialism, Islam and Christianity into major competing forces doesn't hold water anymore," replied Elliott.

Maria had not gone to sleep. "Well, if you think that is the case, I would suggest that you pass out gospel tracts on a street corner in Beijing, and see where it gets you."

Mom continued, "The big issue facing us all is the nature of man. This is particularly relevant in today's world, because of the technological revolution and the opportunity it affords the few to control the masses.

"The Bible's admonition for government leaders is as relevant today as it was in the days it was recorded. It is the answer to all our governmental problems. When David, King of Israel, died, his parting words were recorded in 2nd Samuel, chapter 23, verses 3 and 4. This is good:

He that rules over men must be just, ruling in the fear of God. And he shall be as the light of the morning when the sun riseth.

"Isn't that good? I love that verse."

"It would be a different world if all the leaders would listen to his advice," the Professor added.

"Yes, it would. Listen to Psalms, chapter 2, verses 10 through 12. I like the New King James on this one. I sincerely believe that the entire chapter is a specific word from God to all those in authority in this generation:

Now therefore, be wise, O kings; be instructed, you judges of the earth. Serve the Lord with fear, and rejoice with trembling. Kiss the Son, lest He be angry, and you perish in the way. When His wrath is kindled but a little."

Hubert spoke up, "In my opinion, the thing that made our nation great was that our people feared God. They believed they would be held accountable before God. They tried to do the right thing. That's it in a nutshell."

Mom continued, "Our founding fathers understood the nature of sin. For that reason, they built into the government a system of checks and balances that one branch of government...or to put it more accurately... that one man, or one group of people, would not be able to dominate the others.

"Despotic government by evil men is the real enemy and it comes in many forms. It can be Militaristic, Socialistic, Communistic, Fascist..."

"...Monarch, Dictator, Emperor, Caliphate..." asserted Elliott as he finished Mom's sentence, "I understand this, and we have already developed the technology for 24/7 surveillance by government."

"Yes, that's the point."

"Well, I for one, am willing to give up control of my life if it will keep me from being decapitated or blown to smithereens."

"For some of us it isn't that easy. That's not who we are," remarked Mr. Ike.

"Elliott," Mom resumed, "before we get too happy over the changing face of Socialism, let me read something here that might throw some light on where it is today."

"Go ahead."

"Okay, let me throw some facts at you: Reporters Without Borders, as you know, is the name of a French non-profit organization that defends the right of the public to be informed. Every year it publishes a World Press Freedom Index, which rates the nations according to freedom of the press. In 2014, Russia comes in at number 147 out of 180 countries, slightly ahead of China, which fell two slots to 175.

"I am sure you remember the recent murder of the Putin critic, Boris Nemtsov. He was charismatic. He was outspoken — and he was gunned down in cold blood. The New York Times ran an article with the headline, Fear Envelops Russia After Killing...'"

"I read it."

"Does it not raise a legitimate question as to whether the lethal reprisals of Lenin and Stalin against detractors is returning to Russian politics? The chilling effect on any meaningful opposition cannot be denied."

"But..."

"Let me finish, Elliott. Why should that surprise us? Since 1992, at least 50 journalists have been killed in Russia. In China, the numbers are even more startling. According to RWB for 2014 alone: 66 journalists have been killed; 119 kidnapped and 178 imprisoned.

"Are we immune to the loss of freedom in the United States? In the same index, the United States fell 14 places to number 46 in the ranking of the nations for freedom of the Press. That was an eye opener for me. Are we, as I speak, losing the freedom to express ourselves in the United States?"

A man wearing a straw hat and leaning back with his elbows on top of the iron railing, declared boldly. "Even if we can't fix it, God can. And when we get to the place that we realize we can't, that's when He will step in."

Mom didn't digress. "China is becoming capitalistic? So what? Big deal! China has slave labor camps for dissenters who make fashion clothing for Europeans and Americans.

"Russia is becoming more religious. So what? Big deal! It is still a police state ruled by the former director of the notorious KGB, Russia's secret police. It is still Socialistic and has taken back Crimea, is invading the Ukraine, and is putting boots on the ground in Syria. And this year, Putin is able to boast, for the first time in history, that he has more nuclear warheads in a state of readiness than the United States.

"The clash of the four winds is getting stronger as Socialism continues to grow and threaten the world against the countervailing winds of Christian evangelism and Islamic jihad."

Omar spoke up, "I think that all of us are being reminded, today, of the peril that hangs over the world. Mom, as you know, I am Muslim. Elliott won't admit it, but he's a hard core Marxist. You and your group are, I believe, true Christians."

"Thank you."

Omar continued, "Mom, earlier you answered Hubert's question about the significance of the struggle within Islam between the competing factions in the Middle East. I would like to broaden the question to the conflict between the Christian, Islamic and Socialist nations — or even broader to the clash between civilizations. Where is it going in your opinion? And how does Israel fit in?"

"The only answer I can give, Omar, is the Bible answer."

"That's what I want to hear."

"We have already covered the awful devastation of the Day of the Lord, and the rise of the Anti-Christ. He will unite the world for the first time since Nimrod who built the Tower of Babel. The ideological conflicts will temporarily be solved by bringing Islam, Christianity, Darwinian Secularism and Socialism together. It will be universally hailed as the New World Order. His attempt to mix the diversity of the world will last for a time and then will fall apart. We will discuss that a little later, today."

"And Israel, what will happen there?"

"We must understand that in God's eyes, Jerusalem is the center of the earth. It is the City of God the Great King. The Jews are God's chosen people. A Jewish couple gave the world the Messiah, with the promise that whosoever believed on Him would have eternal life.

"Israel was scattered among the nations because of the sins of the people. But God promised throughout the Scriptures that He would bring them back to their homeland in the last days. They have been arriving in a steady stream since Israel was declared a nation in 1948."

"May I say something?" asked the Pastor.

"Yes."

"Israel's future looks bright. In addition to the huge oil and gas reserves recently discovered, and the developing technology in the country, they are making plans for the construction of the Third Temple. An orthodox group called the Temple Institute has manufactured temple furniture, priestly garments, and hired an architect. It is soon. Very soon."

"Thank you, Pastor. Along the same lines of Israel's great future, let me mention one more thing before we take a break. In light of the present tension between Israel and the Socialist-Islamic coalition of Russia, China and Iran, there is an astounding 2500 year old prophecy found in Ezekiel 38 and 39. It states that Russia will lead a military coalition of Islamic nations against Israel in the last days. The prophecy states that the coalition will fall upon the mountains of Israel. Israel will win the war."

"There you go again, Mom," Elliott spoke up. "What possible chance would Israel have against Russia?"

"Don't underestimate God, Elliott. It will take place just as He said. It is well known, although not officially admitted, that Israel is a nuclear powerhouse with a delivery system that can reduce the Middle East to embers."

"They have everything that the United States has!" I heard myself blurt out as I grimaced and looked around to see if the others knew where the comment came from. It was too late. Omar and Elliott were looking at me quizzically. I knew I had an appointment with a video camera for the details of my statement. I resolved to keep my mouth closed.

"Then the Anti-Christ will summon all nations here to fight against the rightful heir of planet Earth, the Lord Jesus. He will be revealed from heaven with His mighty angels, in flaming fire taking vengeance on them who don't know God and who do not obey the gospel of the Lord Jesus Christ. He is coming back in the clouds to claim title to the world that He purchased with His own blood. The battle will take place here."

I looked out over the great valley. Three tiny specks of reflected sunlight caught my attention. They were coming up the valley straight at us. Three gnat sized objects in tight formation getting larger by the second. Their altitude seemed lower than my vantage point. "Why is there no sound?" I asked myself. I later surmised that they were flying so close to the sound barrier that their sound was barely escaping their speed. Before I could jump to my feet and say, "Look!" the roar of their engines hit like an explosion. Three Israeli Boeing 15 Eagle strike fighters, in tight formation, assumed vertical position right in front of us and with wide open throttles, disappeared over our heads into the clouds.

There were gasps and screams from the crowd, followed by a discussion about where on earth did they come from? Finally, we all settled down.

"Just a little entertainment from the IAF, folks," the Tour Guide explained. "The best trained air force in the world. Nothing to be concerned about. There's a little cowboy in all of us."

I thought to myself, "Israel is getting ready. Will it be enough to hold off the world?"

THE PRIME MINISTER

I looked up and the flight attendant was standing beside me. "Oh, Mr. Chandler, I'm sorry. I hope I didn't startle you. I wanted to tell you that we will soon be in Tel Aviv. Is there anything I can do to make the rest of your flight more enjoyable?"

"No, not really. Thank you."

I had landed at Ben Gurion International Airport several times before. The feeling was always the same. Each time, I recalled the ancient Jewish struggle for a homeland. It all began 3500 years ago when God called Abraham out of Babylon and brought him to the land that would eventually be known as Israel.

"This may be Providential." These were my startled words when I opened a magazine to an article that Maria had insisted I read, "Because it will help you understand the mindset of the Jewish people, and the prophetic role they will play in the last days."

I had no idea how the magazine had gotten into my stuff. I must have thrown it in my bag inadvertently. The article was entitled, *The Land of Israel — Whose Name is on the Deed?*

I looked at my watch and decided I would spend the last thirty minutes of the trip reading. I began:

Abraham was an immigrant from Babylon who didn't own one square foot of the land we now call Israel. He lived in a tent. The Lord spoke to him:

Genesis 15:18 "To your descendants I have given this land." NKJV

The family moved to Egypt to escape a great famine and eventually became slaves to the Egyptians. Over a period of 400 years they became a great nation of some 3,000,000 people. The oppression by the Egyptians became so severe that God raised up Moses to deliver them. He led them out of Egypt to the land that was promised to Abraham — the land of Canaan — today, the land of Israel.

A frightening principle is introduced in the Biblical account of Israel's ancient history. There are no exceptions to the rule. The principle is this: a nation by its sins can forfeit its legal right to its homeland.

God told Abraham that his descendants would not occupy the land of promise until the sins of the Amorites were full. The appointed time came when the sins of the Amorites and the Canaanites filled the cup of God's wrath over 400 years later. That cup was poured out on the peoples when Joshua crossed the Jordan to claim the promise that God had made to Abraham. He conquered the tribes, thus fulfilling the ancient prophecy to Abraham.

From that day to this — 3 and ½ millennia later — there has been no recognized independent state formed on that tiny piece of land except the nation of Israel. Although the Jews were scattered among the nations, a poor remnant remained (Jeremiah 52:14-16). Since the days of Joshua, there has never been a time when Jewish blood did not occupy the land.

God is no respecter of persons. Although they were God's chosen people, Israel was not exempt from the principle that its homeland could be forfeited. God warned them:

> Deuteronomy 4:23 Take heed to yourselves, lest you forget the covenant of the Lord your God which He made with you...25... and do evil in the sight of the Lord your God to provoke Him to anger, 26 I call heaven and earth to witness against you this day, that you will soon utterly perish from the land... 27 And the Lord will scatter you among the peoples, and you will be left few in number among the nations where the Lord will drive you. NKJV

The historical fulfillment of this Scripture is an incontrovertible fact. It cannot be denied. Israel was moved from their homeland and scattered among the nations.

I continued reading:

> But Israel was different from all other nations. She had an express written Covenant with God. He had given them the land. He promised to bring them back:

> Ezekiel 11:17 Therefore say, 'Thus says the Lord God: "I will gather you from the peoples, assemble you from the countries where you have been scattered, and I will give you the land of Israel."' NKJV

On May 14, 1948, the nation of Israel was born, thus fulfilling the Holy Scriptures.

I stopped reading and thought about the miracle of Israel, and how her very existence, was seriously threatened many times over the years. Speaking out loud, I exclaimed to myself, "It looked impossible in 1948. It looked impossible in 1967 when the tiny country defeated Egypt, Jordan and Syria and seized the Sinai Peninsula, Gaza, the West Bank, and East Jerusalem in six days. And it looks impossible now.

"It looks like it may be coming down to a battle even more unfair. Even more disproportionate. And a victory for Israel even more unlikely. Israel versus the rest of the world. It looks impossible this time as it did the times before. The Bible picks the winner. He who takes on Israel takes on God."

I thought of the Scripture found in the book of Zechariah, chapter 2, verse 8 in the New King James Version where the prophet reassures Israel of His love for them, "For he that touches you touches the apple of His eye."

I thought about how the prophet Isaiah who, in very troubling times, told the people that they had nothing to be concerned about. The reference is found in chapter 40, verse 12, of the prophet's book also found in the New King James Version:

(God) has measured the waters in the hollow of His hand, measured heaven with a span and calculated the dust of the earth in a measure... 15 Behold, the nations are as a drop in a bucket...

I was greeted by an outgoing young lady with an engaging smile and firm handshake as soon as I stepped onto the tarmac. "I'm Judy Horton, Administrative Assistant to the Ambassador. Welcome to Israel, Secretary

Flink. It is a pleasure meeting you. Your tireless efforts for peace in the region have not gone unnoticed. I hope you had an enjoyable flight."

"Oh, yes. It was wonderful. Meet Frank and Emery. They have been assigned to me by the Secret Service."

"The Ambassador sends his warmest regards and apologizes for his absence. He won't be able to make it. He said you would understand."

"He isn't going?"

"No."

"Yes, I think I do understand. Thank you."

"Good," she exclaimed, "you're bypassing Immigration and Customs, of course. This is Amos, your driver. Amos is aware that you are on a very tight schedule. I talked to the office of the Prime Minister a few minutes ago. He is at the Knesset this afternoon, meeting with his Cabinet. He is waiting for you."

"That was quick. The Ambassador is wasting no time in getting me to the Prime Minister," I thought, as we pulled away in a Hertz shiny jet black Land Rover. Frank and Emery were following a short distance behind in another one. In front of us were two Israeli police cars with emergency lights flashing, and two motorcycles behind us.

For the first five minutes, neither of us spoke. I guessed the driver was waiting on me to say something. But I couldn't. I wasn't able to pinpoint the cause of my emotional state, except I felt a deep concern that a colossal storm was developing and I was about to be caught up in it.

I shook it off and intentionally tried to think of something else. "This is beautiful countryside and sparsely populated," I declared, breaking the silence. "There is still a lot of room here for development."

"Yes, sir. It's amazing. We have learned to utilize every square inch of our tiny country."

"Amos, if I had to guess, I would say that you are in your early thirties and that you came to Israel from the United States. Tell me a little about yourself."

"I'm thirty-five years old and grew up in New York City. I am married and have one ten-year-old son. I had the good fortune to fall for a Christian lady whose prayers led me to Christ."

His upfront response took me by surprise.

"You are a Christian? A Messianic Jew?"

"Yes, sir. I was educated in New York and I was a freelance stockbroker with an office two blocks off Wall Street. I did that for twelve years."

"What brought you here?" I asked.

"Reading has always been my hobby. I began to see that Anti-Semitism was an even greater international problem than I had been told, and that it was rearing its ugly head in the streets, schools, and even in the churches of America. I decided that it was best for my wife and son to come to what I believe is fast becoming the safest place on earth for the Jewish people."

"You really believe that?"

"I know it. That's why thousands of Jews are arriving here monthly from all over the world. And some of our leading Orthodox Rabbis are saying that the coming of the Messiah is imminent. They are urging Aliyah as soon as possible. Aliyah is the Hebrew word for going up, and refers to immigrating to Israel, which is an action that will bring in the Messiah. They are calling for people all over the world to return to the homeland."

"I'm sure you understand that millions of Muslims that surround you are planning catastrophic disorder to bring back the Mahdi. He will destroy the Jews and Christians. Israel will be the front line."

"I understand."

"That doesn't bother you?"

"No. Not really."

"What about the fact that the United Nations Human Rights Council has issued more resolutions condemning Israel for human rights violations than against all other nations combined? And the UN's current consideration to prosecute your leaders for committing war crimes against Hamas last year."

"So?"

"The UN represents 193 nations. Doesn't that bother you?"

"Haven't you heard? Zechariah the prophet said all the nations of the world would be gathered against Jerusalem... and that the Lord would go forth and fight against them as when He fought in the day of battle. I like the odds. God is on our side. The Rabbis are right. The Messiah is coming! They just fail to recognize that His name is Jesus. But that day is coming soon. Many are turning to Christ."

"It's exciting, I must admit."

"And besides, the employment opportunities are greater here than in the US. Recent oil and natural gas finds in Israel's coastal waters, and even under the land, have finally laid to rest that old joke that Moses took the wrong turn at the Red Sea and left all the oil to the Arabs."

"Definitely. His chosen people will be exporting oil and gas to other nations." And then I asked, "What do you do here?"

"I trained as a night sniper for the IDF, and became active before the tunnels from Gaza were destroyed. I serve multiple roles in all three services. My rank is Second Lieutenant. I'm a platoon leader.

"My primary interest is cyber security, however. I hope to land a job with the German Franhofer Institute, the biggest cyber-tech firm in Europe. They are coming here. On top of that, Microsoft, Google, IBM and almost all the Internet and high tech giants have located research and development centers here already. We are the New Silicone Valley and we are thinking global.

"But today, I am honored to serve you, Mr. Secretary," he stated, confidently smiling.

I began to like him already. His exuberant faith was rubbing off on me.

My mind went immediately to the prophecy of Ezekiel who foretold a Muslim coalition, led by Gog, whom many believe is the Anti-christ, that would invade Israel in the last days. I reached for my New King James

Bible that Maria had bought for me the Christmas before. It was in my carry-on.

"Amos, I want to read you a Scripture. It is found in the book of Ezekiel, chapter 38, verses 8 through 9. Listen, to this:

After many days you will be visited. *In the latter years you will come into the land* of those brought back from the sword and gathered from many people on the mountains of Israel, which had long been desolate; they were brought out of the nations, and now all of them dwell safely. You will ascend coming like a storm, covering the land like a cloud, you and all your troops and many peoples with you...

"Now, if we skip on down to verse 21, we will see the finale of the great battle:

"I will call for a sword against Gog throughout all my mountains," says the Lord God. "Every man's sword will be against his brother. And I will bring him to judgment."

"What a plum she has become," I commented, "the prophecy states that there will be a military invasion against Israel in the last days from the north, and that those who come against her will die upon the mountains of Israel."

"It's fun to watch God work, when He's up to something," Amos exclaimed. "Let me show you something."

He began to point out locations of battles along Highway 1 that would take us up to Jerusalem, including battles for Israel's independence, and ancient wars, as well. War memorials dotted the landscape, which he said were "constant reminders of the awful price our fathers paid for freedom and independence. We must keep constant vigil in our nation's struggle for survival."

He was a reservoir of information, pointing out routes travelled by the Romans, the Crusaders and the Maccabees on their journeys through the land.

"Over there," he pointed, "is where Joshua commanded the sun to stand still and it didn't go down for a whole day, giving Israel a great victory over the Amorites."

"And he will do it again, Amos. The promise He made Joshua was, 'Nothing shall be able to stand before you all the days of your life.' God hasn't changed. He is still the same. The promise is yours as well."

"I know. I'm counting on it."

As we approached Jerusalem, I saw some old rusted military vehicles that were left in place as reminders of Israel's fight for independence in 1948.

I thought to myself, "The biggest fight is yet to come. Thank God that we know who comes out on top. The devil will be defeated and cast into the Lake of Fire."

"Amos, the almond blooms are absolutely gorgeous. There must be trillions of them."

"I know. I don't think I have ever seen them more beautiful."

For the next few miles I took in the dazzling display of God's creation. The almond trees were in full bloom. They lined the streams and were splattered across the green fields. Large groves were planted in neat rows along the highway, awaiting harvest. Delicate white and pink hues adorned faraway mountains. I was unable to contain the words any longer, "Praise God. Thank you, Jesus."

"Yeah, I know what you mean," Amos responded, apparently reading my mind, and went on to say, "Mr. Secretary, do you know the meaning of the almond tree to the Jewish people?"

"Yes, I've heard the story before. But please refresh my memory."

"The almond tree blooms in the dead of winter, heralding the coming springtime and harvests. It is the first to bloom. It is the last to bear fruit. It has special significance to my people.

"The legend began with the prophet Jeremiah. He was little more than a child when God called him to be a prophet. He was told that he would speak the words of God and that the words that he spoke would determine the fates of the nations.

"He prophesied against his own people, because they had forsaken the God of Abraham and burned incense to other gods. He said that kings from the north would invade Judah and set up their thrones in the gates of Jerusalem. And like the holy prophets before and after him, he prophesied the dispersion of Israel among the nations and the regathering in the last days to their homeland."

Amos continued, "God asked Jeremiah, 'What do you see?'

"Jeremiah answered, 'I see the branch of an almond tree.'

"To which God replied, 'I will watch over my word to perform it.' The word *watch* used here is translated from a Hebrew word meaning *to watch or be wakeful.* Just as the almond tree blossom *awakens* the promise of the coming spring, it also signifies that God will stay awake to see that His promises to Israel are fulfilled."

"And the promise, again?"

"That the Messiah will come and rule the world from Jerusalem, and Israel will be exalted to the top of the nations, and there will be peace throughout the earth."

"Now I remember. From looking at the blooms here today, you are going to have a great year."

"Yes, and it also teaches us that we must be patient to reap the harvest. The almond is the last to ripen, at the end of the fruit harvest. The Messiah is our hope. He will come at the appointed time. We will be patient. We will be ready for the harvest."

The scenes went flying by and neither of us spoke for a time. "Hey Amos, Can we take a restroom break at this station coming up?"

A few minutes later, we were standing in front of a cash register with drinks and snacks in hand and I was fumbling for a credit card. "How much are these?" I asked, pointing to almond branches in full bloom, neatly arranged in a large water vase on the counter.

The attendant was an elderly lady who had to be near retirement age, "Aren't they precious?" she said. "I picked them myself.

"And do you know what?" she asked.

"No ma'am. I don't."

"I felt that I should pray over this one here!" She said, picking it out from the group. "It is so perfect. I asked Jehovah God to find it a home in the hand of the person most in need of a miracle."

"I'll take it."

Thirty minutes later, I was being ushered into an office in the Knesset building to meet with Prime Minister Benjamin Netanyahu.

"Would you like some tea? Some coffee?" the receptionist asked.

"No, thank you."

"It just so happens that the Prime Minister is here today. He told me to call the minute you arrived. I am sure he will be here soon."

"This is incredible!" I thought, "I was carrying out my mundane office duties three days ago in the State Department Building, and presto, here I am in the office of the Prime Minister of Israel, caught up in some sort of unknown international maelstrom that affects the world."

Quite frankly, I was perturbed and embarrassed that I didn't know the contents of the message from the President. I grimaced and shook my head. For the last year, I had been the go-to guy in the State Department in matters pertaining to the Middle East. This time I was being left out of the loop and it appeared I would have to settle for the role of messenger boy. I quickly became philosophical and rebuked myself for being so silly, and not being enthusiastic about any assignment that served my country.

I walked to a window overlooking the City of God the Great King — Jerusalem. Nothing could have prepared me for the moment. I thought, "What will we discuss? Am I ready?"

Other thoughts were racing through my mind. "There is the Peace Accord. It has no hope unless the Palestinians are willing to recognize the Jewish State and its right to exist." I reasoned. "Even though Israel has agreed to a two-state solution, the Palestinians haven't budged. Tony Blair did a great job, but he hit a brick wall.

"And there is the Palestinian demand that Israel return to the boundaries pre-dating the 1967 Six Day War. It would leave Israel totally helpless. Can you imagine living in a country only nine miles wide?

"And then there were the times that Israel gave up land for peace. She withdrew from Gaza and South Lebanon. What did she get? Thousands of rockets from Hezbollah and Hamas from the lands she surrendered in her quest for peace."

I chided myself for not being a better diplomat, "Your job is to see both sides and try to work out a compromise."

I thought about statements made by the Prime Minister in past years that showed his resolve. I was thoroughly convinced he was not someone to mess with. At Auschwitz in 2010, he spoke in memory of the 6,000,000 Holocaust victims — one-third of the world's Jewish population — murdered by the Nazis. He reasserted Israel's right to defend itself and warned that new Amalekites were appearing who were once again threatening to annihilate the Jews:

> We will not allow it…We will never forget… I promise as the head of the Jewish State… that never again… will we allow the hand of evil to sever the life of our people.

At Yad Vashem, the memorial to the Holocaust, in January of 2015, he said:

> Those who try to challenge us within our borders will discover that we are ready to respond with force…those who play with fire will get burned.

And again, the historic speech before the joint session of the US Congress in March 2015, he uttered these prophetic words, "Even if Israel has to stand alone, Israel will stand."

"That is exactly what the Bible teaches," I thought. "Israel will someday stand alone — before the United Nations without the United States."

I reflected on the sparse audience in attendance, at the speech of Prime Minister Netanyahu, before the United Nations General Assembly, in October 2015. The State Department reported that Secretary Kerry, and UN Ambassador, Samantha Power, were unable to attend because they were called into a video conference by the President, only moments before the Prime Minister began his speech.

I thought how that for forty-four seconds, Netanyahu looked down on the assembly in total silence, to symbolize the deaf ear that the world was turning to a nuclear Iran — that has sworn to kill every Jew on the face of the earth.

I knew that military analysts had long discussed the defense strategy called the Samson Option — how as a final resort, Israel could unleash on her attackers massive nuclear force, even if it meant her destruction. This prospect would possibly deter rational minds, but with Iran's suicide bomber mentality, I thought how it could be an incentive to attack in order to unleash the chaos that would bring back the Mahdi.

"Where is all this going, Lord?" I asked. "We can only pray that Israel's resolve will remain firm, and that her enemies remember Masada and be persuaded that she will take it to the limit."

I knew from the Scriptures, however, that there would come a time in which it looked so hopeless that the Anti-Christ would persuade Israel to enter into an agreement that would divide the land. And that the Anti-Christ would later break the covenant with them and entice the world to come against them. Daniel, chapter 11, verses 36 and 39; and Joel, chapter 3, verse 2, came to mind from the King James Bible:

And the king (Anti-Christ) shall do according to his will; and he shall exalt himself, and magnify himself above every god, and shall speak marvelous things against the God of gods... He shall magnify himself above all... *and shall divide the land for gain.*

I will also gather all nations, and will bring them down into the valley of Jehoshaphat (judgment), and will plead with them there for my people and for my heritage *Israel, whom they have scattered among the nations, and parted my land.'*

The Bible is emphatic. Israel will be saved in troubled times, during the last days. The New King James Version repeats the words of Moses, to the children of Israel over fifteen hundred years before Christ. It is recorded in Deuteronomy, chapter 4, verse 30:

> *When you are in distress, and all these come upon you in the latter days,* when you turn to the Lord your God and obey His voice 31 (for the Lord your God is a merciful God), He will not forsake you, nor destroy you, nor forget the covenant of your fathers which He swore to them.

Again it states in Jeremiah, chapter 30, verse 7:

> Alas! For *that day is great, so that none is like it; and it is the time of Jacob's trouble, but he shall be saved* out of it.

I began to sense an inner joy over the promise of the deliverance of my people. "My people?" I chuckled, "I never called them 'my people' before."

I had my back to the door. I didn't hear him come into the room. "Greetings, Mr. Flink!" his voice boomed like a cannon. I jumped and turned quickly to see the Prime Minister advancing toward me with his hand outstretched and smiling ear to ear. "Welcome to Jerusalem. It is a pleasure to have you. Can I call you David?"

Catching me totally by surprise, I must have spoken the last thought on my mind. Extending my hand toward him, I spoke earnestly and with a straight face, "I am Jewish!"

"You're what? You're Jewish?" He asked, laughing out loud.

"I didn't mean to say that. I don't know where it came from."

He continued laughing, "It's a new revolutionary approach to diplomacy. I like it. Shows great finesse. Kerry should give you a raise."

He invited me to sit down in one of two office chairs in front of a huge desk. He pulled the other one out from the desk and sat down facing me. After a few questions about my trip and my family, he got to the point. "Why are you here, David?"

I reached for my briefcase and retrieved an envelope with the Presidential Seal prominently displayed. Contrary to my expectations, he broke the seal and opened it in front of me. Unfolding the letter, he looked at the message inside. He showed no emotion. Not five-seconds later, he slowly and deliberately refolded it, put it back in the envelope and stuck it in his inside jacket pocket. Then biting his lower lip, he glanced to the side and slightly downward as if transfixed on some far away object. I knew from his body language that he was deeply troubled by what he read.

I had been fearful of the contents of the letter from the time it had been handed to me by the State Department courier. "I hope I have been a messenger of good news." I stated.

Without responding, he arose to his feet, turned, and walked to the window where I had been standing when he walked in. He stood there silently with his back to me for several minutes without saying a word. Finally, he turned to face me.

His facial features had noticeably hardened. He looked like a different man. He was postured as if to ward off an attack. Yet when he spoke, it was with the quiet authority of a brigade commander who is confident that his battle strategy is working and that victory is hours away. His words were measured and firm, "Thank you very much, David. This message does not require a response at this time. You are free to go. I wish you a safe trip to the US."

"There is one other thing, Sir."

I pulled the briefcase from the floor into my lap. The almond blossoms had been wrapped in white tissue paper and adorned with a pink ribbon. I held it up for him to see.

"The lady who gave me this blossom is like the thousands who flee anti-Semitism each year from many parts of the world. She came to Israel fleeing the Soviet persecution of the '70s. Like those who came before her and after her, she has suffered much. But thanks to people like you, she now sits under her own vine and fig tree in her ancient homeland. She and her husband run a thriving business. She told me that she had prayed over the almond branch and said, 'I believe it will bless a special person, today.'"

He didn't respond.

I kept on, "I have no idea what was in the letter you received from the United States today. I sense in my spirit, however, that the news was not good. I want you to know that there are tens of millions in America who love you and love Israel. And we pray for you every day."

Extending my hand with the almond branch I implored, "Please receive this. Someday when I return to Israel, I will tell her about the man she blessed."

Still silent, he reached to receive the gift. Clutching the stem and looking at the blooms, he said, "I receive this as a sign from God. It reminds us that in the winter seasons, God has promised our best days are ahead. Praise the Lord God of Israel who has renewed our hearts today."

Then he embraced me. "Thank you, David!"

It was as distinct as the sun coming out from behind a cloud. His countenance changed immediately. The brigade commander was back!

"Please relay a message to your President for me."

"Yes, Sir."

"Even if Israel has to stand alone, Israel will not be alone."

And then he left.

I stood motionless for a second and tried to put together what had just happened. It defied protocol. I felt incredibly optimistic. "You know," I said, still looking at the door, "If things keep going like they are now, in five years Israel won't need the United States."

"Where do we go from here, sir?" Amos asked as I settled back into the car.

"Tel Aviv. And let's get there as quickly as possible. I'm exhausted."

"Sure, Mr. Chandler."

I adjusted the front passenger seat, trying to get as close as possible to reclining flat on my back. Closing my eyes, I vowed that I would sleep on the way back. Amos peeled rubber as our car sped away from the curb.

It was no contest. The churning I felt in my stomach told me that I was not going to sleep. I opened my eyes and watched the street scenes slide into the past. I couldn't put my finger on what was causing a deep sadness inside. I knew if I would just wait silently, it would soon surface.

"What is this about, Lord?" I asked.

It only took a few minutes for Him to answer me. I was using the voice memo on my smart phone to jot down some of the major points of my visit with the Prime Minister when it hit me. "I don't want to leave Jerusalem. That's why I'm sad," I said out loud as I sat upright in my seat.

"What?" Amos enquired. "Do you want to turn around and go back? Did you forget something?"

"Oh, nothing. Nothing. I'm okay." I softly reassured him as I lay back down. "Just an identity crisis."

"A what?"

"It's nothing, Amos. I'll be alright."

It was beyond reason and logic. Something I am not able to fully describe. I thought about what my dad said to me once when I was a kid,

"Son, the day is soon coming for all Jews when they will hear the sound of a hiss deep inside them. It will be the call to come home. Someday you will hear it. And when you do, you must obey it."

And then he quoted Isaiah, chapter 5, verse 26, in both Hebrew and English:

And he will lift up an ensign to the nations from far, and *will hiss unto them from the end of the earth; and, behold, they shall come* with speed swiftly.

I remember asking him, "Dad, what is a hiss?"

"Oh, it's sort of like a soft whistle. Like when bees are hissed from their hives. God will call you. He will hiss for you. You will know it, son. You will know it."

I was leaving Jerusalem, but I knew that I would be back. I whispered a prayer for the Prime Minister.

"Amos, I'm going to take a nap."

I closed my eyes and saw my mother standing before our group in Megiddo nine months before. I wanted to hear the rest of her lecture.

THE GREAT MIX DECEPTION

Our group had taken a break and had just resettled to hear more of Mom's lecture. She began, "The Bible predicts that strong deception shall prevail over the earth before Christ returns. It will be a time of embracing delusions and denying the obvious."

"Where is that found in the Bible?" Omar asked. He was now sharing a Bible with one of the group.

"Jesus said that the devil is a liar, and that his lies will increase as we approach the end of the age.

"Omar, would you read II Thessalonians 2 beginning, let's see, with verses 8 through 11, please?"

The lady with whom he shared a Bible said, "Here. I have it right here, Omar." She handed it to him. Omar took it in both hands and cleared his throat.

Maria turned toward me with her mouth and eyes open wide and then whispered, "Do you believe this? Omar is going to read the Bible."

"You look like a tent meeting preacher, Omar," Pastor Tom carefully kidded him.

"I'm not sure, but I think that was a compliment, Pastor. Okay, I have it. It's the New King James. Here it is:

And then the Lawless One will be revealed, whom the Lord will consume with the breath of His mouth and destroy with the brightness of his coming. The coming of the Lawless One is according to the working of Satan, with all power, signs and lying wonders, and with all unrighteous deception among those who perish, because they did not receive the love of the truth, that they might be saved. And for this reason God will send them strong delusion, that they should believe the lie.

Omar looked up from the page. "This is provocative stuff! So, the Anti-Christ will deceive the world."

"Yes."

"I think I get the drift where this is going," Omar stated, "The truth that the world has rejected is that Jesus is the Savior..."

"Right, and the deception they will embrace is that the Anti-Christ is the true Christ – the Messiah – the Savior of the world."

Omar didn't respond. He handed the Bible to the lady beside him.

"In fact, Omar, it will soon get so bad, during what the Bible calls the Great Tribulation, deception will be mandated by law and be enforced by the Mark of the Beast. You either buy into the lie or die.

"The devil is very clever. And he is now preparing the peoples of the world to accept the New World Order, and its ultimate leader and agenda.

"He is doing it gradually. Like the frog in the kettle, we don't realize that we are being boiled alive because of the gradual increase in the heat.

"One of his weapons is the making of globalism chic and associated with that which is pleasant. It has become a craze. You're a member of the Ku Klux Klan or a bigot, if you don't admit that the coming One World will solve all our problems. Globalism has become the dominant theme of our time.

"The devil's end game, whatever it may appear to be, is always control. He wants to control the individual. He wants to control America. He wants to control the world.

"Maria, did I give that list to you about …"

"Yes, I have it here in my Bible."

Mom kept talking as she walked over to Maria, "Someone has published a list of mottos or slogans that are found in our culture that illustrate our fascination with all things global. It probably has no real significance otherwise — other than we are obsessed with the topic — and are being conditioned to accept the idea of the New World Order."

Using one hand because of the Bible she held, and using her teeth, she managed to open the single sheet of paper.

"Okay. Here are a few of the popular mottos and slogans you may recall: The Airline Alliance: One World; American Airlines: One World; and Visa: Go World. And do you remember this one, the China Olympics: One World One Dream?

"Retailers of popular fashion lines for women have marketed: One World Designer Dresses, One World Purses and even One World Pajamas."

Hubert reacted, "Ethel already has a One World purse. She has everything in the world in it."

"The list goes on and on." Mom continued. "Some books published in recent years include those with the following titles: One World One Family; One World One Day; and One World Ready or Not, on and on it goes ad infinitum.

"There is also a World Book Day, Oneworld Publications and a One World Observatory in New York City," interjected Mr. Ike.

"Thank you," Mom replied. "One international group representing over 400 of the world's largest banks is calling for a One World Currency.

The United Nations has been calling for it for some time. It is reported that the G20 nations are committed to that goal."

"Global is the most-used adjective in the news these days," added Mr. Ike. "You have Global Initiative, global challenges, global climate."

Mom cleared her throat, sipped some water and asked, "Are you still with me?"

The reply was a hearty "yes" from the crowd.

"It's what I call the rush to world government. It is happening so fast that it is hard to keep up with it."

"The Pope is certainly advancing the agenda," the Professor commented, smiling. "He is something else. He is calling for a world political authority."

"That sounds like world government to me," exclaimed Hubert.

"Well, in my opinion," Elliott loudly interjected, "this Pope has it together. If you remember, he made the cover of Time Magazine as the New World Pope. From the first day, he has made it clear that the ecumenical unity of world religions is at the top of his priority list. He believes that Muslims and Catholics worship the same God. And he is reaching out to American pastors who are now saying that the protest is over. Some of the pastors of the American charismatic mega-churches have visited him at the Vatican."

"It doesn't stop there," Mom reacted, "he has invited Muslim leaders to the Vatican to pray. He strongly condemns those who say that Islam is a violent religion.

"And what about mainline Christianity? It is embracing Chrislam as Christian leaders make historic concessions with Muslim leaders, trading pulpits, attending ecumenical conferences and saying publicly that they pray to the same God. The two largest religions in the world are coming together.

"What do you say about this Pastor?" Mom asked.

"Thank you. There will be two Christianities in the last days. One will be true and one will be false. The false will rush to mix with Socialism, Islam and materialistic Secularism. The true will cling to the faith that was once delivered to the saints and confront the popular culture with the true message of globalism — that God loves all men everywhere and commands them to repent of their sins."

"And what significance do you see in the Pope's appearance before both houses of Congress?" the Professor asked his old classmate.

"Other than being historic as a first in American history, this has far greater significance than a one world tag on a pair of pajamas at Walmart. This is major league."

"What do you think it means?"

"It's all about getting rid of our differences and coming together in a world community. The sad part is that we have rejected the Good Shepherd and are like sheep scattered upon the mountains. The False Shepherd is waiting in the wings."

The Pastor nodded at Mom indicating that she could proceed.

"Another deception I want to talk about this afternoon is one that has reached epidemic proportions and, like an epidemic, it is spreading rapidly across the world. It is the world perspective that man, in his sinful condition can, without the help of God, peacefully blend together the characteristics that make us different from each other. The characteristics of race, nationality, ethnicity, gender, age and religion.

"God is so beautiful and man is the crown of His creation. He loves us so much with all the beautiful diversity He put in us. But because we have rejected Him as well as His love, we are filled with prejudice, hate and intolerance.

"The best example of the failure of the mix is in the European Union. We discussed it earlier this morning under the heading of multiculturalism. It is failing miserably in Europe. The sum of it is that it isn't working at all.

"Europe was supposed to be the center-piece of multiculturalism. They were blissfully optimistic in the year 2000. That was the year when the European Union adopted the phrase Unity in Diversity as its official motto in all of its 22 different languages. It expressed the hope of unity in mixing the cultural diversity brought on by liberal immigration policies. Today, Europe is hardly the poster child for multiculturalism. They openly admit that it isn't working.

"The Holy Spirit years ago showed me there would come a time when the entire world, for reasons of survival, would seek to resolve its conflicts by attempting to blend world-views."

"Listen up, Omar," pled Elliott, "this is going to be right down your alley. All that stuff about the Last Day."

Omar responded with a slight smile and an affirmative nod.

Mom cleared her throat and took another sip of bottled water.

"We started our study with the Biblical metaphor of winds striving upon the Great Sea and how they are playing out today in ideological clashes around the world.

"Now I want to refocus our attention on the Great Image metaphor in the writings of Daniel, which we discussed earlier."

"The Great Image." Billy stated, sipping a fruit drink he got at the Welcome Center. "Oh, boy! I was hoping we would get to that again."

"You like that, Billy? Well, it just so happens that it has more meaning for you, probably, than the rest of us. As a millennial, the great prophet Daniel will minister to you, today, about the day in which you live, as well as the days ahead."

"That's cool!" he exclaimed, as he high-fived a friend next to him.

"The Great Image is found in Daniel chapter 2. It records a dream of the great Babylonian King, Nebuchadnezzar, and its interpretation by teenager Daniel, who was being groomed by the King's closest advisors to someday advise the King.

"Nebuchadnezzar was scared out of his wits by a great metal image he had seen in his dream. Daniel assured him that God had the interpretation of what it meant.

"Daniel told him essentially that the metal image was a time graph, depicting not only his great empire, but other Gentile world powers which would follow him. It had a head of gold, chest and arms of silver, belly and thighs of brass, legs of iron, and feet of iron and clay.

"Daniel told him that he was the head of gold appearing first in time, and that the feet of iron and clay, appearing last in time, would see the Kingdom of God destroy the kingdoms of the world. I don't know of any serious prophetic Bible scholar who does not agree that we are living in the days just before the kingdom of iron and clay feet manifests.

"Are you still with me?" Mom asked.

After a convincing response from the crowd Mom resumed, "For an overview, let me recap here the kingdoms signified by the different metals:

The Gold: The Babylonian Empire 612-539 BC
The Silver: The Medo-Persian Empire 538-331 BC
The Brass: The Grecian Empire 330-63 BC
The Iron: The Roman Empire 63 BC – 476 AD

The Iron and Clay: The Revived Roman Empire yet to come.

"Next, the Great Image had two iron legs, which foretold the historical division of the Roman Empire into the Eastern and Western civilizations known today as the European Union and the Middle East.

"Okay. Now, could you read from Daniel 2, beginning with verse 41, and read through verse 43, Billy? Do you have a New King James Version? It captures the meaning of these verses very well in my opinion."

"Sure, let's see. Okay, here it is:

Whereas you saw the feet and toes, partly of potter's clay and partly of iron, the kingdom shall be divided; yet the strength of the iron shall be in it, just as you saw the iron mixed with ceramic clay. And as the toes of the feet were partly of iron and partly of clay, so the kingdom shall be partly strong and partly fragile. As you saw iron mixed with ceramic clay, they will mingle with the seed of men; but they will not adhere to one another, just as iron does not mix with clay."

Mom hesitated, as if she was soberly measuring her next words. Finally, she stated, "I say this as humbly as I can. I spent years struggling with the meaning of this verse. Here is what I believe the Lord has shown me. The mixture of iron and clay is found in both feet of the Great Image. The debate in the past has centered on the meaning of what the iron represents and what the clay represents. For example, the iron represented the European Union and the clay represented the Islamic nations of the Middle East."

"What do you think, Mom?" Billy asked.

"Read it carefully. The emphasis is not on what the iron and clay represent. What is stressed is the attempt… the attempt to mix or mingle what will not hold together. And the failure to mix them. That is what it plainly says. It is the attempt to mingle the seed of men — which is the dream of the New World Order — to mingle the nations, ethnicities, cultures, religions and civilizations. In other words, the seed of men. One world. One government. Without God or His Son. That is the plan.

"It is the biggest lie of our time. It is the Great Mix Deception. The idea that we can build a New World Order where Christianity, Islam, Darwinism and secular Socialism can all come together in one big happy family. We can leave God out of the picture and peacefully co-exist.

"Nimrod tried it almost four thousand years ago when he built the Tower of Babel. It ended in confusion and chaos."

"Where do you think it goes from here?" Hubert asked.

"I know what happens next, Mom," Billy exclaimed. "Can I answer his question?"

"What happens next, Billy?"

"Let me read it for you. It is part of the Scripture I read a few minutes ago. Daniel told Nebuchadnezzar what he saw in his dream in verses 34 and 35:

You watched while a stone was cut out without hands, which struck the image on its feet of iron and clay, and broke them in pieces. Then the iron, the clay, the bronze, the silver, and the gold were crushed together, and became like chaff from the summer threshing floors; the wind carried them away so that no trace of them was found and the stone that struck the image became a great mountain and filled all the earth."

"What is the stone, Billy?"

"I think the Stone is…Jesus. He is coming again. He will destroy the kingdoms of this world and set up the Kingdom of God."

THE ANGEL

The time had passed so quickly from Jerusalem to Tel Aviv, that I was shocked when we drove into the entrance of the hotel. Amos said, "Mr. Secretary, we are here. It has been a pleasure driving you, today."

In a few minutes I was in my room. I was bushed. I had been locked in fast-forward for three days with no letup in sight. The bellman was courteous and I tipped him generously before discarding my jacket, loosening my tie and kicking off my shoes. I don't know how long I slept, but it was the first time I had been in a horizontal position for almost thirty-six hours.

The hotel phone rang at 10:10 pm. "Hello," I answered.

"David! This is John. Why aren't you answering your cell phone? Call me. I'm in Vienna."

"I was asleep."

"How'd it go?"

"Not well. The Prime Minister really had very little to say."

John seemed beside himself. "I checked my email and the office in Washington, too. I don't get it. It's a departure from procedure. I didn't get an advance copy of the letter. Do you have any idea what was in it?" he asked.

"I can't tell you what it said. His reaction was stoic. Somehow, I got the impression that he was not pleased."

"We'll talk tomorrow, David. Thanks." He hung up.

It was 10:26 pm. I quickly changed into my jogging pants and Nike's after a quick bath with wet wipes, courtesy of the house. I brushed my teeth, slicked back my hair and headed for the VIP Lounge on the seventeenth floor.

"No problem, sir," stated the bartender. "The restaurant closed at ten but the bar is open until midnight. Would you like a sandwich menu? We are famous for our Pastrami on matzo and our kosher tacos. I highly recommend either."

"Sounds good. I'll take the Pastrami and a Sprite to drink, please."

I missed Maria. I thought, "If she were here, she would not allow the Sprite — too much sugar." Looking at my watch, I resolved to call her before I went to bed.

"The view of Tel Aviv and the Mediterranean are beautiful, sir, and the weather is balmy for this time of year. If you would like, I can serve you on the balcony."

"Excellent."

I took a big bite of the sandwich and then I remembered I hadn't asked the blessing. "Forgive me, Lord. Thank you once again for all the blessings you provide. Amen."

In less than five minutes, I feverishly swallowed the last bite of the sandwich, guzzled the Sprite, and reached for the check.

"Wait a minute, David, what are you doing?" an inner voice seemed to say. "Why don't you relax and take in this beautiful place I have prepared for you?" Still frozen on the edge of my seat, I closed my eyes and slowly filled my lungs with the mild breeze flowing off the surface of the Mediterranean. I surrendered to a deep peaceful stillness that lasted several minutes. It was punctuated only by receding sounds of Tel Aviv nightlife far below.

"David!" a voice burst in with the authority of a boot camp sergeant. "I have been sent here with a message for you. Don't be afraid."

Startled, I arose to my feet and turned in the direction of the voice. Before me, no more than ten feet away in the semi-darkness, beside a wall mounted flickering gas lantern, stood a young man that must have been seven feet tall. He was dressed in a white linen tunic that came to his ankles. Draped around his shoulders was a white cloak, fastened at the neck by a gold chain with clasps at each end attached to eyelets in the cloak. It was mid-thigh in length and gathered by a tightly drawn golden sash around his waist. He was bronze and statuesque. I would guess him to have been about thirty years old.

I was overpowered by an unseen Presence and went immediately to my knees. I bowed my head and held up my hands as if in surrender. "Stand up, David. We must bow only to the Most High God."

He walked out of the shadows and stood by the banister that enclosed the balcony. "Isn't it beautiful?" he added, raising both his arms wide as if trying to embrace the world. "And the Father gave us a full moon tonight, too."

I got up and walked to the balustrade at the edge of the balcony. I could see him better, now. I noticed that there was a large empty sheath that hung from the golden sash around his waist.

"Oh, yes. The view is gorgeous." I answered, trying my best to recover from the shock of the encounter. I must have inadvertently glanced inside the bar to see if anybody was aware of us.

"Don't worry about them. They can't see me," he said, while still looking out over the sea. "The Mediterranean is the nexus of three continents. Europe, Asia and Africa meet here. Its commerce was the glue that tied them together in centuries past.

"Seven world empires have arisen from this region and the last, the seventh, even though it has come and gone, will re-emerge and rule the world in the last days.

"The Mediterranean was known in Bible times as The Great Sea. It will soon become the epicenter of world power under the Lawless One – the Man of Sin – the Seed of the Serpent. The Scriptures say he will come out of the Great Sea."

He seemed to freeze for a few seconds and then continued, "David, I have been sent here to tell you what is coming upon your people. You have been chosen by the Most High to warn them of great catastrophe in the near future. You will not be afraid of them. Your forehead will be made of brass. You will speak all that the Lord commands you. Do you understand?"

I must have hesitated because he turned and looked at me with penetrating intensity. "Do you understand? This question requires an answer, David."

"Yes, I understand."

"Good. A blackout is coming to America. It will be a great catastrophe, and it will be a harbinger of things to come unless your people repent of their sins. North of the big river that runs from east to west, there will be elements that melt with fervent heat. The lights will go out. The rich and poor together will flee to the great highways and, at first, cluster in small groups, waiting for someone to lead them. There will be no cars. There will be no trucks."

"When will this…?"

"It is not for you to know the times and the seasons which the Father has put in His own power."

"What can I…?"

"You are a messenger, David. You will go where the people are. You will tell them what to do."

"But I'm not equipped for anything like this. I am not a survivalist. Neither can I advise them spiritually. I'm not a famous minister or televangelist. The people will not know me. Who will listen to me?"

"The Holy Spirit will tell you what to say. If you are faithful, doors will open for you that no man can shut."

"What if they will not hear?"

"The great highways will fill up and become rivers of people, all of them on foot, to the lands of the South. The migration to escape the catastrophe will be so great that the ramps will be filled also. They will be trying to crowd onto the highways and fierce fighting will break out when the people on the ramps are pushed back by those already on the highway. There will be no room for them."

Passion welled up inside me. I was totally absorbed in his description, "I want to help the ramp people. I want to yell out to the people on the highway as loud as I can, 'Let them on the highway! Let them on! Let them on!'"

"That is exactly what you are commanded to do."

"What does all this mean?" I asked.

"You must pray for the interpretation, David. I can tell you this much. Jesus is coming soon and the hope of His coming will be the thing that sustains the people of God in the days ahead. Tell the people to embrace family. Tell them to praise God for everything. Tell them to let the ramp people on. Some of them will be angels in disguise sent to give you hope."

Then a long silence followed as he turned again and looked toward the West.

I could feel my heart racing. I knew that his message was not over, but I sensed a mood shift. I waited until he was ready. I was totally exhausted.

I turned toward the Great Sea. I looked at the reflection of the moon on its surface and thought, "This is the stuff that art, poetry and literature are made of." But I knew that the calm, peaceful panorama belied the turbulent history of the waters.

It was a tranquil night except for a dry, gentle breeze from the sands of North Africa. To the northwest was the European Continent and behind me was the vast expanse of Asia. The cultures and the commerce of the ancient world all came together here.

Suddenly, I was in the Spirit and in a flash I saw the history of the great body of water come to life.

I saw a teacher in a classroom teaching her pupils that the eastern coast of the Mediterranean was the Cradle of Civilization where history began. I saw a minister of the gospel telling his congregation that life began here in a beautiful garden — the home of Adam and Eve.

I saw the great merchant ships of the ancient nations sail its waters from beautiful port cities. Proud sails of many colors adorned the ports from Tyre to Spain.

I saw camel caravans from the East bringing exotic perfumes, oils and fabrics to the ports of the Sea. I saw great grain and lumber ships returning to home-ports with cargos of slaves, peacocks and monkeys. I saw the beauty of diversity in art, music and dress. I also saw the human tragedy of war, greed and slavery.

I saw seven bloodthirsty beasts rise out of the Great Sea, one after another.

I saw the countries of the Great Sea Basin, all with the same common origin and ruled by a Great Dragon, fall apart like pieces of a giant jigsaw puzzle and then come back together again for a common destiny in the last days.

I saw four winds striving upon the waters until they became a storm that engulfed the world.

I saw the shadow of a Cross fall across the world that ended the rule of evil.

I immediately snapped out of the vision. He was smiling. It was the first time I had seen him smile.

"Oh, my goodness," I answered, and then began to tremble from head to foot.

He stopped me. "You need to get hold of yourself. I am not finished. I have one more word for you."

"Okay. Please go ahead," regrouping as best I could.

"Your leader will rule for three intervals, two of which will soon be completed."

"What do you mean by intervals?" I asked, wiping my eyes with a napkin I retrieved from the table. "Will he be elected for a third term?"

It was as if he didn't hear what I asked. "At the end of the third interval...," he paused for a full ten seconds. He seemed hesitant to finish the sentence and I was not sure I wanted him to.

"...there will be a great tsunami."

"Tsunami! Where... you mean like the ocean... how big...?"

He didn't answer.

I was trying to wrap my mind around it. It took a few seconds for me to frame the next question, "Is there no hope? Is there hope for America?"

"Man cannot fix it. It has gone too far."

"But is there hope?"

"Your country has become as wicked as Sodom and Gomorrah. Only repentance from sin can save America. That's all. Nothing else. The discussion of other solutions is idle chatter. But to answer your question, 'All things are possible with God.' Prayer can change it. It can be a tsunami of mercy."

I wanted him to stay but I knew it was time for him to go. "Sir, I have one final question."

He didn't respond. He just looked at me.

"I don't mean to be presumptuous or disrespectful, but I couldn't help but notice the sheath on your side — that it is empty. Is there a reason for that?"

"Yes, there is. I am sure the Enemy has picked up on it. Tonight, I came as a messenger. The next time I will come as a warrior. He knows that I will be wielding a sword before this assignment is over."

He turned and walked into the shadows beside the flickering gas lantern. He turned again, faced me and stated, "I'll see you in New York."

Then he disappeared.

THE COMMITTEE

As soon as I boarded Etihad Airways Flight #55 in Tel Aviv bound for Dubai and found my seat, I received a text from my secretary informing me that hotel reservations had been made for me, and that I would be staying at the Emirates Palace Hotel.

"Can't you put them on a separate floor," I asked. "I'm getting a phobia. They are with me day and night."

"I can't, boss. Secret Service took charge of all travel arrangements. It's out of our hands."

"Oh, it's okay. Don't worry about it."

I had only one complaint with my reservation — Frank and Emery were in rooms next to mine. To be honest, I was getting tired of looking at them. I was also getting an eerie feeling about them for some unknown reason. I couldn't put my finger on it.

The flight to Dubai took less than thirty minutes. The beauty and the wealth of the city were breathtaking, even from the air.

Once on the ground I requested the taxi driver, "Please get me to the Emirates Palace as soon as possible."

I must have given him an opportunity to show some pride in his fabulous city. "I don't know, but the Dubai Police Force may be the only one in the world that is stocked with Ferraris, Mercedes, Bugattis and Bentleys. We won't try a getaway."

"Are you serious?"

"Yes." He laughed, sensing my unbelief.

"By all means, let's obey the traffic laws. Your jails might not be as nice as your police cruisers."

When I arrived at the hotel, I went immediately to my room, tipped the bellman, and lay down on the king sized bed. I lay flat on my back and stared at the ceiling. A torrent of images and thoughts flooded my mind. I missed Maria desperately. I wondered how she was coping with the stress back home. I knew that she and her friends were praying. That would help. I couldn't get over the look on Prime Minister Netanyahu's face when he turned and faced me after reading the message from the President. The words of the angel were still ringing in my ears, "Only God can save America. She must repent." Had Jonathan finalized mom's arrangements? Were our cousins from West Virginia coming to the funeral? Was my life in danger on this mission?

I got up, walked to the window, and looked at the Burj Khalifa — the tallest building in the world — standing proudly under the Arabian sky. I thought about the heap that once was the Twin Towers. I wondered if God was saying something to the people of the world. Could it be a sign that economic and military power was shifting from one hemisphere to another? Would I have the answer to that question tomorrow after my appointment with the Committee? I clicked the appointment calendar on my phone which I had laid next to my wallet on the TV credenza. The meeting would be, as I remembered, on the 147th floor of the Bruj Khalifa.

"Oh, God, it's all still a mystery. Give me wisdom."

I rested as much as I could the rest of the day, while studying the materials that were supposed to prepare me for the meeting. I went to bed early.

The elevator stopped and the door opened directly into a large waiting room in an office suite. Frank exited first, briefly checked it out from the elevator door and said, "We'll be downstairs in the café off the main lobby."

The gold English letters on the wall above the door that led to the office area told me that I was at the right place. The lights were dim and reassuring. The rich mixture of wood and leather, along with lush scarlet, black, and green carpet conveyed an image of wealth and stability.

In the center of the waiting area was an illuminated black marble fountain that I imagined was an abstract sculpture of a flowing oil well. I squinted to read a small burnished bronze plate at the base of the sculpture. It read, "Congratulations to our friends at White, Grafton and Gillespie on your grand opening — The British Petroleum Company."

A chrome and black velvet pedestal sign welcomed me and told me that I was in a law office and that someone would be with me shortly.

I was immediately engulfed in a huge burgundy leather chair. I relaxed for a moment with my eyes closed, relishing every second the rest afforded my tired body. "How nice," I thought.

Things had been so hectic since the Friday before that I had not had time to consider a question that was troubling me, but I apparently had suppressed. It came to the surface and I looked around the room at the strange surroundings. "What am I doing here?" I asked myself.

Tony Blair had recently resigned as the Big Four special envoy to the Middle East. This added further mystery to the setting of a meeting that had the potential to change the world. He was the first to convene the Committee in his efforts to bring peace to the Middle East. Now he was gone. I surmised that this forum was chosen because it would bring together, in a neutral setting, faces that were familiar with each other and, yet, were competitors in the struggle for leadership in the Middle East.

I still had no idea what the meeting was about, nor who would be attending. John had left a message on my smart phone to scrap the resumes and the agenda — that everything had changed and to, "listen to what they have to say." The only description he gave was, "It's a matter of grave national concern and the President wants you there. Homeland Security and all agencies are on high alert. Internet chatter is exploding."

My thoughts were interrupted by a male receptionist, who must have been a retiree from a rock band and was hard of hearing. He yelled in classic British brogue, "Secretary Flink. Oh, do tell. I am so sorry if I startled you."

"No, no, no! It's okay."

"Mr. Secretary. Welcome to Dubai. It is an honor having you with us today. Would you be so kind to follow me, Sir?"

He led me down a long hallway to a large, empty conference room. Before entering the room, he showed me where the toilet was and then opened the door for me, advising me that Barrister White would be with me shortly. He added, "Can I offer you a cup of tea or a soft drink? I would personally recommend the Turkish coffee. It is excellent."

I thanked him and declined his offer. I turned around to view the place that I was informed would be the site of the historic meeting. As I imagined it would be, there was a large window running almost the entire length of the room that provided another spectacular view of the beautiful Persian Gulf waters. There were two ornate conference tables placed parallel with each other and perpendicular to the big window.

There were eleven chairs. Five were at one table and six at the other, and they were facing each other with a chair at the window for the moderator. Each setting had a pitcher of water, a glass, and a nameplate. I quickly scanned the names of those who would be attending the meeting. None of them were heads of state, but several were chief foreign ministers.

Glancing toward the head of the table, I saw two nameplates I had overlooked. They were the settings for United Nations. One was for the Assistant Secretary General, Gadhadhar Sharmar, and the other for Anselm Horn, Deputy United Nations Special Coordinator for the Middle East Peace Process.

I had experienced the pleasure of meeting both of them before and was greatly encouraged that they would be present at the meeting. I was particularly pleased that Horn would be present, since I had worked with him before as the Special Coordinator. I had found him to be a delightful and intelligent Norwegian with an engaging personality. With some apprehension, I managed to whisper to myself, "This could turn out… okay."

The door suddenly opened and a man walked into the room and positioned himself at the head of the conference table. He smiled and nodded, acknowledging the members of the group as he lay a legal pad on the table. Two men came in immediately and quietly took their places. One sat at the end of one of the tables by stenographic equipment. The other stood behind one of three cameras that had been placed at different locations in the room.

He called them by name, stating sternly, "We will not be recording the proceedings today." They looked at each other and began immediately gathering their equipment.

I guessed the man to be about my age. He was dressed in a dark suit and tie and neatly manicured from top to bottom. It was good to hear his American accent, which I thought placed him from somewhere south of Jackson, Mississippi.

I responded immediately, "I beg your pardon, Sir. My name is David Flink. I represent the United States."

"I am so sorry. Of course, I have heard of you, Mr. Secretary, and saw your name on the roster of delegates. Please forgive my manners. It is so good to have you in our offices today."

"I must insist that these proceedings be recorded and properly certified. However, I have no objection to the videographers being released," I stated.

"Well, then, I should run this by the other delegates. I see no reason they should object."

Extending his hand with a firm handshake, he stated, "My name is Bart White. I am a partner here at White, Grafton and Gillespie. The others should be here in a few minutes. They are finishing up their meeting downstairs."

"Meeting? Downstairs? I don't understand."

"I thought you knew about it."

"This is the first I heard…"

"What about the meeting last night?"

"Meeting last night! What meeting last night?"

"I assumed you knew about it also. It was hosted by Iran. It was in one of the conference rooms at the hotel. My partner attended. I understand that things did not go well."

"What happened?"

"The Foreign Minister from Iran brought a uniformed North Korean General to the meeting, and from that point things went downhill."

"I know what that's about," I thought. "The Ayatollah is flexing his muscles before the others. I can see why that went over like a lead balloon."

It was obviously planned to remind the other Committee members of Iran's long-standing friendship with North Korea. The ears of the world were still ringing from North Korea's announcement that it had developed a plutonium bomb and possessed missile capability to deliver it to the American mainland.

I thought, "Hmm… sentiments are warming up between North Korea and Russia." Both parties had declared 2015 as the "Friendship Year" between them.

Russia was providing arms to Iran, who was arming Hezbollah and the Houthi rebels in Yemen, who were firing Scud missiles into Saudi Arabia. Iran forces were fighting alongside their Shi'ite brothers in Iraq against ISIS. In addition, Iran had hammered out a nuclear deal with major nations of the world. Russia had boots on the ground supporting the Shi'ite regime in Syria. With that circle of influence, Iran's star was certainly rising in the race for the most powerful country in the Middle East.

And it was well known that China and North Korea had also been good friends since the Korean War.

My thoughts ran wild. "What about that outrageous circus the night before? A North Korean General in full uniform at an Islamic family gathering. I'd like to have been a fly on the wall in that meeting."

I was sure that the meaning of the good general's presence was not lost on the other Committee members. When you put the package together... Iran, North Korea, China and Russia... it represented a power axis that could intimidate the bravest.

"Are the Secretary General and Special Coordinator here?" I asked. "Did they attend the meetings?"

"Yes, they're here. No, they did not attend the meetings. They just arrived this morning from Brussels. They are in the office lounge. I filled them in on the meetings. They have talked to Secretary Kerry. I think they are sticking around to see what is going to happen next."

It was all beginning to make some sense, now. It explained the text I had received from John a couple hours earlier. "Stick it out. See what they have to say. I'll explain, later."

The greetings were cordial as the delegates filed into the room. The first to arrive were Gadhadhar Sharmar and Anselm Horn. We embraced, exchanged greetings, spoke briefly about the upcoming American elections, and listened to Horn's latest joke. After a round of laughter, each of us took our designated seats.

Delegates from Saudi Arabia and Turkey arrived next. The Turkish envoy looked quite western in a dark business suit and tie. The Saudi was in full cultural dress with keffiyeh headdress and an ankle length thawb covered by a white cloak with gold stitching. Each carried a briefcase. They entered the room with much aplomb as they took their seats.

The delegate from Iran was last to arrive, greeted everyone in the room except me and took his seat without looking my way. He also was dressed in traditional Middle Eastern clothing.

"Gentlemen! Let me introduce myself. My name is Bart White and I am a senior partner here at the law offices of White, Grafton and Gillespie. Welcome to Dubai. It is an honor to host a meeting of such distinguished guests. Please feel at home. We are here to serve you.

"I am not sure as to the purpose of our meeting here today. I was contacted a week ago by the Deputy UN Special Coordinator for the Middle East, Anselm Horn, who is with us as you know along with the distinguished Assistant Secretary-General, the Honorable Gadhadhar Sharmar, of the United Nations."

Everyone enthusiastically applauded the two UN officials. The Secretary-General spoke a few words about the need for peace in the world and that there was no reason it could not begin with peace in the Middle East, adding, "It is my hope that it will begin here. In this room. Today."

After a standing ovation, he graciously smiled and took his seat.

Special Coordinator Horn made some opening remarks and had something personal to say to each delegate. I mentally noted, "The atmosphere is getting more relaxed. Maybe some good will come out of this after all."

Then, White turned to the Vice Minister of Foreign Affairs for Iran and stated, "Amir-Mohammad Ahadi, of the great Islamic Republic of Iran, you requested this meeting today. Why are we here?"

The Vice Minister seemed taken aback by the question so early in the proceedings and fumbled for a few seconds with some notes. He cleared his throat, acknowledged the dignitaries in the room and looked straight at me.

"I will get to the point. The main reason I am here is to announce the obvious. America is no longer the world's great superpower. Iran's good friend China is now the number one industrial power in the world. China and Russia are each developing militarily and will soon, if present trends continue, both overtake the United States as the world's leading military powers."

He spoke very good English and I detected a certain western air about him. But it was apparent when he opened his mouth that it was only skin deep.

"In fact, it appears that America is hopelessly imprisoned in a capitalistic Christian system whose death is far overdue. In its place will soon bloom the glorious partnership of a united Islam, our dear Socialist brothers around the world and, perhaps, someday, a more enlightened Christianity."

I thought to myself, "Sounds like he has been spending time with Putin and Pope Francis."

He paused for a moment, looked away from his notes and our eyes locked. Then, he added, "The time has come for new world leadership. And you, America, and your Zionist imperialistic outlaws have raided us for the last time."

He cleared his throat nervously and went on, "The Islamic Republic of Iran has a very strong friendship with both China and Russia."

"As well as North Korea," I added.

I was furious. I was certain that steam was coming out my ears. I mumbled to myself, "This is not a good start. This may be the shortest diplomatic gathering in history. He wants hardball. Hardball he's going to get!"

"Yes, we have been close friends with North Korea for many years."

"You have been so close that presently you are regularly and extensively exchanging information on nuclear warheads and ballistic missile systems. And you have been since 2013. Isn't that correct?"

"No. That isn't correct."

I got very specific to let him know that Iran was not beyond the reach of US Intelligence. "And isn't it a fact that in 2015, while you were still negotiating the Nuclear Treaty with the US, there were four different missile and nuclear teams that came from North Korea to Tehran? And in the last delegation there were nine experts?"

"I don't know where you are getting your information…"

"And isn't it true that your friend, North Korea, has tested a new type of missile launched from a submarine and developed a nuclear weapon small enough to be mounted on a long-range missile?"

"I know that they claim that."

"And isn't it true that you have every intention of developing a nuclear weapon and a missile system to deliver it? To Israel? To the United States? In spite of the nuclear deal with the Five plus One world powers?"

"Mr. Flink! I did not come to Dubai to be insulted by you nor by the US State Department! I came to warn you!"

"Gentlemen!" Mr. Horn interrupted, "Why don't we take a break for a few minutes and let our tempers cool. We aren't achieving anything this way."

"I'm sorry. I apologize honorable Coordinator." My next words were very difficult to form through clenched jaws and pursed lips, but I managed to pull it off. "I apologize, Amir Ahadi."

He nodded affirmatively and added, "I guess we both were a little tense. No problem."

"Thank you."

I didn't move. I sat in my seat. I looked through the huge window at the blue western sky…toward America.

I was not surprised at North Korea's recent announcement that it had developed a plutonium bomb small enough to mount on a ballistic missile. I knew that the North Koreans had been messing around with plutonium since the 1970s and that it was just a matter of time. The shape of the bomb was the last big obstacle in perfecting it.

I had been told by a nuclear physicist that a plutonium bomb properly designed, and not much larger than a roll of paper towels, would have the same yield and destructive force as the bombs dropped on Nagasaki and Hiroshima. He said, "When it crosses the Mexican border, it's all over."

When I came to myself, I was still looking out the window.

"David. May I speak with you privately?" It was Anselm Horn.

"Sure. Where?"

"Barrister White said we could use his office."

"Close the door, Matlock," he stated. "By the way, that was excellent cross-examination, but the worst diplomacy I have seen in a while." He spoke with a concerned smile.

"I know."

"I know he sounded obnoxious and rude. But, David, you need to hear what he has to say. After all, you came halfway around the world."

"It was inexcusable. I will do better. Thank you for the advice. But I have a question."

"What's that?"

"When did Iranian Shi'ites start talking about a partnership with Christianity?"

Then I remembered the Professor's lecture at Armageddon. He said, "Christianity must be massively overhauled to become the more enlightened Christianity demanded of the New World Order. It would require the sacrifice of everything we hold dear."

A few minutes later we were back in the conference room. Mr. Horn seemed excited. "Gentlemen! I believe we are ready to proceed. After Amir has spoken, we will allow time for a response from each of you. If there are no objections, then I defer to the esteemed delegate from the Islamic Republic of Iran."

He began, "I come to this assembly, today, with a spirit of great heaviness and urgency. It is not only urgent for the United States, but for the world. ISIS has two plutonium bombs and they were openly displayed by ISIS fighters, somewhere near Mosul three weeks ago. They were in the bed of a pickup truck and were examined by Turkish officials and a nuclear inspection team from NATO.

"If anyone knows how the bombs were acquired or from whom, they are not saying. Apparently, there has been no leak of the event to the press.

"It has now been confirmed by the Ministry of Intelligence of the Islamic Republic of Iran that ISIS has successfully placed these two bombs inside Central America, and they are now on their way to the United States through channels offered by the Mexican drug cartels."

The delegate looked at me after he finished, as if expecting some reaction. But I merely tapped a pencil on my notepad, yawned, and sipped some water. That did not mean that I was not deeply concerned.

The Turkish Minister immediately followed and it was obvious that Iran's boast of power would not go unchallenged. "We are saddened by this tragic news and sympathize with our good friends in the United States. As the Sunni homeland of the great Ottoman Empire and the last Caliphate on earth, we are destined to lead the wave of Islamic resurgence around the world. Our close association with Europe, as well as our ties with the Muslim Brotherhood give us a worldwide forum as the nation most suited to lead Islam into the future."

I expected a similar monologue from the Saudi prince, extolling the purity of the Wahhabi Sunnis, his country as the location of Mecca and Medina, and Saudi as the oil capital of the world. But he simply asked a question, "Honorable Delegate from Iran. Surely, you didn't invite us here to tell us that there is going to be a nuclear attack on America. Why are we really here?"

"I have asked you to come for two reasons: One — the time has come... no, let me rephrase...I am making an urgent call for Islam to unite across the world. This will be necessary to bring the world under Sharia law and to establish the World Caliphate. I am calling for an international forum of all Muslim nations to study the possibility. We can be divided no longer.

"Let's be honest, today. There is only one common sentiment that is strong enough to compel us to forget our differences and come together. We have been shamefully dispossessed of our land and our heritage. There is only one way to remove the shame and restore our honor. We must take back our land.

"Let me repeat, there is only one way. Israel must be wiped from the face of the earth. The nation of apes and pigs must be annihilated!"

"Allah Akbar! Allah Akbar!" Exclaimed the minister of the Turks. While the Saudi, with a clenched fist, ground his thumb into the table smiling as he said, "Little Satan. Little Satan — must be crushed!" Then the Saudi prince exclaimed, "In the name of Allah! In the name of Allah!" They shouted and laughed like Pentecostals.

The Iranian minister abruptly sat down and began to calmly sip ice water from his crystal glass. And then he stated, "Two — America is the problem. Secretary Flink, you represent the most powerful nation in the world. You are also the most unpredictable. You are unpredictable because of millions of obstinate Christians in your midst whose stubborn beliefs are unacceptable to Islam and the Socialist brothers. They are hand in glove with the strong American nationalists who call themselves patriots and swear by your irrelevant Constitution. Other terrorists, cut from the same cloth, are the Ku Klux Klan and the Black Panthers.

"There are tens of millions of them, and come the 2016 elections they can take control and change the direction of current American policy in the Middle East and the present trend toward a united and peaceful world. Overall, we are pleased with the leadership of your present Administration, but there is no guarantee that its policies will endure."

I felt a lump in my throat, but managed to ask, "Can you not dispense with all the embossed language about the New World Order and stick to the point? What do you propose?"

His tone was flat and direct, "These dissident elements must be brought under control. America must end all of its imperialistic aggression. And with the rest of the world it must surrender its sovereignty to the will of the emerging global community. This is the road to peace for the world."

I looked at the UN officials. There was no visible reaction.

I thought to myself, "You hypocrite," as well as a few other words that shouldn't have crossed my mind.

Then I went on to say, "The kind of peace your good friend, Putin, is advancing in the Ukraine and Syria? And by the way, how do we bring the Christians and the patriots under control?" I asked.

"That is your business. But I will be frank."

"You mean to tell me that you haven't been?"

"America is a nation without walls. I am not making a threat, neither am I telling you something you don't know. I have a list prepared by Iranian intelligence, which I copied from my laptop this morning. It points out the gaping holes in your national defense. They are known to the enemies of America around the world. I want to put this as delicately as I can. So, here it is. You are finished. To put it in the words of one of the prophets, 'you have been weighed in the balances and are found wanting.' Shall I go on?"

I wanted to get up and punch him out. But the better part of reason and a silent prayer compelled me to listen to what he had to say. The more he talked the more I might learn.

"Certainly." I replied.

"Your electrical infrastructure is as fragile as a glass jar. It is a fact known all over the world that an EMP (electro-magnetic pulse) emitted from a multi-megaton neutron bomb 300 miles over Kansas could fry electrical components across the American continent. Smaller areas could be disabled by smaller bombs at lower altitudes."

He was reading from the notes on his laptop. "It could be launched from land or sea. China is known to have three submarines armed with nuclear missiles. Or, a bomb could be launched from an innocent looking merchant vessel a few miles off the American coast, with a Scud missile that costs $100,000."

"A neutron bomb at high altitudes?" I wanted him to know that I knew what he had been up to. "Is that the reason that Iran was firing high altitude missiles from watercraft in the Caspian Sea fifteen years ago? Getting ready to attack America?"

He continued, "In either case, whether low or high altitude, there would be no light, heat, water, fresh food, gasoline, cell phones, TVs, radios or internet. All the trucks would stop and your car wouldn't run. America would be blown into the Stone Age. Estimates of Americans who could die of starvation and disease are off the charts. Up to as high as 90%.

"North Korea now has the plutonium bomb. It has an extremely higher yield ratio in size and weight when compared to the uranium bomb. They say they now have the missile capability to deliver it to the mainland of America."

I was bluffing, "They say they have the ability. That doesn't mean they have it."

"Don't give me that, Secretary Flink. A suppressed report that leaked to the media in April 2014, from your own Department of Homeland Security, found that North Korea could deliver on its threats to destroy the United States with a nuclear electromagnetic pulse attack.

"North Korea has now placed a satellite in orbit at an altitude of 300 miles. There is no defense if it were to carry a bomb. It could be detonated in orbit over the United States. It is indefensible once it gets in orbit. To defend against it will require that it be shot down at liftoff.

"And I thought I mentioned a few minutes ago that 2015 is the Friendship Year between North Korea and Russia. The top foreign minister of the country just made diplomatic rounds that included Russia and Cuba.

"And have you forgotten that a North Korean ship was caught red handed trying to smuggle missile system components from Cuba through the Panama Canal in 2013?

"Your own National Security Agency has advised the US Congress that China and two or three other countries have the cyber capability to take down the US power grid.

"And it was hot news when the US media told the world that recent studies have shown that the utility companies have 55,000 electrical substations across the United States. If a coordinated attack were to knock out nine of the key installations, it would cause a national blackout that could last up to eighteen months. It has been demonstrated by a handful of vandals in America, out to have a good time, that it is possible to disable a substation with a high-powered rifle. Think about it."

"I appreciate the seminar on how to destroy America, honorable Amir. Let me remind you that we are still the strongest military force in the world. And I assure you that we have not only the ability to defend ourselves, but have the means to retaliate and to utterly devastate anyone who would be so foolish as to attack us.

"Now," I added, "let's get off this topic and get to the reason for this meeting. I am sure that you will agree with me that none of us want to walk down the nuclear road."

I took a minute to gather my emotions. I looked up and all eyes were fastened on me. I wanted to do something outrageous, like stand to my feet and sing out "Oh, say does that Star Spangled Banner yet wave…"

Instead, I asked again, "What do you propose?"

"Promises are a dime a dozen," he replied. "America has zero credibility with our peoples. There is only one way that you can convince the world that you mean what you say."

"And what would that be?"

"America must immediately withdraw all support of Israel, including financial aid, weapons and defense systems sales, as well as training in their use. A boycott of all Jewish goods and services by American government and businesses, sanctions imposed on countries that do business with her, and the termination of all tourist traffic to Israel.

"The world needs your support for petitions to the United Nations to prosecute the thugs, like Netanyahu and others in Israel, for war crimes against Hamas and the people of Gaza that took place in 2014. We expect the same penalties that were carried out at Nuremburg. Finally, we will need your support for Palestinian statehood and the return of all land unlawfully granted to Israel in 1948 pursuant to the Balfour Declaration."

"My Lord, it's a pack of wolves," I thought, "does he realize whom he is taking on? The Bible is plain. He who takes on Israel takes on God."

I glanced again at the nameplates across the conference table. This time it startled me. I hadn't noticed it. The names on the plates were almost an exact list of the invaders of Israel prophetically recorded in Ezekiel 38 and Psalms 83. These scriptures describe an end time coalition of nations prophesied to invade Israel in the last days. The spirit of those who sat at the table with me had been captured by the Psalmist almost 3,000 years ago word for word. Psalms chapter 83, verse 4 in the New King James it reads:

Come, and let us cut them off from being a nation; that the name of Israel may be remembered no more.

"You have not answered my question, Amir. How are you going to control th Christians and patriots in America?"

"It will not be an easy task. America must be transformed. Those who refuse the values of the transformed America must be isolated and re-educated to accept the policies that are more conducive and less offensive to the global community at large."

"How will you do that? Internment camps and brainwashing?"

"Secretary Flink, you are not being easy to work with."

I replied as calmly as I could, "Do you realize that the Christian evangelical community represents 40 percent of the American population? I can tell you now that they have no intention of working with you or any group you may put together. I don't think you realize whom you are talking to. I am the officially designated representative of the United States for this meeting."

"Secretary Flink! I have spent the last 45 minutes explaining to you that America cannot survive an outright war with her adversaries. You may

have the power to annihilate them in return, with the same old mutually assured destruction doctrine of the Cold War. But will you or your
Christian brothers be the first to pull the trigger? We don't think so. Two
plutonium bombs in backpacks will soon cross your border. Whom will
you retaliate against? ISIS? Send a few more bombers over to strike their
positions in Iraq?

"Please take the message back to your President that Turkish officials
have established contact with leaders of ISIS. There may be time to avert an
international financial crisis that would be sure to follow a nuclear attack
on America. Submit to our demands expressed here today and insure that
the world transitions peacefully into a New World Order."

Special Coordinator Horn stood and spoke calmly, "Gentlemen, I see
no reason to continue these discussions today. It is my recommendation
that we adjourn."

There was no objection and everybody began immediately, without
comment, to gather their papers and laptops. I was the first to get up and I
expressed my good wishes to all that were in the room.

Bart White was talking to the Saudi delegate. He looked up. With a
smile and a thumbs up, he loudly exclaimed, "Have a blessed day!"

After a brief visit with Special Coordinator Horn and the Secretary
General, I left. The envoy from Saudi Arabia and I met at the door. He
graciously gestured for me to exit first.

"Thank you. I have a question, please?"

"Yes?"

"Would you happen to know Omar Al-Kazak. I met him in Israel last
year. I understand he comes from a very prominent family in Saudi Arabia.
I thought you might know him."

"Are you talking about the news reporter?"

"Yes, that's him. You know him, then?"

"Oh, yes. Our families are close. I have known him since childhood. At
one time we were classmates in America."

"Hmmm! What are the chances of that?" I thought. "Would you know how I could get in touch with him?"

"I'm sorry. I can't help you. He dishonored his family."

I wasn't sure what he meant, but I feared the worst. "Do you know how I could reach him?"

"Do you not understand? He blasphemed Allah, dishonored Mohammed and shamed his family. He became a Christian. Do you not understand?"

In the taxi back to the hotel, I remembered an article I had read the previous year that came out of the highly regarded Atlantic Council, a think tank in Washington. The gist of it was that an "extraordinary crisis" was needed to preserve the ideal of the New World Order.

And then there is the statement widely attributed to David Rockefeller, "All we need is the right major crisis and the world will accept the New World Order."

"Crisis. New World Order."

"Lord, please guide my steps in the days ahead. Let me obey you and do what is pleasing in your sight."

THE TEST

Frank walked in my room ahead of me and came back with the announcement that it was clean. I told him to cancel everything for the rest of the day, including the invitation of the Foreign Minister and his family for a night cruise on his yacht in the Persian Gulf.

"I don't feel good, Frank. Just tell them I'm sick. Just tell them I'm sick. You know what to say. Please extend my sincere regrets."

The Secretary was waiting for my call. I didn't want to talk to him. In fact, I didn't want to talk to anybody. I stood there looking out the hotel window at what seemed a surreal world that had all but cancelled every meaningful experience of my life.

An image came into view of an old black and white photo I had seen when I was a child. The picture was in a book by Ernie Pyle, the famous World War II war correspondent. It was taken from his front line coverage of the war in Europe. The photo was the face of a middle-aged Frenchman dressed neatly in a dark suit and tie. He was standing in a crowd in Paris as he watched goose-stepping Nazi occupation troops pass by in victory. The look on his face was more eloquent than a thousand words. For a moment I think I shared his anguish — a deep sense of being violated — raped — by a band of complete strangers.

But this was my country and it was now — not France 70 years ago. A Scripture had been on my mind since Tel Aviv. It would not go away. I had memorized it when I was a child. Was God trying to speak to me? II Chronicles, chapter 7, verse 14, rolled off the tip of my tongue:

> If my people, who are called by my name, shall humble themselves, and pray, and seek my face, and turn from their wicked ways; then will I hear from heaven, and will forgive their sin and heal their land.

I looked at my watch and realized I had been standing at the window for twenty minutes. It was time to call the Secretary. I was ready now.

For the next hour I answered questions. Then, he took a deep breath and spoke in a quiet somber tone, "Frankly, I don't know what to do with this one."

Then, his voice changed as if commanding a perfunctory office function, "I will contact the White House to see if there are any changes in your schedule. If you don't hear from me, be ready for a debriefing in New York. I may be canceling the rest of my trip. I may fly back myself. I will try to reach the President."

He hesitated and then continued, "But I am very hopeful that an agreement between Israel and the Palestinians will soon be history. If we can bring peace to Jerusalem, then maybe we can bring it about in the rest of the world.

"Which hotel is it, David? I have been so tied up in the Peace Accord and the ISIS threat that I can't always keep the details straight."

"It will be at the Millennium UN Plaza Hotel in Manhattan."

"Oh, yes. I've stayed there before. It's right next to the United Nations Building."

"John, I'm curious as to why the meeting is in New York."

"The President is on his way back from Hawaii with the First Lady. He said that he would send a team up from Washington. That's all I know."

The Secretary paused a minute and then went on, "I don't know... frankly, I don't know... it would be sheer speculation for me even to guess... Oh, my God. All we need is a news leak. That would be disastrous. I need to call home." He hung up without saying goodbye.

I could sense the frustration of the Secretary. For one who typically was on top of everything, he seemed as uninformed as I about the details of the mission.

My phone rang. It was Maria on Face Time. She was drinking coffee someplace in Washington. I quickly calculated the time difference. It was 9:27 a.m. there.

"Honey, you look great." I exclaimed. "I can't wait to see you live and in person."

"What's wrong?"

"Now, what does that mean? Nothing is wrong."

"You don't fool me for a minute, David Flink. You look like you've been run over by a truck."

"Have you talked to Jonathan?"

"Yes, he just left here fifteen minutes ago. He insisted we meet for coffee. He didn't touch his coffee. Obviously depressed. Said that he has to talk to you as soon as you return. Before you talk with anyone else."

"I have an appointment that I have to keep in New York tomorrow night at 7:00. Let's see. I will be flying into Newark International on a private jet from Dubai."

"New York? What's with this New York stuff? I thought you were coming to Washington. Uh...I guess it doesn't really matter. I will take a flight early tomorrow," she stated, switching to her country music twang, "I will stand by my man."

"Arrival time is around 10:30 a.m. If you and Jonathan can meet me at the airport — that should give us some time to talk before my evening meeting. Did he tell you why he needed to talk to me?"

"He said, 'Something is coming down — big time.' Thinks it may be connected to your trip to the Middle East. I didn't tell him anything except what little I know — that you had high level meetings in Israel and the United Arab Emirates — in Dubai."

"Honey, we're talking high level. You won't believe how high level one of the meetings was."

"You met an angel! I knew you would. It is the same one that spoke to you in Mom's room at the nursing room. He said he would meet you again. Don't you remember?"

"Now what on earth made you think that?"

"David Flink. From the time you called me last Friday morning and said that you were going to Tel Aviv, I felt that God would give you a message for America before you got back."

I felt goose bumps from head to toe. I managed to reply, "Yes, honey, there was an angel."

"Jonathan says that America is on the brink of destruction."

"I'm eager to hear why he believes that."

"Oh, by the way, what suits do you have with you?"

"I only brought the black one. Why?"

"What color is your tie?"

"I have two ties with me. One is green, and the other is red. Maria, why do you ask?"

"We can talk about it tomorrow. Try to get some sleep, sweetheart. I'll see you in the morning." She paused and then stated, "I love you and I will be praying.

"Why me, Lord? Why am I the one that has to take this message back to America?" I asked sitting on the edge of the bed. I slipped off the bed and got on my knees. I began to pray for my country… until I fell asleep.

Convincing them was not easy but, finally, Frank and Emery consented for me to leave Newark International with Jonathan on the way to the hotel. The stated reason was true, in that he and I needed to discuss the final arrangements for my mother. They knew Jonathan and that made it easier for them, I think. They would follow us to the Millennium UN Plaza from the airport. We would meet in the lobby later in the evening at precisely 6:45 p.m.

Maria was waiting with a luggage cart. "Oh, Baby, you are back. Thank God, you are back." She shrieked as we embraced, "I thought you would never get home."

"The flight was great, Sweetheart. I think I am ready for my meeting tonight. I feel rested for the first time since leaving here last week. It is so good to see you. You are more beautiful than before I left."

"Please tell me more," she said, gripping my hand.

"Where is Jonathan?"

"At the Cellphone Waiting Lot. I've called him already."

She had a concerned look on her face. "David, Jonathan is not okay. I hate to tell you, but the loss of your mother has left him devastated. And that isn't all. He won't talk to me about it, but apparently he has received information regarding a meeting in New York and he thinks it is the one you are attending. He says he has to talk to you this afternoon. He drove all the way from DC. Where are we going, now?"

"To the Millennium UN Plaza."

"I know where it is. I used to work in Manhattan."

"Uh-huh."

"You don't remember."

"What?"

"I knew it. You are someplace else. We met in Manhattan. That's where you proposed."

I recognized Jonathan's car as he pulled up to the curb, "There he is. There's Jonathan, 'Hey, Jonathan.'"

"You guys need to talk. I'll see you at the hotel," Maria volunteered.

Maria was right. I could tell by looking at Jonathan as soon as I got in the car that he was stressed out.

"Here, let me drive," I exclaimed. "You must have driven all night. Besides, I am better acquainted with New York."

I thought I would try to lighten things up a little as we left the airport, "Jonathan, do you remember that old '59 Impala Dad bought you and me? I saw one just like it while…"

"I know what you're trying to do, little brother, but we need to get to the matter at hand."

"I know."

"There is a meeting in New York tonight with close advisors to the President. In my position in the office of the Chief of Staff, I see a lot of very sensitive stuff that has to deal with national security and the plans of the Administration…"

"I know all that, Jonathan. I am your brother and, like you, an employee of the US Government. I know how it works."

"I sounded like I was interviewing for a job in the private sector, didn't I?" he chuckled. The atmosphere relaxed.

"What happened?" I asked.

"Nobody knows anything for sure. It's all hush-hush. But the word is getting out in the White House that a national security threat a hundred times bigger than the Twin Towers is looming.

"It started while you were gone. At first, I didn't pay much attention to it. But frankly, the whispers are coming from too many sources not to be seriously considered. My supervisor was called to the Oval Office three times yesterday. Homeland Security and Pentagon officials also came and went. Two different members of the White House Press Corps asked me what was going on during lunch yesterday. I don't think there has been an actual leak, but rumors are flying in all directions."

"Where are we on the Homeland Security Advisory?"

"We're on blue. 'Guarded.' The normal risk category. If we're in danger, they don't know about it at DHS."

"What else do you know, Jonathan?"

"I got an email. I was copied by mistake. It originated in my office without my knowledge. The Lord must have wanted me to see it."

"What did it say?"

"It is the attachment that's important. It's the agenda for tonight's meeting in New York. I have a feeling you will be at that meeting."

I laughed, "Jonathan, you know the definition of compartmentalized and classified don't you? You know I can't talk about those things."

"That means you will be there, right?"

Before I had time to answer, he lurched for a leather folder on the back seat and with some difficulty retrieved it. Then he handed it to me, "Look, at this."

"I'm trying to drive out of this mess so we don't wind up in Hoboken… just hold it where I can see it!"

He pulled a large pamphlet from the folder. It read, MULTI-AGENCY RESPONSE TO AN EVENT OF MASS DESTRUCTION. Its source was printed below, Federal Emergency Management Agency — Department of Homeland Security.

"What's up with this? I would expect that we would have something like this in print ahead of time, in case of a national catastrophe."

"Yes, but…," as he turned to the cover page.

"Okay, I've read it. It says, 'Prepared for The President of the United States by the Office of the White House Chief of Staff' with the subheading, 'Bureau of Strategic Planning' and … and it looks like it was published last week. I don't get it, Jonathan. What is unusual about this?"

"David, this came from my office. This is what I do. I coordinate the scheduling of events for the President. This pamphlet showed up in my email by mistake yesterday morning. I am the one personally responsible for its publication. And I didn't know a thing about it until yesterday."

"That is strange. Wonder why?"

"I have worked with Betty for five years. She is my personal secretary. I called her into my office and asked her about it. I would have trusted her with my life."

"What did she say?"

"She walked to the door and quietly closed it. Then she started crying. She said, 'Jonathan, I don't have any idea what is happening. But two ranking members on the White House Staff came to my office and told me to put the pamphlet together.'

"'Why, didn't they come to me?' I asked?

"'These were their exact words,' she replied, 'Jonathan is to know nothing about this. It is classified. A cloud has developed on his security clearance.'"

I responded immediately, "A cloud on the security clearance of Jonathan Flink? That's impossible. Preposterous. What reason did they give?"

"They said that I was an evangelical Christian, and that as a member of that persuasion, I had been classified by the Department of Homeland Security as a potential terrorist."

Maria was waiting for us in the lobby of the hotel. "What took you guys so long? Did you West Virginia boys get lost in the big city?"

"Put us in the woods and show us a creek and we'll find our way out," remarked Jonathan with a smile. "Big cities give us country boys the creeps."

"That's more like it, Jonathan. Both of you. Cheer up. This is the day that the Lord has made — we will rejoice and be glad in it. He is in command!"

We were in the room in fifteen minutes, performing the routine functions of settling in for the night in a hotel. I lay down in the huge king-sized bed. Maria collapsed in a leather chair nearby and Jonathan remained standing with the leather folder he had his papers in. It was so good to feel the comfort of family — just to be with them. The ten minute vacation filled with laughter and chatter came to an end much too soon.

"This is really hard for me," Jonathan began, "but I have seen it coming for some time. I don't know when I first began to question...millions of us...no...tens of millions of us put our faith in him. He was so charismatic... intelligent... articulate ...persuading...the obvious answer to the problems of America...maybe, even the world."

"What are you talking about, Jonathan?" I asked.

Maria looked at me silently moving her lips, "He's talking about the President."

Jonathan continued, "The Bible tells us not to speak evil of our rulers. To honor and pray for our leaders and to be subject to the higher powers."

"I think he is going to say something bad about the President." Maria looked my way and smiled. "Are you, Jonathan?"

"No, of course not. But that doesn't mean that we can't make decisions regarding what he believes and thinks. We do it every day when dealing with people."

"And," Maria added, "that doesn't mean we are to be silent if he is in the wrong."

"Maria is right, David. As a Christian and an American citizen, we have the duty to enquire into what drives the man. After all, based on his promises, we have entrusted him with our most priceless treasures. I have a wife and three children. And a grand-baby on the way."

"I understand your concern, Jonathan. No informed person can debate the present peril we find ourselves in. But how can we know what drives him? It's sheer speculation," I stated.

He replied, "We have staked it all...our hopes...our futures...our families...our freedom...our children and grandchildren...on the integrity of a man whose integrity has been brought into question by broken promises. Don't you think it is incumbent upon us to enquire into the motives of that person? Only fools would do anything else.

"Jesus gave us the fruit inspection test. It is found in Matthew, chapter 7, verses 16 through 20. It says in the New KJV:

You will know them by their fruits. Do men gather grapes from thorn bushes or figs from thistles? Even so, every good tree bears good fruit, but a bad tree bears bad fruit...therefore by their fruits you will know them."

"And how exactly do we inspect the fruits?" I asked.

I mused over my question for a second or two and answered it myself, "I can only think of one way. Compare what a person says with what the person does. If they don't match, there's a problem."

"That's it. Jesus is also telling us here to judge the inner man by observing the outer," Maria exclaimed.

She went on, "I saw a list the other day. I can't remember who published it. It was a list of twenty some promises the writer felt had been broken by the President. Some of those included were ones we have heard his critics mention many times. They are, for example:

'If you like your doctor, you will be able to keep your doctor. Period.'

'My administration is committed to creating an unprecedented level of openness in government.'

"But the promise that got my attention was the last one on the list. I believe it is the first one on the list for most American people. I'm sure you'll recognize it when you hear it. The promise was, 'I solemnly swear that I will execute the office of president of the United States faithfully and will to the best of my ability, preserve, protect, and defend the constitution of the United States.'"

I didn't respond.

Jonathan began to loosen his tie, unbutton his collar and roll up his sleeves.

"Are you going to war, Jonathan?" I asked.

"No. It's nothing like that. It's a little warm in here. That's all."

Maria jumped up and walked toward the thermostat exclaiming, "The fruit inspection test! When you think about it, Jonathan, it's the test that makes the world go round.

"I'm putting it on 69 degrees, Jonathan."

She continued, "Business in the real world would not be possible if we did not apply the fruit inspection test. Who would enter a contract? Who would get married? Who would hire and fire? There has to be objective tests to verify that people are who they say they are. If not, civilized society would collapse."

I drew on my law school background, "You're right, Maria. Any attorney knows that every crime requires proof of a criminal mental state before there can be a conviction. If criminal intent is not found by the jury, the accused goes free."

Jonathan replied, "All three of us learned that in Criminal Law 101. Our entire criminal justice system would fail if juries could not determine the motive of the heart by words and actions of the accused."

"Don't worry about it, Jonathan," Maria intervened. "The President is not the highest authority in this country, anyway. He is subject to the Constitution. Every elected official, including the President of the United States, takes an oath before God that he will defend the Constitution. It is our sole authority. Not the President. Not the Supreme Court."

"Yeah," Jonathan exclaimed, "if they don't abide by it, they can be removed."

"But the Courts get to tell us what it means," I said. "It really doesn't matter that much. His term expires in 2017."

"I hope you're right." Maria replied.

"You guys have him all wrong. He is doing the best he can." I tried to reassure them. "He has the most difficult job in the world."

"Don't get me wrong," Jonathan instructed, "I am not accusing him of anything, David. I am only asking questions."

I looked at my watch, "Okay, you guys, let's dispense with the preliminaries and get to the subject matter of our concerns. We don't have all day, Jonathan. Get to the point."

"Two years ago, I began to study Islam and I couldn't help but make a connection between what I read and my observation of the policies of the present Administration."

"What have you found out?" Maria asked.

"This is very difficult for me to say…and actually I can't believe I am asking it…but…but is it possible that our President is a Muslim? And not only a Muslim, but a Muslim jihadist? And does it explain the actions taken by this Administration?"

He stopped and glanced back and forth at Maria and me with a tense look on his face, as if to measure our shock at the questions.

"Call the thought police!" Maria exclaimed, "This is outrageous."

"Get serious, Maria," I implored.

"I am serious," she answered. "Jonathan, if you had asked me those questions a year ago, I would have told you that you were crazy. But not anymore. I believe that untold millions of Americans are seriously asking themselves the same questions, today."

Jonathan raised his hands with palms out in a defensive gesture, "I'm just asking a question, that's all. But it is one that I believe should be seriously considered. The question is simply this, 'Do his words and actions support a reasonable theory that he is advancing Islam toward its goal of worldwide Sharia? At the expense of the security of the American people?' That is the question."

Instinctively, I reacted, "He's a follower of Christ, Jonathan. He's a Christian."

Maria cupped her hand over her mouth, rolled her eyes back and looked toward the wall. Then she spoke, "Don't mind me. Just keep on talking."

It was one of those moments that I had experienced a few times in my life. When there was something inside…something troubling that I didn't allow to surface. I couldn't put my finger on it.

"No, Jonathan! No. It is not true," I spontaneously exclaimed. "Do you have any idea what you are saying? You are saying that the man in whom we have placed our trust is intentionally dismantling our Constitution, our government and our way of life."

He continued, "I am not saying that he is. But I am asking the question, 'Is it possible?'"

"I understand."

Maria said, "This may take a while. I'll raid the refrigerator. There may be something healthy inside."

Jonathan replied, "Jihad is the holy war of Muslims against all non-Muslims. There are two types. The first is made up of those who employ the sword and incite terror wherever they can. They are ISIS, Al Qaeda, Boko Haram, Hamas, Hezbollah, Al-Shabaab and other splinter terrorist organizations.

"The second form of jihad is 'cultural' in nature, utilizing social, economic, and political means to accomplish the same goals as the terrorist. Most Americans do not know it exists. Its adherents are imbedded deeply in American society and practice social, economic and political jihad every day. Each openly denounces the integrity and methodology of the other, eventually causing confusion among their enemies. This confusion serves well their common purpose — the world dominance of Islam.

"For over thirty years, rich families in the Middle East have sent their sons and daughters to America to be educated in Ivy League schools like Harvard, Yale, and Columbia, establishing relationships with future leaders of America."

For a second I had a flashback of Omar. A sad feeling came over me when for a second or two I relived that day with him and the group at the site of Armageddon.

Jonathan interrupted my thoughts, "They became doctors, lawyers, bankers, educators and high-ranking military officers. It is widely believed that many of them are in corporate management and private business, buying up our motels, convenience stores and truck stops. Others are in high-level government positions where, today, some are advising the

Administration on such sensitive issues as national security. Much like termites working quietly…from the inside out."

"I want to get back to the question you framed a few minutes ago, Jonathan," Maria softly stated. "I don't understand why we cannot publicly ask if our President is a Muslim."

"Or, if he is a jihadist, for that matter," Jonathan added. "It doesn't mean we hate him."

"The test is simple," Maria concluded.

"What is it, honey?"

"What we say and do, is the only measure of who we are."

LEADING FROM BEHIND

"**I** have an experiment that I would like to try on you guys." Jonathan paused, made eye contact with each of us, and then he proceeded, "I promise. It won't take fifteen minutes."

I looked at my watch. I knew my exasperation was showing. "There's a chair over there, Jonathan. Are you going to stand there all day?"

"I'm fine, David, thanks."

"So, what's next?"

"Okay, I have here in my hand three copies of a written exam I have prepared."

Maria reached for her copy, exclaiming, "Oh, boy! I can't wait!"

"Are you being sarcastic?" he asked.

Maria tucked her head down sheepishly between her shoulders and replied, "I'm sorry, Jonathan. I know this is important to you."

Jonathan handed a copy to me, and then one to Maria. There were several pages. I scanned the first page, quickly. Maria seemed engrossed in the content.

Maybe five minutes went by, and then "Wha…? Do you…?" Maria and I spoke at the same time.

"Did you guys plan that?" Jonathan asked.

"You go first, honey," she said.

"You want us to answer these questions?"

"Yes, you will be the first to take the test."

"Then what?"

"I want the public to be informed," Jonathan began. "Most Americans are too busy with jobs and family to look into what is happening in the country. There is a lot of stuff that the mainstream media does not cover. Consequently, most Americans do not know all that is going on. I have researched the facts presented in these questions. They can be easily verified on the Internet."

"What's next?" I asked.

"I have decided to post the test on my personal web site and Facebook. I'm hoping that it will go viral. As you can see, the three main questions are: 'Is the President a Muslim? Is he advancing Islam at the expense of the interests of the nation he has sworn to protect? And does he intend to extend his Presidency beyond two terms?'

"What about your job, Jonathon?" I asked.

"I have no job, remember! My security clearance has been compromised. I'm a Christian. It's just a matter of time."

He continued, "The stated goal of the Islamic jihadist is to replace the Constitution with the Koran and to fly the Islamic black flag over the White House. The death of thousands of Americans on American soil that began with 9/11 is a grim testimony of their determination to terrorize and annihilate all people who will not convert to Islam."

"My goodness, Jonathan! Can't you find heavier subject matter than this? And don't you think this is just a little too harsh? Too much?" I asked.

"David, there is a sizable undercurrent of American sentiment — millions of people, if we will be honest, who are asking the same questions. But for fear of losing their jobs, being prosecuted, or being branded a bigot or racist, they are afraid to speak out. We are no longer living in the culture of a free society if we are afraid to question those who rule. It will no longer be America!"

"He's right, David." Maria joined in, "There is no legitimate reason these things cannot be openly discussed in public. As Americans we must speak out. As Christians we must pray."

"But can't you tone it down, Jonathan?"

"Okay. Back to the three questions. They are set out on the materials you have in your hand. "

He paused and looked away as if pondering some mysterious apparition outside the window. Then he seemed to shake it off, "I am not attempting to advocate. I am not for, or against, the President."

"But the issues raised by these questions are such, that if enough people would honestly respond, it could affect the future of this country."

"I want you to be objective, and most of all, I want you to be honest."

"If we are to going to evaluate the President," Maria exclaimed holding the test papers up in the air, "I will be honest, but I'm afraid it's too late for me to be objective."

"Take the test, anyway, Maria. There are facts contained in it that you may not know or you may have forgotten. Who knows? You may change your mind.

"Above all, be honest. A particular set of facts may not prove anything. Only God knows for sure what is in his heart. The goal is to bring the issues out into the open...for open discussion."

"I don't know how on earth he can deny anything," Maria replied as she looked over the test, "what can he say? 'I didn't say these things. I didn't do these things. It didn't happen.' This thing was not done in a corner, but in the open for all the world to see."

"Maria," I asked, "how can you say that? You haven't seen the facts, yet!"

"Keep an open mind!" Jonathan cautioned, "If possible, lay aside all preconceived notions and biases."

I thought about all the years I had spent in the State Department, and wondered if it would affect my ability to be objective. It is so easy to believe what you are told when the pay is good.

Jonathan resumed, "Now, as you will see on the papers you have in your hands, there are three major questions. After the questions, certain facts are set out. These facts are statements that have been made by the President, or specific actions that have been taken by him. Do you see these?"

"Yes."

"Okay. Look at each fact and after each one you will find two responses. I suppose you would call it Multiple Choice, except there are only two possible options. Do you see that?"

"Yes."

"Just take a few minutes, look at the facts, and encircle your choice based on which one the facts tend to prove."

"I have borrowed the Federal Rules of Evidence as the measure to guide you in your selection. Under Federal Rule # 401, the test for relevancy for any evidence is:

a. it has any tendency to make a fact more or less probable than it would be without the evidence; and
b. the fact is of consequence in determining the action.

"Thus, for the first question you must determine, 'Does the fact tend to prove that the President is a Muslim or a Christian?'"

"Remember that proof is cumulative. There is a final response. Don't make up your mind until all the facts are considered. The final response takes into consideration all the facts. It will be your final answer to the question presented."

"You sound like the judge instructing the jury, Jonathan. Do we get paid for jury duty?" Maria asked.

"Okay. The first question," he replied:

1. Is the President a Muslim or a Christian?

"There have been several polls taken of the opinions of the American people on the issue, many articles written and thousands of blogs on the Internet. This is my own poll.

"On the first question we know there is no legal reason that a Muslim cannot be president. The facts that I have set forth are the statements of the President himself. Statements made by him over a period of time. Authenticity is not an issue since his statements have been made to the world, and can easily be found on the Internet."

I started to say something and forgot what I was going to say. I was back in Tel Aviv on the hotel balcony overlooking the Mediterranean.

"David! You're gone. Earth to David. Honey, are you okay?"

"I was someplace else. I'm sorry."

"David," Maria responded with concern in her voice, "why don't you tell us what happened in Israel. What did God say to you?"

"God gave me an assignment that was confirmed in Dubai. To warn America that a great catastrophe was going to take place unless we confessed our sins, turned away from them, and plead with Him for mercy. That time was running out!"

Jonathan always had liked to play the big brother role because I was born 10 minutes after him, "Little brother, Maria and I knew, somehow, that you were coming back with a message from God. If this is from God, if you are to sound the alarm, then He will give you a big trumpet. He will send friends to help. You will not be alone. You will need to speak boldly what He has put in your heart."

"I'm sorry. Let's go on."

"Are you sure?" he asked.

"I'm okay, thanks."

Jonathan resumed the test, "Okay, the President has made the following statements about Islam and Christianity. I have divided the statements into three categories: the President's view of history; his US government policies; and what inspires him. The issue is whether he is a Muslim or a Christian:"

View of History — Islam:

"We will convey our deep appreciation for the Islamic faith, which has done so much over the centuries to shape the world including in my own country." Turkish Parliament, April 6, 2009

CHRISTIAN   MUSLIM

"As a student of history, I also know civilization's debt to Islam." Cairo University, June 4, 2009

CHRISTIAN   MUSLIM

"Islam has a proud tradition of tolerance." Cairo University, June 4, 2009

CHRISTIAN   MUSLIM

"Throughout history, Islam has demonstrated through words and deeds the possibilities of religious tolerance and racial equality." Cairo University, June 4, 2009

CHRISTIAN   MUSLIM

"The future must not belong to those who slander the prophet of Islam." UN General Assembly, September 2012

CHRISTIAN   MUSLIM

View of History — Christianity:

"During the Crusades and the Inquisition, people committed terrible deeds in the name of Christ... In our home country, slavery and Jim Crow all too often was justified in the name of Christ." National Prayer Breakfast, Washington, DC February 2015

CHRISTIAN   MUSLIM

Government Policy — Islam:
"Islam is not part of the problem in combating violent extremism — it is an important part of promoting peace." Cairo University, June 4, 2009

CHRISTIAN   MUSLIM

"We will encourage more Americans to study in Muslim communities." Cairo University, June 4, 2009

CHRISTIAN   MUSLIM

"I consider it part of my responsibility as President of the United States to fight against negative stereotypes of Islam wherever they appear." Cairo University, June 4, 2009

CHRISTIAN   MUSLIM

Government Policy — Christianity:
"Which passages of scripture should guide our public policy? Should we go with Leviticus, which suggests slavery is okay and that eating shell fish is an abomination? Or we could go with Deuteronomy, which suggests stoning your child if he strays from the faith? Or should we just stick to the Sermon on the Mount — a passage that is so radical that it's doubtful that our own Defense Department would survive its application." Call to Renewal, June 2006

CHRISTIAN   MUSLIM

Maria interrupted, "Stop! There is no place in the Bible that endorses slavery or killing your child if he strays from the faith… that is ridiculous. It just isn't true. I've seen politicians use this technique before. He made up a false representation of the Bible and then attacked it. To people who don't know the Bible he has done a grave disservice. He has turned them away from the truth. I hope God forgives him."

"Honey, don't be so critical. We don't know the whole story. Maybe he is relying on somebody else's interpretation. Maybe he hasn't read it."

Personal Inspiration – Islam:
The Muslim call to prayer is "one of the prettiest sounds on earth at sunset." NY Times, March 6, 2007
CHRISTIAN   MUSLIM

Personal Inspiration – Christianity:
"I looked and could not find similar warm and heartfelt statements regarding Christianity," Jonathan explained. "I'm not saying they are not out there, just that I could not find them."

"If he had praised Christianity, it would be available on the Internet," Maria replied. "In July 2015 the President and his wife sent a tweet to Muslims around the world wishing them a happy Eid-ul-Fitr, which marked the end of Ramadan. This was two hours before the Chattanooga terrorist attack by Muhammad Youssef Abdulazaaz that left five US Service members dead. Only after much criticism did the President order flags flown at half-mast — five days later."

Criticism – Islam:
"I could not find any critical remarks of Islam made by the President."
CHRISTIAN   MUSLIM

Criticism – Christianity:
"Remember that during the Crusades and the Inquisition, people committed terrible deeds in the name of Christ." Washington Prayer Breakfast, 2015
CHRISTIAN   MUSLIM

"When I listen to less than loving expressions by Christians, I get concerned. But that's a topic for another day." Easter Prayer Breakfast 2015
CHRISTIAN   MUSLIM

Maria nudged me when we read this one and remarked, "What did he mean by that? 'Topic for another day?' That's creepy."

"What he meant by that is sheer speculation, Honey."

Then we were all quiet. Maria broke the silence, "This comment is not a criticism of the President, but, in my opinion, there is a real problem with any religious persuasion that advocates the overthrow of our Constitutional government. And Islam is committed to a worldwide Caliphate with the forceful overthrow of all government not based on Sharia law. It boils down, in my opinion, as to whether this President is a Muslim who is dedicated to the world conquest of Islam. And, if so, does it affect government policy?"

"We'll get to that question in a minute, Maria, but draw a circle around what you believe the statements prove about the President's faith. Is he Christian? Or, is he Muslim?"

"Are we to consider the fact that he claims to be a Christian?"

"Sure, Maria. I would weigh it along with the other facts. It is impeachable, however, since it could be self-serving.

"Finally, let me point out one more statement. It was made two years before he was elected President. The statement was:

"I will stand with the Muslims should the political winds shift in an ugly direction." This statement is found in the President's best – selling book, *The Audacity of Hope*, written in 2006.
CHRISTIAN   MUSLIM

"Now, I am going to ask you to consider all the facts. As if your decision would determine the future of America. Is the President a Christian or a Muslim?
FINDING: CHRISTIAN   MUSLIM

I could tell that Maria was upset. She took a deep breath, stood up, and walked to one of the large windows that overlooked the UN building. She appeared to be staring at it. It was more like she was speaking to herself, than to Jonathan and me, "I don't see how the political winds could shift in a more ugly direction than they are now. I believe he has already taken his stand."

Jonathan was still focused on the test, "Maria, your point is well taken. That's the next question — whether or not he is a jihadist."

She turned around and added, "Can't you see that even his non-governance has been a tool to disrupt and confuse? To foster mayhem? He doesn't have to instigate chaos. He can create chaos while advocating peace. As the leader of the free world, all he has to do is to refuse to lead. To lead from behind. Instability has resulted. We are in the time of chaos. Order will eventually come. But it will be a different world. A new world. A New World Order. He knows that."

"I'm sorry, but I don't think that is his purpose. He just wants the US to play a lesser role in the world. What you are saying is a bit too radical for me, Honey."

"You used to teach, didn't you, David?" she asked.

"Yes, I did some substitute teaching in Middle School. You know that. What's the point?"

"What did you get when you left the room for fifteen minutes?"

"Chaos."

Nobody said a word for a few seconds. Maria turned back and looked out the window. Then she commented, "If you want my opinion...the President left the room seven years ago!"

THE CHAOS STRATEGY

Maria suggested a break. We stretched our legs, talked about the Big Apple, and I made some decaffeinated coffee. After a discussion about the pros and cons of coffee as a health benefit, we retreated to our respective positions. Maria insisted I lie down on the bed again to alleviate the pain caused by a skiing accident on Whiteface Mountain years before.

Maria sat down near me in the leather chair with her feet upon the bed. Jonathan was standing where he had been since we came to the room.

"I don't know why you have to get so macho with the coffee pot, David," Maria complained, "this stuff is strong enough to kill a horse."

She then reached out and squeezed my arm, "Honey, I love you. But please tell me that you had nothing to do with that memo produced by the State Department."

"Which one?"

"The one that said that the way to combat ISIS was to offer them jobs. I'd like to see the employer's face who read that resume. The idea gives a new meaning to workplace violence."

"Okay. Its time to get started," Jonathan ordered. "In my recent studies of the Islamic faith, I made some astounding discoveries. One of them is the parallel prophetic themes that run through both Christianity and Islam, when the subject matter is the Last Days."

"One of the main doctrines of Islam is the Last Day or the Day of Judgment. They believe Allah will judge the world at that time. Muslims teach that it will be preceded by a time of moral corruption, great chaos, anarchy, utter confusion and disorder. Wars, massacres and great bloodshed will prevail and there will be a great earthquake. Great cities will disappear in one day as if they had never existed."

"Sounds like the Book of Revelation to me," Maria spoke up.

"Yes, it does, I agree." A flashback to my childhood brought back some scary memories. "I will never forget the evangelists who came to our church when I was a child. They preached about the Second Coming, the Anti-Christ, the Mark of the Beast and the Great Tribulation. They warned us to be ready. They said the Lord was coming as a thief in the night."

"What's wrong with that?" Jonathan asked. "We need more of that, today."

"Don't give me that, Jonathan. You were as scared as I was. I agree we need to warn others of the Lord's return, but it was the theme of every sermon back then."

Jonathan pulled his tie all the way off and hung it on the closet door-knob. "Okay," he continued, "the Imams teach that during this time of trouble the Islamic Messiah, the Mahdi, will appear. That he will have the solution to all the world problems and rid the world of evil. He will establish a World Caliphate. Sharia law will be forced upon all people."

I looked at Maria and moved my lips dramatically with a small whisper, "Omar would enjoy this."

Maria smiled and nodded affirmatively.

"Here's the scary part," Jonathan continued. "This is fact and not fiction. True Islamic jihadists believe that terror and chaos will bring in the Mahdi — and that it is their solemn duty to employ whatever terror tactics it takes to bring him back."

"Let me add something here, Jonathan," I interjected, "this is the reason that every Muslim country in the Middle East, as well as Israel, is resisting Iran's efforts to obtain nuclear weapons. They have no doubt that she will use them. A nuclear race in the Middle East is all the world needs. That is where we are headed."

"Jonathan, are you going to tell us that the President is implementing chaos as a weapon in the advancement of Islam?" I asked.

"I am merely posing the question, that's all."

"What do you think about all this, Maria?" I asked, "Never mind, I know what you... "

"The sword has been the way of advancing Islam from the beginning," she replied. "Marxist Socialism is the same. They both can be summed up in one word — genocide. May God help us. They are now joining forces in an attack on our freedoms."

"Little brother, just use the Internet and search for chaos and Islam. See where it takes you. I think you will be surprised. It's a major part of their teaching on the topic of the Last Days."

"Now, David, let's assume you wanted to affect political change in a particular region, other than by legally prescribed means, of course. What would be the first thing you would do?"

"That's easy, I would bring about as much instability as I could. I mean, that's Revolution 101. Protests! Riots! Civil war!"

Jonathan continued, "The study of the Islamic Last Day doctrine brought me, as I said earlier, to some very sober questions about current US policy.

"That brings us the second question about the President":

2. Is the President an Islamic jihadist, and is he using his office as President of the United States to foster chaotic conditions in the world that advance Islam, all in violation of the laws and welfare of the American people?

"Now, on the syllabus, you will find facts that can be reasonably considered as relevant to this question."

"The issue in each case is whether or not the facts set out have any tendency to prove, or not to prove, that the President is employing chaos as a weapon to advance Islam."

"After each fact presented you will select between ORDER and CHAOS. If you encircle CHAOS, then you are saying that the fact tends to prove that he is a jihadist and is employing a chaos strategy to bring back the Mahdi. If you encircle ORDER, then you are saying that fact does not tend to prove the issue."

"The facts are listed in two sections. The first list is under the 'Domestic Front' heading and the second list is under the 'Foreign Front' heading."

"Finally, you will encircle YES or NO indicating your conclusion as to whether he is a jihadist."

"Jonathan, can we comment as we go along?" Maria asked.

"I don't see why not. Even a jury deliberates."

"I am asking all my friends to forward the questions to all their friends on the Internet. With a request that their replies be sent back to my email address. I hope to get a true sample of what people are thinking," stated Jonathon.

"You're serious about this aren't you, Jonathan," I responded.

"Yes, let's look at the list. Let's try to keep talking to a minimum. David has an important appointment to keep tonight."

DOMESTIC FRONT
Militant Islam in America

Fact: In spite of 9/11 that killed over 3,000 Americans; the Fort Hood shootings that killed 13; the Chattanooga, TN shooting that killed 5; the Garland, TX attempt; and the Boston Marathon bombing that left 3 Americans dead, the FBI did not mention Islamic terrorism as one of the 10 most dangerous domestic threats to US national security. It was listed as a foreign threat only.

ORDER   CHAOS

Fact: The President, The FBI, the Department of Homeland Security, the State Department, the CIA, the Pentagon and the National Security Council do not officially recognize Islamic extremism as a threat to the American people.

ORDER   CHAOS

Fact: The Oklahoma beheading of an employee, and the stabbing of another at a food processing plant in Oklahoma in 2014 was investigated by the FBI as workplace violence and not a terrorist attack. This was the case even though the attacker had recently converted to Islam, tried to convert his fellow employees and had several photos of Osama bin Laden on his Facebook page.

ORDER   CHAOS

Fact: The President has consistently denied the existence of Islamic terrorism, stating that ISIS speaks for no religion. That, 'no religious faith teaches people to massacre innocents.'

ORDER   CHAOS

Jonathan added, shaking his head, "Do you really think that he believes that?"

Maria responded with a question, "How can anybody say that there is no such thing as Islamic terrorism? What if President Franklin D. Roosevelt had told the American people after Pearl Harbor, 'This was not an attack by the Japanese. We know that the planes came from Japan. Hundreds of aircraft bore the emblem of the rising sun. The government of Japan is boasting that it was their planes. But we know better. The Japanese would never do anything like this.'"

"I'm not sure this is the same thing," I countered, "the Japanese were driven by extreme nationalism. The President is just saying that, 'no faith teaches people to massacre.'"

"David, they were motivated by religion," Maria replied. "The Japanese had their own suicide bombers. They were the kamikaze pilots. They gladly sacrificed their lives for their deified Emperor. It was the Shinto religion that motivated them, just like Islam motivates the terrorist to die while killing others."

Jonathan responded, "Yes, and everybody knows that Mohammad taught that the only way to know for sure that you will be received into Paradise is to die killing infidels. Plus, you get 72 virgins in the afterlife to boot.

"ISIS makes war under these illusions that come directly from the Koran and the Hadith. Paradise in an afterlife? If that isn't religious teaching, I don't know what it is."

"I guess you're right," I admitted. "I've never thought of it that way."

Maria added, "I never feel comfortable when everybody in the room agrees with me, but I think everybody in the world knows, except the US government, that the ISIS warrior is Muslim. Militant jihadists, whatever they are called, are the true Muslims. They are the real thing — the reincarnation of the first Muslims that marched under Mohammad."

Fact: While the US government denies that Islam is a national security threat, a widely published Pew Research Center poll of Muslims in America, found that 26% of Muslims between the ages of 18 and 29 affirmed that there could be circumstances that would justify suicide bombing.

ORDER   CHAOS

Fact: In August 2015, it came to light that the FBI had circulated an intelligence bulletin to Federal, State and Local law enforcement warning against attacks on mosques, Islamic centers and Muslims by militia extremists.

ORDER   CHAOS

Fact: Jeh Johnson, Secretary of the Department of Homeland Security, admitted that his grandfather had been interrogated by the House Un-American Activities Committee under Senator Joseph McCarthy in the 1940s on suspicions that he was a Communist. Reportedly, Mr. Johnson has vowed to protect Muslims from the same kind of "persecution" that his grandfather went through.

ORDER   CHAOS

"I have a question, Jonathan."

"Go ahead, Maria."

"How is it possible to defend against an enemy whom we cannot identify? How do we separate the terrorist threat in America from the 2000 plus Islamic mosques in the country, many of which are radicalizing their young people? How do we separate the terrorist threat from the Islamic enclaves that are rapidly forming in many of our cities? How can we presume that there is no connection between the hundreds of thousands of Muslims that we are bringing into the country, and the violent advance of Islam around the world? To separate terrorism from the ideology that drives it is certain death."

"I am glad to report that there is some good news on this front," I stated. "A terror suspect from Somalia, who now lives in Minnesota, has been kicked out of two different mosques up there. The reason stated was because he was suspected of radicalizing their youth."

"Yes, I saw that," replied Jonathan, looking wistfully toward the window, "Maybe, there is hope…if, somehow, we can all work together."

Immigration

Fact: In a recent study, the Center for Immigration Studies reported that between the years 2010 and 2013, nearly 300,000 immigrants, mostly from Muslim countries, entered the United States bringing the total number migrating to the US from predominantly Muslim countries to 2.4 million.

ORDER   CHAOS

Fact: As of June 2015, 93% of the Syrian refugees resettled in US since the beginning of the civil war in Syria, have been Muslim. 4.9% have been Christians. The FBI has admitted that the immigrants are impossible to screen because the US has no boots on the ground in Syria, and because it is a failed state.

ORDER   CHAOS

I raised my hand.

"What, David?"

"I was just going to say that I have closely watched the Iraq and Syrian refugee resettlement program. The big problem there is that there is no way to vet them. Their records are in regions now controlled by ISIS. In addition, in the past we have been hesitant to accept refugees from Syria because many were radicalized Muslims."

Fact: Many Muslims have migrated from Somalia, which is one of the leading terrorist hot spots in the world. Once in the country, they can be joined by family members.

ORDER   CHAOS

Fact: Approximately one-third of the Somalis in America live in Minnesota. Minneapolis-St. Paul has more Somalis than any other city in America. At a press conference in April 2015, Andrew Luger, a US District Attorney for Minnesota, stated that Minnesota had a terror recruiting problem.

ORDER   CHAOS

Fact: One hundred ninety communities have been selected for Middle Eastern refugee re-settlement, and were on a secret list in the State Department. Information has been difficult to get from the government by the cities selected. They received no forewarning other than the fact that relief organizations came into town to set up offices. Early cities identified were Spartanburg, SC; Twin Falls, ID; Dallas, Fort Worth, and Houston, TX; Chicago, IL; San Diego, CA; Louisville, KY, as well as many others.

ORDER   CHAOS

Fact: The President's Task Force for New Americans has unveiled a plan to integrate millions of immigrants and refugees into welcoming communities across the United States. The plan is to get the program institutionalized so it cannot be reversed. It was announced in April 2015 that boots were on the ground in 29 states to welcome and provide services for them. The Mayors of Atlanta, Chicago, Los Angeles and Nashville allegedly are on board welcoming the immigrants into their cities.

ORDER   CHAOS

Fact: It was alleged that the President, at the same time that he created the task force to integrate millions of immigrants and refugees into America, announced that he would bypass Congress and grant amnesty to 5 million illegal immigrants and child migrants.

ORDER   CHAOS

Fact: Immigration and Customs Enforcement (ICE) reported that 68,000 illegal criminal immigrants were released in 2013 back into society and were not deported. A congressional committee investigated — twenty-five percent of them were first level crimes, like murder and rape.

ORDER   CHAOS

"I think it's a shame," opined Maria. "While the floodgates are open for unscreened Muslim immigrants by the hundreds of thousands, Christians are being deported. I don't know if you saw this or not, but a federal judge recently ordered the deportation of 15 Iraqi Christians who had fled to the United States from ISIS. They had been detained in a San Diego detention center run by ICE for six months awaiting a judicial ruling."

"Let's stop just a minute here," Jonathan announced. "What I am going to say is that we don't have to be afraid of the new America that is taking shape. I believe the Lord is showing me that it will offer us the greatest mission field in American history. Christians have had great difficulty penetrating the 10/40 window. God is bringing it to us. I believe many Muslims will come to Christ in America and return to their homelands as Christian missionaries."

"We receive that! Praise God, Jonathan!" exclaimed Maria as she stood to her feet. "I believe what I am about to say is prophetic. I sense the anointing of the Holy Spirit. As part of the great outpouring of the Holy Spirit promised in the book of Joel, chapter 2, the Church will begin to love the strangers in our midst. We will follow the example of our Lord interceding for the lost and taking the message of God's love into the streets, the homes and the marketplace. What a different America it will be. It is going to get exciting."

Fact: On December 18, 2015, the President signed into law the 1.1 trillion dollar Omnibus bill. It was passed overwhelmingly in both houses of Congress 316 - 113. Congress funded the big ticket items the President asked for including full funding for 300,000 visas for migrants from Muslim countries in 2016 alone by funding every US immigration program in existence, as well as, expansion of the President's resettlement of Syrian refugees. The President was so elated that he invited the new House Leader, Paul Ryan, for dinner at the White House.

ORDER   CHAOS

Southern Border

Fact: In July 2014, a top US General in charge of the Southern Border, said he has been unable to stop the flow of illegals, weapons and drugs crossing the border. In less than a year, 100,000 migrants, mostly children, crossed the border. Some 50,000 children had, at that time, been referred to the Department of Health and Human Services at great cost to the American taxpayer. It was estimated the number could reach 90,000 for the year.

ORDER   CHAOS

Fact: In 2012, Sixty-two percent of the households headed by illegal immigrants in the US were on welfare.

ORDER   CHAOS

"That was almost four years ago," exclaimed Maria. "It has to be worse today with the hundreds of thousands that have come in since 2012."

Fact: Judicial Watch, an organization that monitors the government, has issued a report that it has learned that ISIS is running a camp about eight miles from the Southern Border — near El Paso, TX. The warnings conflict with claims by the Department of Homeland Security that there is no imminent danger from ISIS across the border.

ORDER   CHAOS

Fact: A Department of Homeland Security bus was reportedly caught on video, on May 7, 2015, transporting a busload of Somalis and other Africans who had illegally crossed the Mexican border into the United States. They were taken to a detention center near Victorville, CA. The only English word they had to know for entry into the United States was the password 'asylum.' The windows of the bus were covered to hide the occupants.

ORDER   CHAOS

Fact: A US Congressman from California, Duncan Hunter, recently warned that ten ISIS members have been caught crossing the Mexican border. The Department of Homeland Security claimed his assertions were false. He stood by his statement saying that he got his information from border patrol agents. He added that if they had caught 10, there could be dozens who had not been caught.

ORDER   CHAOS

Fact: ISIS announced it was close to buying a nuclear weapon from Pakistan and smuggling it across the Mexican border using established drug routes used by the drug cartels. The ISIS spokesman said, "it's just a quick hop through a smuggling tunnel and, hey, presto, they're mingling with another 12 million 'illegal' aliens in America with a nuclear bomb in the trunk of their car."

ORDER   CHAOS

Fact: In the Supreme Court case Arizona vs United States (2012), the President filed a lawsuit against the state of Arizona. The issue was an Arizona statute, which allowed Arizona to enforce its own laws governing immigration. The US Supreme Court decided in favor of the Federal Government under the theory that federal law pre-empted state law. The effect was that the states lost control of their borders, granting control to the Federal Government.

ORDER   CHAOS

Fact: The President has resisted all efforts to seal the border or to enforce the laws that are in place.

ORDER   CHAOS

"Did you hear what the President said to 2015 graduates of the US Coast Guard Academy at the graduation ceremony?" Jonathan asked.

"No! I missed it. They said it was telecast. I heard about it."

"Instead of inspiring them to secure the border, he talked about climate change and how it constitutes an immediate risk to our national security."

"I hope the cadets will be well armed." I chuckled.

"You guys," Maria replied, "get serious. This is not Don Quixote attacking windmills to bring back the days of chivalry. This is the Commander-in-Chief of the Armed Forces of the United States telling the branch of service charged with securing our borders that they are irrelevant. That they don't matter anymore. That there will be no national boundaries in the New World Order.

"After all," she continued, "with his record on border security, what could he say? Any exhortation to secure our borders would have been patently hypocritical."

"Maria, I just think he sees global warming as the bigger threat than the immigration crisis," I countered.

Race

Fact: To a racially divided America, after hearing the verdict of George Zimmerman by a Florida jury acquitting him in the shooting death of Trayvon Martin, a black teenager, the President said, "Trayvon Martin could have been me thirty-five years ago."

ORDER   CHAOS

Jonathan explained, "I brought up the race issue, not because it directly relates to whether the President is a jihadist, but because it relates indirectly. The statement was considered by many Americans to be inflammatory at a time of great tension between the races. I thought it spoke to the issue of creating an atmosphere of instability that Muslims believe will prevail preceding the Last Day. I felt he definitely identified with the black side of the controversy against law enforcement by this very personal and emotional statement. It had to resonate deeply with the black community. I guess what I am trying to say is that it was divisive at a time when our nation needed healing."

"It was gas on the fire, Jonathan, but it is stretching it too far to say that it was an act of jihad," I stated.

"But David, division leads to anarchy. Jesus said, 'A house divided against itself cannot stand.'"

Maria turned to me and said, "David, I know you believe in him. But don't forget that as a Community Organizer in Chicago it has been reported that he lectured on principles taken from Saul Alinsky's infamous book, *Rules For Radicals*. One of the rules contained in the book is 'change is brought about through relentless agitation and trouble-making of a kind that radically disrupts society as it is.'"

Financial Collapse

Fact: The President claims that we do not have a spending problem. His fiscal policy reflects this opinion. He insists on growing the size of government and the national debt. It is now official. The Director of the Congressional Budget Office recently predicted, before Congress, that the debt is unsustainable.

ORDER   CHAOS

Fact: The massive immigration that will result from the President's policies will cost the American taxpayer trillions of dollars per year providing food stamps, medical cards and housing allowances. If present entitlement trends continue, this money will come from a dwindling taxpayer base and fewer employment opportunities.

ORDER   CHAOS

Fact: The US Government will be $20 trillion in debt when the President leaves office. The debt will increase at the rate of over 2 billion dollars per day.

ORDER   CHAOS

Fact: By the time the President is scheduled to leave office in January 2017, he will have accumulated more debt for the American people than all the Presidents before him combined.

ORDER   CHAOS

"What are you about to say, Maria?" Jonathan asked. "You can put your hand down."

"I was just going to say, 'it's called crashing the system.' You make the problems so massive that they are unmanageable. It guarantees a collapse — and a rebuilding from the ruins."

FOREIGN FRONT
Withdrawal from Iraq

Fact: The withdrawal of ground troops from Iraq, against the advice of our military experts and generals, has created a vacuum that is now irrefutably filled by ISIS. The Iraqi troops deserted their positions, which left behind billions of dollars in American military equipment and ammunition. It cannot be denied that it is directly related to the rise of militant Islam in the Middle East, with untold suffering for millions of people.

ORDER   CHAOS

Arab Spring

Fact: The President's support of the Arab Spring has been enthusiastic with covert weapons shipments to Libyan rebels through Kuwait and other third party countries. These arms found their way into the hands of al-Qaeda and ISIS. Our involvement in Libyan arms deals is believed to have led to the Benghazi tragedy.

ORDER   CHAOS

Fact: The Arab Spring began in Tunisia in 2010 and spread across the Middle East, leading to widespread protests, demonstrations, and civil war. The Arab Spring has resulted in the overthrow of stable governments in Tunisia, Libya, Egypt, and Yemen, as well as civil war in Syria. Millions of refuges from the war-torn areas have fled from Iraq and Syria and are stretching the resources of less affected Middle Eastern countries, the European Union, and the United States. The Middle East is a tinder box and on the verge of a nuclear arms race.

ORDER   CHAOS

Fact: According to the United Nations High Commission for Refugees, there were 60 million refugees and internally displaced persons that had been driven by violence from their homes by mid-2015. Almost 20 million of them were refugees, and a third of the refugees came from Iraq and Syria. The ongoing conflict in Syria is seen as a major contributor to the record numbers.

ORDER   CHAOS

Fact: The number of refugees and internally displaced persons has exceeded the 50 million people who were displaced in World War II. Many see the Arab Spring, the US withdrawal from Iraq and the rise of ISIS as major contributors to the dramatic increase in refugee migrations.

ORDER   CHAOS

Maria began to cry. Jonathan fetched a tissue from a box on the end table and handed it to her. She smiled slightly, wiped her eyes with the tissue and said, "Please forgive me for being such a softie. I have seen the plight of these people on TV. God help us to remember that these statistics represent 60 million individual human tragedies. We should be praying for them. Jesus must be weeping."

I bowed my head and sensed the awesome magnitude of what was taking place. It was changing the face of the world. The world would never be the same again.

Jonathan interrupted the spell, "I don't mean to rush, but let's please go on the next item on the syllabus."

Alliances

Fact: Forsaking long-time Middle Eastern allies like Mubarak's Egypt, Saudi Arabia, and Israel, the President has turned to their common enemy, Iran. Iran's leaders have sworn to destroy Israel, as well as the United States.

ORDER   CHAOS

Fact: The President has joined Shi'ite Iran, in bombing Sunni ISIS, in Shi'ite Iraq. At the same time joining Sunni Saudi Arabia, in bombing the Houthi insurgents in Shi'ite Yemen. While at the same time he is negotiating with Shi'ite Iran who is supplying weapons to Hezbollah in Lebanon, Houthi rebels in Yemen, Hamas in Gaza and Assad in Syria. He has negotiated a nuclear agreement with Iran, whose Supreme Leader is publicly calling for "Death to America."

ORDER   CHAOS

"Jonathan, I will have to admit that it's a mess. Nobody can tell whose side we are on," I stated.

Maria spoke up, "That's because you are analyzing US policy from old assumptions that no longer hold water. We are assuming that the Administration wants to engage ISIS and win when he has repeatedly said that the goal is to contain them."

"I don't think the President intentionally is forsaking our alliances in the Middle East," I stated, "it's just a very complex situation over there."

"Yes, Honey," Maria replied, "but the Saudis did not advise the President that they were launching a major attack on the Yemen insurgents until the day of the attack. This is a clear sign that a strategic country, in maintaining a balance of power in the Middle East, no longer feels she can depend on the United States.

"We have abandoned our role as the stability factor in the Middle East. Putin has been reported as saying, 'we must seize this window of opportunity.' This is what he has been waiting for. He is now occupying Syria and threatening us."

"Whether we like it or not," added Jonathan, "we must admit that the vacuum created by the withdrawal of the United States is now being filled by Russia."

ISIS

Fact: The White House has announced our war strategies ahead of time: our intention not to put boots on the ground; to maintain and not to defeat ISIS; setting time limits on US involvement in Iraq and Syria; and advising ISIS and the world when we would attack Mosul.

ORDER   CHAOS

Fact: Retired United States Air Force Lieutenant General Thomas McInnerney stated on Fox News Radio, "There is no question we are deliberately losing to ISIS."

ORDER   CHAOS

Fact: Former Secretary of Defense, Bob Gates, who served under Presidents Bush and Obama, recently stated on MSNBC, 'we don't have a strategy at all' in defeating ISIS.

ORDER   CHAOS

Fact: General Barry McCaffrey was America's most decorated General when he retired in 1998. Interviewed on MSNBC News, he described the President's action against ISIS as a 'political gesture' and a 'pinprick.'

ORDER   CHAOS

Fact: In September 2014, the Pentagon announced that the US was carrying out an average of 5 strikes a week against ISIS. Congressman Ed Royce was said to have compared the number of US airstrikes with those in Kuwait during the first Gulf War. He reportedly stated that over a period of several weeks the US conducted 116,000 air strikes in Kuwait.

ORDER   CHAOS

Fact: In a program launched by the President in 2014, Congress approved 500 million dollars for training Syrian rebels against ISIS. The goal was to have 15,000 trained fighters by 2017. As of July 2015, the US had spent the one half billion dollars and trained only 'four or five' actual fighters.

ORDER   CHAOS

"Yeah, that's right, Jonathan," I replied. "The stated reason is that less than 1% of the volunteers could be vetted."

"What does that tell you about the tens of thousands of immigrants coming into the country from Syria?" Maria asked.

"I'll have to agree with Maria that the government is minimizing the threat of ISIS," Jonathan remarked. "If they never succeed in becoming a true Islamic State with national boundaries, their continued existence is a rallying point for Muslims all over the world. ISIS is the first Islamic group to announce a Caliphate since 1924. This alone will attract millions to the vision of a global Caliphate. They are inflaming the passions of radical Islam."

"I have a question," Maria posed. "It's about the great mystery of ISIL. Is it possible that the White House has a motive in calling the terrorist group, ISIS, ISIL?"

"I don't know. Why do you ask?"

"ISIS is, as you know, the acronym for the Islamic State of Iraq and Syria. While ISIL stands for the Islamic State of Iraq and the Levante. I'm sure you remember the big debate in the Media when the President chose to use ISIL to identify the terrorist group."

"Its definition varied from time to time, but the Levante was a much larger area in the Middle East encompassing almost the entire region. It included Turkey, Jordan, Lebanon, Palestine, Syria, Egypt and Israel."

"Israel?"

"Yes."

"You have to be kidding."

"Where are you going with this, Maria? You always scare me when you take off on a tangent."

"Maybe it isn't a tangent. As I understand it, ISIS called themselves ISIS. But for some reason, the Administration and the United Nations decided to call them ISIL and they have never bothered to tell the public why."

"So!? Get to the point!"

"The name ISIL, in my opinion, adds substantiality and legitimacy to their claim as the rightful heirs of Islamic leadership in the entire region of the Middle East. They become the Islamic State, not just of Iraq and Syria, but of the entire Middle East, including Israel."

"Get outta here! I knew it. I knew it. It's dangerous to leave you alone for 5 minutes. I..."

"If you have a better explanation, David, I'd like to hear it."

"I don't need an explanation. It's sheer speculation on your part."

Fact: The world watched on TV as the waters of the Mediterranean turned to blood when ISIS beheaded 21 Christians in Libya. No response from the US as Libya pleaded for help. The White House did not mention that the murderers were Islamic, nor that their victims were Christian.

ORDER   CHAOS

Fact: The President wrote in his bestseller, *The Audacity of Hope*, that, 'if things ever get nasty, I will stand with the Muslims.'

ORDER   CHAOS

Fact: In the most striking show of solidarity against Islamic terror since 9/11, in an event that will go down in history, leaders from 40 nations, including presidents and prime ministers, locked arm in arm with 1,600,000 people and marched through the streets of Paris after 17 people were killed by Islamic terrorists in the Charlie Hebdo attack. Neither the President, Vice President nor Secretary of State John Kerry attended the event. The schedules of the President, and the Vice President were open for the weekend.

ORDER   CHAOS

"The President's absence spoke loud and clear," Maria stated. "If I were ISIS or any other branch of militant Islam, I would have read this as a US statement to the world, 'Don't count on the United States in a battle against radical Islam.'"

"Surely you don't think, Maria," Jonathan asked, "that his absence was intended to send a message to ISIS...?"

"Come on! You know the attention given to detail in diplomatic formalities when it comes to international relations. Why else would you miss an event like that?"

Refusal To Call It What It Is

Fact: The President called the Paris Kosher Deli attack 'random shootings that killed some folks.' The shooters were screaming 'Allah Akbar' and announcing that it was in revenge for the prophet Mohammad.

ORDER   CHAOS

Fact: The President denied ISIS as a significant threat. He called them 'the JV team, which if they were to don Laker uniforms would not make them a Kobe Bryant.'

ORDER   CHAOS

"In all fairness, don't you think this statement could have been an honest mistake in assessing the threat of ISIS?" I asked.

"Yes, I suppose it could," Jonathan replied.

Maria replied, "But it certainly would embolden the adversary, if they thought they were being underestimated."

Fact: Contrary to the President's assessment of ISIS, on September 8, 2014, while being interviewed on MSNBC News, former Secretary of the Department of Homeland Security, Janet Napolitano, said that ISIS foreign fighters living in the United States and fighting for ISIS are the number one threat to the United States.

ORDER   CHAOS

Fact: ISIS is spreading to many parts of the world, using the Internet and Social Media to recruit young people in Britain and the United States. They are flying on commercial airlines back and forth from their homes to fight for ISIS in Iraq and Syria. Others are being arrested by the FBI for trying to join ISIS. The President has said that ISIS is not a significant threat to America.

ORDER   CHAOS

Fact: As of May 2015, some forty jihadist groups in various parts of the world had pledged allegiance to ISIS.

ORDER   CHAOS

Fact: The President denies that ISIS is Islamic.

ORDER   CHAOS

"Let me say something," Jonathan announced. "I believe that ISIS is the reincarnation of true Islam taken directly out of the Koran and the Hadith. It is a carbon copy of the religion founded by Mohammad. They are literalists who take the sacred writings seriously. I have met militant Muslims who converted to Christianity. They take the Bible literally. They make wonderful Christians."

Fact: The State Department released figures in 2015 showing worldwide increase in terror in 2014. Terrorist attacks went up 35% over 2013. Fatalities went up 81%. The President maintained that the world was becoming a more tolerant and peaceful place.

ORDER   CHAOS

Guantanamo Bay Prisoners

Fact: The Guantanamo Bay terrorists, called the Taliban Five, were released in exchange for Sergeant Bowe Bergdahl, who had left his unit in Afghanistan to join the Taliban. He has now been indicted by the military for desertion.

ORDER   CHAOS

Fact: A report from James Clapper, Director of National Intelligence, stated that 116, or almost 30 percent of the 647 of the released Gitmo detainees, have either returned to the fight or are suspected of doing so.

ORDER   CHAOS

Fact: Sergeant Bergdahl converted to Islam while in captivity for five years. The President celebrated his release with his parents in the Rose Garden before a televised world audience. A smiling President stood by the side of the elder Bergdahl, who was praising Allah by quoting the most famous war cry of Islam, "In the name of Allah, the most gracious, the most merciful."

ORDER   CHAOS

Maria interjected, "What about the six soldiers who died searching for Bergdahl? Why didn't they get a Rose Garden ceremony?"

Israel
Fact: In March 2015, shortly after Prime Minister Netanyahu gave his speech to Congress against the nuclear deal with Iran, the White House abruptly declassified and made public details of Israel's nuclear program. According to Israel National News, the top-secret document had never been formally disclosed. It was classified in order not to cause a regional nuclear arms race.

ORDER   CHAOS

Nuclear Treaty with Iran:
Fact: Israel's Prime Minister Netanyahu says that the nuclear deal with Iran will pave the way to a nuclear Iran and will spark a nuclear arms race. It has elevated Iran to a new status of respect in the world community. Iran has forced the leading world powers to the council table and, most Americans believe, has walked away with a clear victory.

ORDER   CHAOS

Fact: The US State Department has stated that Iran is the number one state sponsor of terrorism in the world.

ORDER   CHAOS

Fact: While the US and world powers were removing sanctions and unfreezing 150 billion dollars of Iranian assets — which can be used to sponsor terrorism around the world — Russia was arming Iran with an anti-ballistic missile system that could make an attack on her nuclear facilities almost impossible.

ORDER   CHAOS

Fact: While negotiations were in progress, the Supreme Leader of Iran, Ayatollah Khomeini, speaking to an audience in Tehran, exclaimed, 'Death to America.'

ORDER   CHAOS

Fact: In August 2015, two hundred retired Admirals and Generals signed a letter to Congress requesting them to reject the Nuke Deal with Iran, because it was a threat to national security. The President remained undismayed.

ORDER   CHAOS

Jonathan commented, "I think I'm the neutral guy here, but does it not matter that 65 precent of the American people, when informed about the details of the Iran Nuclear Deal, have said they are against it?"

"Of course not, Jonathan," Maria replied. "He will do what he wants to do. It doesn't matter that Iran demands a 24-day notice before nuclear sites are inspected. It doesn't matter that Iran will self-test for any suspected violations of the agreement. It doesn't matter that sanctions are removed, granting Iran billions of dollars to promote terrorism. It doesn't matter that Iran has been identified by the US State Department as the number one promotor of terrorism throughout the world. It doesn't matter that while nations were hammering the agreement out in Vienna, the Ayatollah and the rallying masses in Tehran were shouting 'Death to America.'

"Nothing will stop him. Can't you see that? Not 200 Admirals and Generals. Not Congress. Not the American people. He will do what he wants to do."

"Maria," I responded in disbelief, "I don't believe you are saying that the President wants Iran to acquire the bomb… or are you?"

"Do I think he wants Iran to get the bomb? Yes, I do. Do I think he wants to blow up the Middle East? No, I do not. His ultimate goal is to unite the region. He wants to blend the world. In my opinion that's what it's all about. I think he believes a nuclear Middle East will force the countries to the negotiating table to survive extinction. He wants to be the man. And he would like to pull it off with the Kerry Peace Accord."

"Honey, this is far out! Too far out!"

Jonathan entered the conversation, "You know, David, each of the Middle East leaders would like to be the one, I think, to lead the way in uniting Islam under his leadership. The competition is fierce between them. It may take an outsider to make it happen."

"Here's what I think," Maria stated, sitting up in her chair and holding her hand up like a traffic cop motioning a motorist to stop, "Let me talk!"

"Mom always said that we were in the beginning days of the chaos stage which, she believed, the President was actively promoting to dismantle the world. At the same time, he was pushing a New World Order that would emerge from its ashes — a world order that blends the principal antagonistic ideologies of the world today, which means godless Darwinian Secularism, Socialism, Islam and a revised Christianity — a Christianity without Jesus, the Cross and the Supernatural."

"I don't believe he has this in mind," I replied.

I remembered the words that Mom had written in her Bible. "Oh!" I yelled, "Let me show you something!" I scrambled for the Bible lying on the end table by the bed. "I haven't shown you this. This is Mom's Bible."

"I recognize it! Where did you get it?"

"She gave it to me ... uh, oh, let me put it this way... it was given to me the day that I left for Tel Aviv. Look at what she had written on the cover leaf. Look!"

THE HOLY BIBLE
THE KORAN
THE COMMUNIST MANIFESTO
THE ORIGIN OF THE SPECIES

"And then under it you will notice in her own handwriting":

No Resolution — they won't mix

Jonathan spoke up, "Maria, Mom's view is contrary to what you are saying that the ideologies will blend together. She said that they wouldn't mix."

"No, it isn't, Jonathan," I replied before Maria could answer. "There is one more step. The prophet Daniel said they would attempt to mix ideas, but they wouldn't mix. The key to understanding this is that the attempt to mix will fail and one of the ideologies will prevail over the others."

Maria finished my sentence, "At the head will be the Islamic Anti-Christ who will have undisputed rule over the world for 3 and ½ years. He will be destroyed by Jesus when He returns."

"Maria, do you think the President has a role in the future of the Middle East?" I asked.

"I'm not sure that he has a Biblical role. But if he can bring the Islamic factions together, it will be prophetic, indeed. Whoever calms the Middle East and unites it with the European Union will be the Anti-Christ. The Roman Empire will rise from the dead."

"David," Maria spoke up, "I believe the desire to unify Islam explains his entire foreign policy. It explains his leading from behind. The retreat from the red line with Syria, and his half-hearted war against militant Islam in Iraq, Syria and Yemen. He backs off every time. I don't believe that it's because he is weak and impotent. He doesn't burn bridges with anyone in the Middle East. He has made no lasting friendships there. Neither has he made permanent enemies. He believes he will pull it off — be the guy that puts it all together."

"It certainly would secure a legacy and a place for him in the last days drama," Jonathan concluded.

"I don't know about all this, but one thing I know for sure. America has been taken hostage. I have been given an assignment to warn the American people.

"Now," Jonathan concluded. "All the evidence is in. Consider all the facts soberly as if your decision would determine the future of the American people. Then express your finding based on the evidence.

"Is the President an Islamic jihadist who is using his office to foster chaotic conditions in the world that advance Islam in violation of the laws and welfare of the American people?

FINDING: YES   NO

"Shall we take a break?" Jonathan asked.

"Let's eat!" exclaimed Maria.

We were all starved and Maria ordered a Pizza Supreme from a shop not far from the hotel. It lived up to the reputation she had given it. For fifteen minutes we relaxed, shared memories, cracked some jokes, talked about whether Elvis made it to heaven, and then bantered back and forth on who was the greatest basketball team in the NBA.

We all missed Mom. We missed her soft quiet strength, her dry sense of humor, her zero tolerance for sin, and, most of all, her love for her family.

FUNDAMENTALLY TRANSFORMING AMERICA

Jonathan grabbed the trash and the empty pizza box and headed for the garbage can, talking as he went, "I'll take care of the clean-up. You guys focus on the third question."

He continued as he tidied up the kitchenette, "You were never good at keeping things neat, David. Look at this mess."

"We just got here a few minutes ago, Jonathan, remember?"

Maria asked, "Okay, here's the third question:

3. Does the President intend to extend his presidency beyond two terms and to continue it indefinitely?"

Jonathan decided to sit down. He smiled slightly and said, "Okay, are you ready?

The rules are the same. The answers are YES or NO."

"It isn't possible, Jonathan," I advised. "The 22nd Amendment limits him to two terms in office. To repeal it would require a 2/3 majority in Congress, and ratification by the states. That would take years, if he had the votes."

"David!"

"Don't look at me like that Jonathan. I know what you're thinking. He could sign an Executive Order in a five-minute ceremony. I'm just not sure that he would."

"Maybe you're right. But you haven't seen all the facts, yet."

"I know. But even if he signed an Executive Order, its constitutionality would be immediately challenged in Federal Court."

Jonathan lowered his jaw, cocked his head and looked at me with a 'when did you fall off the turnip truck' look. I had seen it since eighth grade when I said something he thought was stupid.

"I know what you are thinking, brother. That the Constitution was tossed out the window when a majority of the men in black robes exceeded the powers granted to them by that document. When the Court mandated same sex marriages in all 50 states."

"No, not really. I may have been foolish. I just assumed the Supreme Court would not go along with an Executive Order that extended his Presidency. What I was going to say was, 'If he doesn't pay any attention to Congress, why should he regard the Supreme Court?'"

"You're beginning to sound like my fiancé."

National Security Force

Fact: The President, while campaigning for office in 2008, called for a civilian national security force that is just as powerful, just as strong, and just as well-funded as the US Military.

YES   NO

Maria was sitting in the chair with her eyes closed shaking her head from side to side. I was sure she was going to comment. I decided to beat her to it, "You must be aware, Maria, that many people have raised questions as to what the President actually meant when he made this statement."

"David, this is exactly what he called for. Anybody can check it out on YouTube. The question I have is this, 'Who were the enemies in our midst in 2008 that would have required such a massive civilian national security force to contain them?' I don't think he had 11 million illegal immigrants in mind. Neither do I think he had the hundreds of thousands of invading Muslim immigrants in mind. If neither of these, could it possibly have been 325 million freedom-loving Americans?"

"There you go again, Maria. You are speculating about the purpose he intended."

"Then tell me why he wants it, David."

Fact: According to the White House visitor logs, Al Sharpton has been a White House guest 61 times since 2009. During the Baltimore riots in 2015 he made the following statement, "We need the Justice Department to step in and take over policing in this country."

YES   NO

"Al Sharpton is not the President," I stated.

"No, he isn't David. But do you actually believe he was not expressing the sentiments of the President? What did they talk about when they got together? How to give power back to the states?"

Gun Control

Fact: The Second Amendment to the Constitution gives the American people the right bear arms. The President has relentlessly pushed to control or ban guns since his election in 2008, against the will of Congress and the American people.

YES   NO

Fact: In his 2014 State of the Union Address the President promised that he will get his gun control agenda with or without the consent of Congress.

YES   NO

Ammunition Purchase

Fact: One recent effort by the Bureau of Alcohol, Tobacco and Firearms proposed a ban on the sale of .223 caliber ammunition for the AR-15, the most popular rifle in America. The Administration dropped the proposal due to overwhelming opposition from the public.

YES   NO

Fact: In 2014, several Federal agencies, including the Department of Homeland Security, the FBI, the Department of Agriculture, the IRS, and the US Postal Service ordered some two billion rounds of ammunition over a six-month period.

YES   NO

"Hey, Jonathan," Maria interjected. "Using my phone calculator, I just did the math — two billion rounds of ammunition ordered over one six-month period is enough ammunition to shoot every person in America six times."

"And they are trying to take the ammunition away from the people," Jonathan replied. "What's wrong with this picture?"

Arming Local Police Departments

Fact: Under the Clinton Administration, surplus property was made available to local police departments. Under the present Administration, the Pentagon is arming local police departments around the country with military grade equipment as never before. Upon request and without cost, police districts are receiving armored vehicles weighing as much as 30 tons each and built to withstand land mines. M-16 rifles, silencers, machine guns, night vision equipment, and Black Hawk helicopters are available.

YES   NO

"You know, Jonathan," Maria asked, "that the President discouraged the use of heavy military equipment by local police after the Ferguson protests, don't you?"

"Yes."

"The stated reason was that it could lead to an undermining of public trust in the police," Maria opined. "Personally, that's hard for me to believe that the present Administration is concerned about a negative image of the police." She paused a minute, then added, "Could the real reason be that the presence of the big armored vehicles has a chilling effect on the protests and the riots?"

SWAT Teams

Fact: SWAT is an acronym for Special Weapons and Tactics. It stands for military style weapons and specialized tactics in high-risk operations outside the scope of regular police units. They are often equipped with submachine guns, assault rifles, riot control agents, stun grenades, body armor, armored vehicles, ballistic shields, and night vision optics. And they are increasing rapidly at all levels of law enforcement across the nation.

YES   NO

Fact: Not only the Secret Service and Bureau of Prisons, but other federal agencies such as the Department of Agriculture, the Railroad Retirement Board, the Tennessee Valley Authority, the Consumer Product Safety Commission, and the US Fish and Wildlife Service have organized their own SWAT teams.

YES   NO

"SWAT teams for the US Fish and Wildlife? What on earth for? Somebody caught fishing without a license? The Railroad Retirement Board? Somebody lie about their age on a government form? Come on, give me a break." Maria scoffed.

"I will admit that the whole country was horrified," I added, "when we witnessed on television 200 Bureau of Land Management paramilitary agents armed to the teeth in a standoff with old man Cliven Bundy, and his wife. Over cattle grazing rights in Nevada? Come on. The message was certainly clear enough!"

"What's that?"

"Don't mess with the Federal Government."

"Yes, but the pushback of the whole country delivered its own message."

"What's that?"

"Don't mess with the American people."

Urban Warfare Exercises

Fact: Military Operation Jade Helm 15 was a military exercise in urban warfare that began in July 2015 in seven western states. The purpose was to train US troops in urban warfare, like that employed in Iraq. It combined all four branches of the US military, the FBI, the DEA and local police departments.

YES   NO

"Jonathan, I think I know the meaning of urban warfare, but exactly how does it differ from other types of warfare?" Maria asked.

"Did you see the American Sniper, Maria?"

"Oh, yes. David and I saw it. It was a great movie. We both liked it."

"Well, that's urban warfare. It was the combat employed by US forces in Iraq in urban areas. It is to hunt down and kill from building to building with civilians in the combat zone. It is altogether different from training combat troops defending against ground invasion."

"I may be showing my ignorance, but I will ask the question again," Maria scoffed. "Who is the enemy? I'm sorry. Maybe, I'm paranoid. But is the enemy the American people? Think about it. Who else inhabits the houses and buildings of America? Who else, other than the American people, can offer armed resistance against attack? The whole concept anticipates armed resistance that will be dealt with from community to community. Why else employ local police departments and equip them with heavy military arms and Black Hawk helicopters?

"I have another question. What is the reason for massive transports of military equipment across the US? At or near the time of Jade Helm 15 — all over the country: South Carolina, Virginia, Indiana, Kentucky, and Louisiana, just to name a few. Train loads as far as the eye could see: tanks, armored personnel carriers, supply trucks, ambulances and all it takes to make war. You can see it on the internet.

"Am I the only one? Doesn't it raise legitimate questions about the purpose of Jade Helm 15? What is the purpose of this gigantic movement of war machinery? It doesn't make sense if the military resistance is from house to house. Could it be strategic placement in the event of civil war?"

"Maria, all that has settled down, now. That hasn't been on the news in months."

"What does that prove?"

Maria paused, took a deep breath and looked at me. Her eyes were softer, now. She shrugged her shoulders and said, "Honey, if I'm out of line, just smack me. I don't know. Am I crazy? I'm just concerned about our country."

I took her by the hand and tried to comfort her, "No, sweetheart, you aren't crazy. If you are crazy, then millions of Americans are crazy too. I don't know what the answers are either. The truth is that nobody knows for sure whether we are training troops for overseas combat or to hunt down dissidents in the US. The only person who knows for sure is the man in the Oval Office. He is the Commander-in-Chief. The real question is, 'Do we trust him?'"

Fact: As of October 2013, The Blaze and Breitbart reported that 197 ranking military commanders had been fired by the President.

YES   NO

Internment of the Population

Fact: During the 1950s, at the height of the Cold War with Russia, government documents reveal that in case of attack an FBI program entitled Plan C would be activated. Some 13,000 people affiliated with subversive organizations would be apprehended.

YES   NO

"Can it happen in America? Look at this next fact on your syllabus," exclaimed Jonathan.

Fact: In 2012, a U. S. Army training manual entitled 'Civil Disturbance Operations' leaked to the outside world. It dated from 2006 and described how American soldiers would be authorized to show deadly force and even kill Americans. It contained a directive 'a warning shot will not be fired.' Dissidents would be taken to internment camps for re-education in a new appreciation of American policies.

YES   NO

Fact: A Department of Defense Document entitled 'Internment and Resettlement Operations' or 'FM 3.39-40,' leaked to the public in 2013. It details the procedures for the internment of Americans and psychological officers for indoctrination of the internees and the identification of political activists. An escape attempt justifies the use of lethal force.

YES   NO

Fact: In 2014, Supreme Court Justice Antonin Scalia, while lecturing law students at the University of Hawaii, condemned the internment of Japanese-Americans during World War II, but went on to say that, 'You are kidding yourself if you think it couldn't happen again.'

YES   NO

The Media

Fact: In 2012, the US Department of Justice secretly and illegally seized phone records of Associated Press reporters, presumably to uncover their 'confidential news sources' regarding government activities. The government would not say why they seized the records.

YES   NO

Fact: In 2014, the Federal Communications Commission (FCC) launched a new study, in effect, to decide what the public 'needs' to know, rather than the news the public 'wants' to know. It is called the 'Multi-Market Study of Critical Information Needs.' The FCC is sending researchers into radio and TV newsrooms across the country to determine how news stories are decided and the politics of the reporters and owners. The FCC has the power to license or not to license broadcasting stations.

YES   NO

"Guess who gets to decide what the 'critical information needs' of the public are? I'll give you three guesses and the first two don't count!" Maria remarked.

Fact: The President made a statement on May 13, 2015 in a panel discussion at Georgetown University, which amounted to an attack on a major news network. He said, 'the only way we are going to change how the body politic thinks is to change how the media reports (the news).'"

YES   NO

"This one frightens me. At first glance it seems so harmless. Just a conversation with some university students. But the implications could shatter the foundations of a free society. Putin couldn't say it any better," Maria intervened.

Fact: Falling thirteen spaces from the year before, in 2014 the United States ranked number 46 among the 180 countries of the world in a comparison of freedom of the Press. The Press Freedom Index is published by Reporters Without Borders, an organization located in Paris, France. The group has consultant status with the United Nations.

YES   NO

The Internet

Fact: The Internet remains the one free forum where every American can express his or her views without some form of government control. In February 2015, the President succeeded in persuading the FCC to impose a sweeping regulation plan on the Internet. The commissioners voted 3 to 2 in favor of the regulations. When asked why they made the decision, the answer was, "The President told us to do so."

YES   NO

Fact: In cases of national emergency under the Communications Act of 1934, the President has the power to "suspend or amend… the rules and regulations applicable to any or all stations or devices capable of emitting electromagnetic radiations within the jurisdiction of the United States."

YES   NO

Jonathan lamented, "The Internet empowers the individual more than any other medium in the history of the world. It gives the individual the same platform as the President of the United States. Its control is a must before the New World Order can emerge!"

"I remember, Jonathan, the controversy that arose over the Collins-Lieberman Bill introduced in the Senate four or five years ago. It was over the so-called 'Kill Switch' bill, which gave the President power to control the Internet with some minor limitations and hoops to jump through. It didn't pass. I don't think it ever went to the floor. You know what that means, don't you?"

"Yeah! I think I do! But tell me!"

"It means that the 1934 Act is still the law. In case of national emergencies it gives the President control over 'any and/or all stations or devices.' That means all radio and TV stations, cell phones, computers, and servers that control the internet."

Fact: In December 2015, EPIC, the Electronic Privacy Information Center, filed a brief filed in the Supreme Court in support of its motion to order the government to reveal its policy for shutting down cell phones for whatever reason it may have. EPIC reports that the President signed an executive order that granted the Department of Homeland Security "the authority to seize private facilities, when necessary, effectively shutting down ... civilian communications." The government is resisting disclosure of its secret plan to kill cell phone service. Limited exercise of the government's authority has already taken place in New York and California cutting off cell phone service in what were deemed emergency situations.

YES   NO

"Certainly no one questions the technological capability of the White House to shut down all or part of the internet. And cell phone service, too! Mubarak did it in Egypt in 2011 during the protests. You couldn't talk to anyone unless you were in the same room with them," Maria added.

"The question to me is, 'what is a national emergency?'"

"That's easy!" Jonathan stated, "It's whatever White House lawyers say it is!"

Anti-Christian Bias

Fact: Evangelical Christians have been classified as 'potential terrorists' by the Department of Homeland Security.

YES   NO

Fact: Instances have been reported where United States military personnel have been instructed, that well-respected Christian ministries such as the American Family Association should be classified as domestic 'hate groups' along with the Ku Klux Klan, Neo-Nazis and the Black Panthers.

YES   NO

Fact: Other reported military briefings have classified Christians and Catholics as 'religious extremists' as well as law enforcement agencies using a list compiled by Southern Poverty Law Center, which wrongfully identifies traditional family organizations.

YES   NO

I had now heard enough evidence on all three counts that I was beginning to realize that Jonathan was not over reacting. I heard myself asking out loud, "Is there an attempt underway to condition the US military, ideologically separating them from the American people? If so, this is huge."

"Where there's smoke, there's fire!" exclaimed Maria.

"Yeah! That's what concerns me!" I stated. "All these isolated reports appear to reflect a pervasive and growing culture of hostility against Christians in the military. The only reason we know about these is because a trainee dared to speak out. How much indoctrination is there out there that is not coming to light?"

Fact: The Washington Times ran an article on April 15, 2015, entitled 'US Military Hostile to Christians...' It quoted a defense attorney who was representing two chaplains facing punishment for conducting counseling sessions reflecting their religious views. The attorney said, 'People of faith are going to stay away from the Military... I would have serious reservations about my own kids joining.'

YES   NO

Maria looked at me with a concerned look on her face. "Honey, are you all right?" she asked.

"I'm troubled by all this, I guess. I already was aware of much of what Jonathan has said today. But, it just hit home, I guess. That's all."

"This attack on Christians is what troubles me," she said. "At what point does this branding of evangelicals become the official position of the United States Military Forces? I think this becomes even more pertinent in view of the fact that official documents of the US government have come to light naming them as 'hate groups' and 'potential terrorists.' And, on top of that, the FBI refuses to recognize Islamic terrorism as a domestic threat in the United States."

Surveillance

Fact: We found out years ago that the National Security Agency, under the Patriot Act, without a warrant signed by a judge required under the Fourth Amendment of the Constitution, had been illegally collecting phone records of Americans.

YES   NO

Fact: The FISC is a top secret Federal Court that meets behind closed doors. Its records are not open to the public and its decisions are not subject to review by a higher court. In a 2014 action, Verizon challenged the right of the NSA, under the present administration, regarding the mass collection of the phone records of American citizens. The Court ordered Verizon to turn over the records of 100 million subscribers to the NSA. They were further ordered not to advise their customers of the surveillance.

YES   NO

Fact: Edward Snowden reportedly stated that the government was recording the content of our communications as well as the parties, numbers and length of calls.

YES   NO

Fact: The National Security Agency (NSA) now has a data facility that can take in 20 billion 'events' a day and analyze them in 60 minutes. The Utah Data Storage Facility, near Salt Lake City, was finished in 2012. It has 1.5 million square feet and an electric bill of 40 million dollars a year. It was estimated to use 1.7 million gallons of water a day to cool the massive collection of servers it houses. The stated purpose is cyber-security, but its precise purpose remains classified. It is reported that the technology in possession of the NSA is able to process 'all forms of communications, including the complete contents of private emails, cell phone calls, and internet searches, as well as all types of personal data trails — parking receipts, travel itineraries, bookstore purchases, and pocket litter.'

YES   NO

"There's no place to hide!" Maria acquiesced, "Even the GPS on my car tells them every place I go. Including visits with my friends, church meetings and political rallies."

"What about the drones?" Jonathan asked, "Drones used by the President overseas as weapons are now being used by law enforcement for surveillance in the United States!"

Fact: The NSA was established after 9/11, under the Patriot Act, to fight terrorism. It has been illegally spying on Americans for years. The government lied to the American people about it.

YES   NO

"As you know, the American Freedom Act has replaced the NSA as the data collection entity, and the nation's electronic records are now being collected and stored by the phone companies. The government now has to go before the FISC to show cause for the records." I remarked.

"At least that preserves some semblance of the Fourth Amendment!" Maria stated.

"Before we throw a party to celebrate," Jonathan commented, "the CISA bill was attached to the Omnibus Bill and was signed into law by the President on December 18, 2015. It allows the big corporations to share private information gleaned from their business transactions with US citizens — to share personal information with the Federal Government and its agencies.."

"So what?" Maria snapped, "it all goes by the wayside, anyway, if martial law is declared. The government will do what it wants to do."

I couldn't help but ponder out loud, "How is it that what began as innocent intelligence gathering by the government to protect the American people after 9/11 has become a monster that can enslave us all?"

"Yeah. It's true. It all depends on who is in control. That will determine which way the train will go." exclaimed Jonathon.

"Now! Here is the final issue to be decided. Remember, consider all the evidence. Then express your finding.

3. Does the President intend to extend his presidency, if at all possible, beyond two terms and to continue it indefinitely?"

FINDING: YES   NO

Jonathan sighed deeply and then asked, "What drives him, David?"

"I'm not sure. The whole world is puzzled! We've all heard the commentators. They are confused. The conjectures are endless: 'He's trying to please his constituents.' Or, 'He's trying to build a political base for his party.' Or, 'He's an ideologue who is merely doing what he believes is right.' Or, 'He wants to leave a legacy so he'll make millions off his books and speaking tours.' Or, 'We don't understand him because he is different from us.' Or, as one Congressman put it to me, 'He changes his mind. We can't trust him.' The truth is that nobody knows for sure."

"Some say he is weak and indecisive."

"Don't count on it, Jonathan. He ignores Congress and issues Executive Orders like trump cards in a Rook game. On massive issues! Like immigration and amnesty. Like the nuclear talks with Iran and resuming diplomatic relations with Cuba. If he wants it, he does it. He doesn't ask anybody. He has many faults, but weakness is not one of them."

Maria's impersonation skills came into play, 'I've got a pen, and I've got a phone. And I can use that pen to sign executive orders … that move the ball forward.'

"To put it in his own words that were spoken just before the 2008 election, 'We are five days away from fundamentally transforming the United States of America.'"

Jonathan continued, "Back to the question, 'Is he planning to continue his presidency beyond two terms?'"

"Jonathan, he can't pull it off!"

"Don't count on it! That's all I'm going to say. With all that's happened since he took office, he has retained almost a 50% approval rating with the American people. Anyway you cut it, that's sheer political power. And when it comes to a showdown — you know as well as I do — power attracts power."

The events of the day before in Dubai were fresh in my mind. "In my opinion, Jonathan, the only way that this would happen would be a major national catastrophe. The people would actually want the government to step in and take over — and do what it takes to restore order! Even if it were to mean martial law and the temporary suspension of our rights under the Constitution."

"A catastrophe? The day that happens we will be only two Executive Orders away from the end of democracy."

"I know what they are," Maria soberly volunteered. "Martial law — and the postponement of next year's Presidential elections!

"I don't claim to be any smarter than the average bear, but I have some gut feelings about the coming year and I believe they are from the Lord."

"Are you turning prophet on me, Honey?"

"I believe that the President will speak words that appear to move him toward the center of the political spectrum mesmerizing and silencing many of his critics.

"I believe that in 2016, protests, riots, attacks on the police, natural disasters, super bugs, food shortages, and Islamic terror will increase in America.

"I believe that the President will step in and alleviate much of the suffering caused by these events. By the exercise of his executive power and personal charm he will appear as the great benefactor to many of the American people. There will be much talk about the constitutionality of a third term and an effort will be made to get him to run.

"With the ISIS and radical Islam threats looming worldwide, with hundreds of thousands of unvetted Muslims pouring into our cities, and the gun control fight still ahead of us, do not expect the Administration to back down on any of its initiatives. I predict that 2016 will be a year of highly publicized token concessions that supposedly demonstrate the good will of this Administration to protect the people. Many will fall for it. But it will only mask the determination to erase our borders, make us more dependent and take away our guns.

"Let me continue. I'm not through," she implored. "God knows my heart and I am not trying to be mean. But how many times have we heard people say, 'He isn't like us!'

"I have a question! How could we possibly expect him to be?

"I'm not trying to put a moral value on his heritage. I am only saying that he is different. His father and step-father were both Muslims. His mother was a Communist and an atheist. In his formative childhood years, he attended an Islamic grade school in Indonesia where he studied the Koran."

"I know! But he converted to Christianity, Maria."

"Look! David! I am not trying to demean him. I am only trying, like millions of other Americans, to understand. Two years before he won the

2008 election for President, he published his New York Times bestseller, *The Audacity of Hope.* That was in 2006. This book was titled after a sermon by Jeremiah Wright with the same name. In the book, he listed Malcolm X as one of four heroes who had spoken into his life.

"As you well know, Malcolm X was a Muslim cleric and civil rights activist who challenged the more peaceful civil rights movement led by Martin Luther King. He exhorted Blacks to break the shackles of racism 'by any means necessary,' including violence. It was Malcolm X who shocked the country when he said that John F. Kennedy's assassination was an example of America's 'chickens coming home to roost.'

"Jeremiah Wright mentored the President for twenty years. Like Malcolm X, Wright commemorated the loss of 3,000 Americans in the Twin Towers. Instead of mourning over the loss, he quoted Malcolm X almost word for word, 'America's chickens! Coming home! To roost!' 'Not God bless America! God _____, America!'

"Apparently, these men were his heroes. This is where he came from. I believe that what they were is who he is!"

"It sounds so radical!"

"Sometimes, the facts are radical, David. That doesn't mean we should stop up our ears. That we should gloss over the facts. By his own words and actions these were the people who molded his life."

Maria walked to the window and stared in the direction of the UN building. She turned around and spoke softly, "You know what's crazy?"

"No, what, Honey?"

"I pray for him and his family every day. God loves them so much!"

Stepping over to me, she smiled sadly. "I'll see you later tonight at the Diner. I love you. Don't forget to wear your red tie," she whispered as she kissed me lightly on the forehead. Hugging Jonathan, she said, "See you later." And then she left.

Neither Jonathan nor I said a word for a couple of minutes as he gathered his papers. Finally, he broke the silence, "David, we don't have to do anything. We don't have to go through with this."

"I know. But all of us have to do everything that we can to survive as a nation. And we have to do it now!"

As he left, Jonathan stuck his head back through the door before it closed. And with a big smile and a thumbs up shouted, "See you tonight, little brother. I got your back!" And the door closed.

I lay back in the king-sized bed and stared at the ceiling, pondering our future in a very uncertain world. Mentally rehashing the previous two hours and our plans to meet later that evening at the Diner in Manhattan, I recalled that it held special meaning for me. It was the little 'hole in the wall' where Maria and I first talked about a life together.

I reached for Mom's Bible, closed my eyes and opened it. Placing a finger on an unknown text, I prayed that God would speak to me. Normally I didn't seek answers that way because at the times I had tried it before, I would get something like 'there is no hope for the wicked.' But this time I felt that God would speak to me.

"Here goes!" I thought and then prayed again with my eyes closed and my finger still on the page, "Lord, thank you for my family being around me at this time. But I don't remember ever feeling more alone than I do tonight."

I opened my eyes and my finger had fallen on New King James Version of Acts 18:9-10. It read:

Do not be afraid, but speak, and do not keep silent; for I am with you and no one will attack you to hurt you; for I have many people in this city.

THE COUNCIL

"**O**h, no," I thought, as I walked past four security guards into a large room with a conference table. "This reminds me of another room I've been in this week. I hope I am better received here than in Dubai."

I was immediately escorted by security to a seat next to a podium directly opposite to, and facing, the table about fifteen feet away. The atmosphere in the room was casual and friendly as those present laughed and joked with each other and talked about the upcoming Super Bowl. They paid little attention to me as I entered the room.

I could tell that they were very tired. In fact, they looked like they had slept in their clothes the night before. I imagined that it was because they had spent many long hours in deliberation.

There were sixteen men and three women in the room. I recognized three members of the President's Cabinet and I thought I recognized three or four more senior officials whom I was trying to place but couldn't. Among them was an Army Colonel in boots, camouflage pants and jacket whom they called, "General." I had no idea who the others were.

I had always been suspicious of rumors about secret organizations that wielded great political influence at the highest levels of our government, including the presidency. Czar types that reportedly advised and acted for them had surrounded presidents in the past. For the last seven years we all had lived with a rumor that there was a clandestine group very close to the President who acted as his personal think tank and were among his closest advisors. I was not sure that such a group existed, but I had a feeling that if it did, I was looking at it.

A man appeared from behind a curtained partition and walked to the center of the table. "It is time to resume the meeting. Take your seats, please," he commanded.

"Due to the present emergency, for the last three days, we have worked day and night on the coordination of government agencies and private institutions to bring about the goals outlined in the White House pamphlet, MULTI-AGENCY RESPONSE TO AN EVENT OF MASS DESTRUCTION."

I thought, "Uh, oh. I've seen this before."

His direct manner and the absence of any formalities caught me by surprise as I heard my introduction, "Deputy Secretary of State, David Flink, my name is Abdel. I am chairman of this council. I understand you have some pressing news for us. We are eager to hear your report on the meeting in Dubai."

I would guess he was about my age. His ruddy complexion, dark wavy hair, and piercing black eyes combined to form a striking appearance that would fit the Middle Eastern stereotype of someone named Abdel. The room grew quiet. I stood to my feet and took the podium.

"Thank you, Mr. Chairman, fellow Americans. It is with great heaviness that I speak with you tonight. I bring bad news from Dubai." For the next hour, I related the facts of my assignment, my trip to Dubai, and the details of the meeting with Middle Eastern leaders. After a session of questions and answers, I asked if I were needed further. Abdel insisted I stay for a few more minutes.

"So, Secretary Flink," A young panel member said, "If I may summarize the message you bring to this council tonight. America has been taken hostage, and you have brought the ransom note back with you. Is that correct?"

"I am not sure I would put it exactly like that…but…I guess…essentially, that is an accurate depiction."

"And the ransom is the sacrifice of all dissident groups who do not subscribe to…I don't know how to finish this sentence except to say it like it is…the sacrifice of Americans who stand in the way of the immediate blending of world religions, cultures and the implementation of global government."

"Christians will be the first in line," laughed the panelist sitting next to him.

He added, "Looks like we're going to take Project Nero off the shelf again." A fellow member spoke up, "Blame it on the Christians."

"Finally, the last step before the beginning of the glorious New World Order," Abdel said quietly and yet very seriously.

I quickly scanned the faces of the council members from left to right to see if I could detect any dissent from the prevailing mood of the group. While a few were enthusiastically expressing their approval, most seemed indifferent, exhausted or somber.

One of the members intrigued me, however. He was a tall, slender, rather frail black man who looked to be in his fifties. He had been intently observing the proceedings, looking over small rimless eyeglasses perched on the end of his nose. His scowl was convincing evidence that he was resistant to what was going on.

The Chairman continued, "I know you are tired. We have been here for days. But I want to conclude by emphasizing in broad terms the spirit we must all have when dealing with the Americans after the event. It can be summed up in a few words. 'The terrorists are attempting to destroy you. We are here to help you.'

"When disaster strikes, we can fully expect that the first thing that the President will do is sign an Executive Order that will declare a national state of emergency. He will declare that martial law has been imposed over the entire country, and the temporary suspension of all rights of the people under the Constitution. Successive Executive Orders, I understand, have been drafted and will be immediately executed."

"That should have happened years ago," a panel member spoke up.

"The Internet and cell phone service will be the first to go. The only communication between the people will be with those in the same room.

"Our goal is to bring all radio and TV stations under the direct control of the government within a period of two weeks."

A very distinguished older man wearing a coat and tie raised his hand to be recognized. "May I say something, Abdel?"

"Go ahead. Be brief."

"I cannot emphasize enough how important it is that every government worker and volunteer constantly stress that the harsh measures being taken are temporary and for the protection of the people."

Abdel nodded in agreement and continued, "Data collection under the Patriot Act, before it ran out, has given us the name and whereabouts of almost every potential insurgent in the country. Harshest measures will be taken first to eliminate those employed in the military and in local law enforcement who resist the Final Transformation. All federal, state and local law enforcement agencies will come under the joint control of the FBI, the US Justice Department, and the four branches of the military under the authority of the Commander-in-Chief. All guns and ammunition of the general population will be seized. Much has been done already in preparation for this. Remember, the President will settle for nothing less than absolute gun control. All weapons must be confiscated.

"For those who fit the elderly, disabled and potential terrorist profiles, they are to be taken into custody and advised that FEMA vans will be arriving within the hour to pick them up. Emphasize that they will be transported to camps where the government will take good care of them until they can return to their homes.

"Emphasize constantly that the catastrophe is an act of terror and that the terrorists are fundamental Christians, Nazi skinheads, the Ku Klux Klan and patriotic political groups. Allow no distinctions between them. Lop them all together. Brand them all as terrorists and enemies of the state."

"If this is done right, I don't think there will be substantial resistance by the population," the older man replied.

"Exactly. How will they communicate? Smoke signals? All communication will be under our control."

The Chairman paused. Then all at once he began to loudly declare, "It has to be done and it has to be done now. We have no other choice. We have waited much too long for this!"

The black man in the rimless eyeglasses was on his feet. "I beg your pardon, Mr. Chairman. Just a minute, now. What do you mean by it has to be done now? What do you mean by specifically targeting these groups? This is something new."

Abdel didn't answer.

"Two years ago, I was asked by the President to be part of this council. The purpose was, as explained to me, to mobilize and unite the nation beforehand in the event of a significant national disaster. As a minister of the gospel, my specific assignment was to lay the groundwork among the churches and the faith-based organizations across the country in case their services and facilities were needed."

He was speaking loudly, "I have listened to you for three days now, and I get the distinct impression that you are interested in one thing and one thing only. And that is taking matters into your own hands. We are advisors to the President only. Not the decision-makers. He will want a well-reasoned report upon which he can act in the event of a disaster. This will take some..."

"We don't have time. Don't you understand? Two nuclear bombs are on their way to the United States, now. At this very moment. If ISIS detonates the bomb, we won't know when or where until it happens. And then... "

"We lose control of the damage," a member exclaimed.

"Precisely. Any damage from an outside source will be indiscriminate, widespread and could potentially blow America back to the Stone Age. A controlled event from within, followed by martial law and the quashing of dissident elements, is the only agenda. There is nothing else to talk about."

"Who is going to present this to the President?"

"Leave that up to me. He is a very pragmatic man. Sometimes wisdom requires that we choose the lesser of two evils. Besides, it is my job to convince him that when the smoke clears, the American people will thank him. It will secure his legacy as America's greatest president. Popular demand will dictate that he continues to rule for years to come. I assure you that history will be kind to him if he listens to us."

The older gentleman chuckled and then stated, "Nothing surprises me anymore." He paused, breathed deeply, and went on to say, "We all are well aware that Ban Ki-moon's term of office as Secretary General of the UN is up on December 31 this year. And there is the rumor that the directorship of the regional headquarters of the UN in Erbil, Iraq, will soon be open. Wouldn't it be something if the President were to consider one of these positions? Either way, he would continue to greatly influence the crafting of the new Middle East and the future of US policy, especially if the UN were to assign troops to the location as some have advocated."

Abdel quickly responded, "This is not the time or place to talk about alternative plans. We must focus on the next season for America. His job is not finished in Washington."

"Maybe, he could do all three," someone joked.

"Yeah," remarked another, "and they said that he was just another lame duck president."

"What about Hillary?" the older gentleman asked. Abdel answered immediately, "that will be taken care of ...I assure you."

"How can you control a catastrophe?" a member spoke up.

"We've been through that a hundred times. It doesn't have to be huge, just big enough to convince the stupid American gophers that a change at the helm is unthinkable at this time."

"There's a risk."

"Of course. If we fail, they will hang us all."

"Yes. One at a time," came an exclamation, followed by nervous laughter.

"I cannot agree with this," objected the man in the rimless eyeglasses.

"What do you mean? You don't agree? Where have you been for the last hour and a half? Did you not hear the Secretary's report?

"Must we endure again the long list of inadequacies in our national defense? Do you need reminding that electricity is the lifeblood of our nation? The infrastructure that supports it is as old as the hills and we do not have the money to fix it. It is all connected. If one part goes, the rest will go like dominos. America goes black. For years to come."

The man didn't budge. He replied, "You can bet your life that the CIA is already on top of this." This is not the time for this council to advise the President to take over the country."

It was obvious that the Chairman was losing his temper. "Are you blind to the fact that there are other scenarios just as deadly as two suicide bombers attempting to smuggle bombs through Mexico? Can't you see that we don't have the cyber capability to keep China from raiding the US government and stealing personnel records of 20,000,000 employees? What makes you think they could not shut down our public utilities?"

"I want to be totally up front with you Abdel, and this council. My task has been impossible to carry out. The churches, as well as the country, are so divided over the policies of this Administration that it is impossible to unite them in any common endeavor that the President initiates. Even the blacks can't agree among themselves."

He added, "Since the Civil War, the country has never been this divided. I don't like saying things like this, but sometimes I wonder if the President isn't intentionally dividing this country. He needs to heal the country and he needs all our prayers to do it. It isn't too late. We can still sit down together. We can still love one another.

"Instead, he lights up the White House in rainbow colors to celebrate same sex marriage and the gay lifestyle. Not only dividing the country even further, but alienating God by flaunting in His face one of the sins for which He destroyed Sodom and Gomorrah."

The man obviously had the respect of the group. I would have thought the meeting would have been in an uproar by now. But instead, the others remained silent except for a few growls of discontent.

He went on, "What is happening in our country is the judgment of God for our disobedience. Please don't look at me like that. Yes, you heard me right. The judgement of God.

"There may still be hope for us if we as a nation confess our sins, ask His forgiveness and turn from our idolatry, immorality and violence. It can start here. In this meeting. Tonight."

I could see anger in the eyes of some of the council members. Others were exchanging glances, while one or two bowed their head as if shamed or embarrassed.

Abdel continued as if the man with the rimless glasses had not spoken. He showed no emotion. "Look, all of you. Your advisory role to the President makes you among the most powerful people in America. Some of you work behind the scenes. The public doesn't even know you exist. And yet you have been selected to address the issues before us."

I knew I had to speak up. I had to stop this man if I could. "Mr. Chairman! I urge you and this council to consider the possibility that the whole story of ISIS and the two bombs is an international hoax. They may think to trick America, into capitulation of its world supremacy and sovereignty. I was there. And I am not thoroughly convinced, myself."

"It's your report, Mr. Secretary."

"The report is an accurate account of what I saw and heard in Dubai. I do not vouch for the authenticity of the claims made. How do we know that the Dubai thing wasn't a stage production to bring me to this room tonight? How do we know? How will we explain to our children that we gave their freedom away because we were afraid of a ghost? I was there, but I can't stand here and say that the whole thing was not a ruse...that it is not a hoax to deceive us into handing over the sovereignty of the United States to world government."

I saw no indication that he heard what I said. He continued in a low decibel monotone and seemed to be on the edge of tears. "We all are very privileged to be in this room tonight. We have been charged to coordinate all branches of the public and private sectors in the event of a national disaster. We have been working on this for two years now and we should be ready. To be handpicked to transition America through its most hazardous hour, and into full membership in the New World Order, is an honor beyond comprehension."

He paused and then went on, "Next year's elections can dismantle everything we have worked so hard for. The dream of global government hinges on what we do here tonight."

"I cannot and I will not betray my country." The man in the rimless eyeglasses stood to his feet.

The older distinguished-looking gentleman stood to his feet, exclaiming, "It is obvious to me, Sir, that you distrust the President! There is no more qualified man on earth to bring in the New World Order and peace to the world.

"He is the only man on the world scene that brings together the forces that threaten to blow our world apart. He is a Christian by his own admission. He has vowed allegiance to the Islamic faith. He is a Socialist by political philosophy. He is the highly evolved secularist. He is black. He is white. He is the child of three continents. He is the perfect "Blended Man" who can mix together all the things that divide us."

"I am sure," the man in the rimless eyeglasses responded, "that he could even mix iron and clay?"

"What...?"

"I don't believe he is the one who is to come ... but he is certainly leading the way."

"What are you talking about?"

"Never mind. You wouldn't understand."

The Chairman clenched his fist, hit the table and shouted, "I will take nothing back to the President from this council, except a unanimous recommendation for martial law at his discretion in the event of a threat to our national security!"

"The threat to our security?" the man responded. "Threat? That's a very low threshold don't you think? That means he could drop the hammer tonight."

The Chairman continued to shout, "The recommendation of this council must be unanimous. It protects us. It protects the President. We have waited fifty years for this night. We cannot let it go by."

"What about the American people?" the man exclaimed loudly, sitting back down.

"There is nothing to discuss. Before we go one step further, I want a commitment from every person in this room that you are irrevocably pledged to do whatever it takes to bring about the fundamentally changed America promised to the American people. If you cannot make that pledge, I am asking you to stand to your feet."

I closed my eyes, wondering what my presence at the meeting would mean for my long-term health. The room grew silent. I heard a slight noise as a firm object slid on the carpet. It was followed by faint nondescript sounds that told me someone was standing up. I opened my eyes.

It was the man with the rimless eyeglasses. He said, "I don't think the President wants to be a rubber stamp of this council. If he does, count me out. I believe he wants a recommendation based on a reasonable debate. I will not be a part of any attempt to hijack this council and the will of the American people!

"One thing further. I do not think it would be out of order to call upon God for direction. The possibility that our country will not survive is very real. We should all be on our knees asking Him for mercy. The Bible says," he continued as he reached for and opened a large, well-used Bible,

2 Chronicles 7:14 If my people, which are called by my name, shall humble themselves, and pray, and seek my face, and turn from their wicked ways; then will I hear from heaven, and will forgive their sin, and will heal their land."

He looked around, meeting the eyes of each person in the room. "As a nation and as this council, we would be well-advised to heed this promise tonight."

After a short pause he continued, "I'm sorry, but I am on my way to Washington. If I am granted an audience with the President I will ask him to lead the nation in repentance for our sins. You know how to reach me when you decide to resume intelligent discussions."

I think I was the only one who saw what happened next. The others were focused on the man who had the courage to stand on his convictions. He began to collect his papers, putting them into his briefcase. Standing at the podium, I had a perfect vantage point.

The Chairman stepped back from the table into the shadows between two curtain panels. Showing no emotion, he methodically and silently pulled a 9 mm handgun, with a silencer attached, from beneath his jacket. An audible gasp was all I had time to muster ...

"Pffffft! Pffffft!"

The execution was carried out in a most orderly fashion. The man's spectacles flew across the room as his body jerked and he fell back onto the floor.

It was almost as if no one was caught by surprise. There were some slight instinctive reactions. Two or three panel members started to get up, but quickly sat back down. Some turned their heads to see what had happened while one or two did not even flinch. Quickly, the realization settled in as to what had taken place. Then, all of us froze.

The Chairman put the gun back in the holster. He rotated his head as if to cure a kink in his neck, walked back to the table, and spoke to one of the panel members, "Let the record reflect that Reverend Philpott was not present for the council meeting tonight."

He resumed talking, pointing to papers on the table, "The Report and this council's recommendations are in this folder. The State Department Report of the Dubai Committee discussions has been graciously provided by Secretary Flink. They are attached.

"Let's see. Yes. The signature page is… page 36." He went to the end of the table and handed it to a council member. "Please sign and pass it down the table."

No mention was made of the man on the floor. No one got up to help him.

My heart was pounding. I stood up and began to gather my things.

"Where do you think you are going, Mr. Flink?" the Chairman asked.

"My mission before this council tonight was to deliver this report on behalf of the President. I have finished my assignment. I'm on my way to Washington."

"You don't understand. Nobody leaves this room."

"I understand very well. You are the one who doesn't understand. I was handpicked by the President for this mission, and my orders are to be in the Oval Office at 8:30 tomorrow morning. I will report directly to him. And the Secret Service is downstairs to see that I get there!"

"The Secret Service? You mean State Department Security don't you?" His piercing eyes looked directly into mine, "Secret Service? I don't believe you. Who assigned them?"

"The President."

"I don't believe you! Go get them!"

He stepped to the door and whispered to a security officer stationed there. The officer looked me over from head to toe and then followed me to the elevator. We joined an Oriental gentleman who smiled as we stepped inside.

I was never one to start a fight. But tonight it would be different. I guessed the security officer to be 220 pounds, with a thick neck and big hands that if balled into a fist could put you to sleep. I had no choice. I asked God to forgive me for what I was about to do.

I had never sucker-punched anybody in my life. In fact, I hadn't punched anyone since high school. I glanced at the officer. He was standing ramrod straight with his head resting on the wall of the elevator and his chin jutting slightly forward. With everything my 200 pound frame could muster, and with my whole body behind the punch, I practically lifted him off his feet. It knocked him out cold. He fell face forward into the elevator floor. I quickly relieved him of a .38 caliber handgun from a shoulder holster and stuck it under my belt.

The gentleman on board the elevator who had greeted us in English was now speaking accelerated Chinese in a loud voice. I asked for his cell phone, which he quickly retrieved from a coat pocket. The elevator stopped two or three times on the way down but no one seemed inclined to get on. I dialed 911 and advised the dispatcher that a man had been shot on the 17th floor of the hotel. I handed the phone back to its owner. The officer on the floor was beginning to move when the elevator door closed behind me as I was leaving.

I quickly determined the location of the lobby and ran in the opposite direction. Turning a corner in a long hallway, I spotted an exit sign and ran as hard as I could toward it. I soon realized that it was an emergency exit that would sound an alarm, but it did little to slow me down. I rammed it as hard as I could. The alarm went off and I bolted into the parking lot.

Totally disoriented. I began looking for my rental car, the make and model of which I couldn't remember. I ran around the hotel and spotted a taxi that was pulling out from the entrance. Hearing my screams, he stopped and I jumped in the back seat. People were coming out from the hotel entrance with the emergency alarms still blaring. Within seconds, I was off the hotel property and on my way to the Diner.

I said a prayer for the man in the rimless eyeglasses.

THE CHASE

We soon arrived at the diner. I went inside and immediately spotted Maria. She was sitting at the far end of the diner facing the main entrance, frantically waving a menu. I sat down in the same booth next to her where we could both watch the entrance.

Dispensing with her normal affectionate greeting, she asked, "Did you forget something?"

"Don't scare me like that. What?"

"Don't you remember? Where are you supposed to sit?"

"Oh, my goodness. You're right."

I quickly jumped to my feet and sat down across the table from her. Jonathon had insisted that we exchange places at the diner in case we were followed, in order to create confusion as to our identities.

"Have you seen Jonathan?" she asked, quickly getting to the business at hand.

"No. I haven't seen him since we last talked. He will be bringing us the contact information soon, I hope."

"Maria."

"Yes, Hon."

"Do you think we should go through with this?"

She looked up from the menu she had just opened. Her eyes were like searchlights, "What's in your heart, David? Are you having second thoughts?"

"I don't think so. But it's like Frost's 'road less traveled by.' My concern is the difference it could make in our future together."

"David, you have only one decision to make. You know what it is. What does God want you to do?"

Maria ordered two waters and I opened the menu.

"David!" Maria whispered alarmingly. "Don't look up, but Frank and Emery just walked in."

"You're kidding."

"I wish I were."

"You don't know them!"

"I met them at the airport, remember?"

I turned and looked back over my shoulder. They were getting seated near the entrance. Frank waved his big hand at me and with a snide look on his face smiled, as if to say, "Aha, I gotcha!"

I didn't wave back. I had been informed by the State Department that Secret Service protection would no longer be provided after the New York meeting. It caught me by surprise.

"We said our goodbyes earlier. I thanked them for their help. It was a big production. I don't understand. Why are they here?" I whispered.

"I don't like this, David."

"Neither do I."

"Oh, no!"

"What?"

"Jonathan just walked in!"

"The plot thickens," I said with a faint stab at humor.

The next thing I knew, Maria was on her feet running through the diner screaming "David! David! My Love!"

She threw both arms around Jonathan, then frantically and all but physically dragging him to our table, sat down, scooted across the seat and pulled him in beside her.

Immediately sensing a grave situation, he whispered, "What's going on?"

"Sssshh. Look behind me," I answered.

"You mean the two A-type dudes in dark suits?"

"It's Secret Service. That's Frank and Emery."

"I've seen the big one around the White House."

Jonathan reacted quickly. He shifted in his seat toward Maria and loudly exclaimed, "Honey, it's so good to see you. It has been too long."

She responded, "I know."

Without saying another word, Jonathan got to his feet and walked to the front of the diner. It was an in-your-face question that came out forcefully enough that I could hear without turning around. "Why are you here? You guys have been my shadow for almost two weeks, now. I wanted a little private time with my bride-to-be and you show up."

Frank answered, "Our assignment has been extended for 72 hours. You are still our charge." Jonathan wheeled around without saying another word, returned to the table, and sat down by Maria.

"Okay," I exclaimed, "What's with the black suit and red tie, Jonathan? The question is directed to you, also, Maria!"

They exchanged glances and soberly looked at me. I was mad, and I knew that it showed. Finally, Maria broke the ice, "It was Jonathan's idea."

"Jonathan?" I looked at him sternly.

"It's like I told you this afternoon, little brother, 'I got your back.'"

Nobody said a word. It seemed like one of those times when silence has more meaning.

Finally, I whispered, "Okay, guys, here's the deal. We all know the peril of this meeting tonight. A long prison term may be the least of the possibilities. But here we are."

"In a nutshell," I whispered, "a major catastrophe has been planned for America."

"Who by?" inquired Maria.

"Until a few minutes ago I thought I knew. This much I can say for sure. North Korea and Iran are holding our country hostage at this very moment."

"How?"

"By the threat of significant nuclear destruction."

"Do they have the capability to do that?"

"Believe me, Maria. If I learned anything in Dubai, it is the vulnerability of the United States to nuclear attack, and the resolve of our enemies to destroy us.

"I've said too much already, but there is no question from what I have seen and heard in the last 48 hours that they have the capacity. I talked to the Secretary on the way over. He had just talked to the President. Law enforcement at all federal levels has been advised. The governors have been contacted and the National Guard from all branches of Armed Forces are being mobilized as we speak. State Police Departments and local police units across the country are being placed in a state of readiness. FEMA and the Red Cross. US Forest Service. All of it. They are preparing for the worst. For a major national disaster."

Jonathan interrupted, "I just got word a few minutes ago. The President is conducting a press conference tomorrow morning."

I continued my thought, "If the hit occurs, it will be a big one. We can expect widespread chaos. Martial law will likely result to restore order. Constitutional rights suspended."

"David, this whole thing is crazy. If he is…I mean…surely he wouldn't attempt a takeover … It won't work…will it?" Maria responded.

"Let's be realistic, guys." Jonathan whispered. "He maintains a 50 percent approval rating no matter what. A permanent majority is not an impossibility. It isn't too far out, in my opinion, to conceive an Executive

Order postponing the 2016 elections until the country is stabilized. The public will be reluctant for change in a crisis of great magnitude."

She cautioned, "David. You're shaking. Your blood pressure. Please settle down."

"I'm okay."

No one commented further. Finally, Jonathan broke the silence and whispered, "Okay, here's the plan. I don't have time to get into it right now, but the original news network we discussed as being the most likely to air this story… you know who I'm talking about?"

"Yeah, I know."

"I didn't go to them. They are fine folks, but I don't know them well enough to know if I can trust them to get into the specifics with them. They look at me with suspicion, anyway. They think I'm from the other end of the spectrum. But listen to me, David. We have an alternative. I really believe that God has opened a very wide door … listen to me."

"Sssshhh!" Maria cautioned.

"I know the right person to help us."

Jonathan was getting emotional. He reached over and took both our hands again, and held them tightly in his. Tears were welling up in his eyes… "David, you don't have to go through with this, you know, you can abandon the whole thing right now. No one will ever know."

He waited for me to say something. I didn't react. "How silly of me," he said, trying to fake a smile. "I knew what you would do. You were always the stubborn one. Everybody knew it. The whole family."

"What's the deal?"

"Okay, here it is." He slipped a small post-it across the table.

"So, what is it?"

"It's the address of a parking garage you are going to when you leave here. Go to the third level. There will be a taxi waiting for you. It's just a few blocks from here. The driver's name is Roy. He will take you to the Studio."

"Let me see," Maria interrupted, snatching the post-it from my hand. "Uh... this street is not far from here."

"Okay, Jonathon. Dispense with all the mystery," I demanded. "Who are we going to see?"

"I gave them my word that if for some reason this mission failed, that you would have nothing on your person that would involve them in this venture. Besides... you might abandon the mission if you knew who they were. But, I really believe they are on the up and up."

"You don't expect me ..."

"Please, trust me on this, brother. I'm betting my life and reputation on this as well as you are. They want to hear what you have to say."

"What is that?" Jonathan asked, interrupting himself and pointing at something shiny in Maria's hand.

"It's a little gold cross and chain. I found it in my purse when I went to the restroom a few minutes ago. I don't know how it got there. I never saw it before in my life."

"Has anyone been in your purse?"

"Not that I'm aware of."

Jonathon grabbed the pendant from Maria and examined it closely. He then stuffed it in his jacket pocket, "You won't need this."

"Jonathon?"

"Give me your cell phone, David."

"Why?"

"Don't give me no lip. Just give me your cell phone."

"Now, your credit cards. Both of you!"

"I am very confused." Maria raised both hands as if to surrender, "Wha...?"

"Sssshhh! Shut up. Just do what I say. The cross is chipped. Look."

It was obvious that the little clasp on the back contained what appeared to be a small electronic chip. "It's an RFID chip. Somebody planted it in your purse. They know your location even as we speak. Stay away from open areas tonight. Do the alleys and backstreets." He held up the cross, the cell phones and credit cards. "Without these they have no way to track you … except visually — line of sight. That's it."

"Tell us all you know, Jonathan. What's going on?"

"I don't like it. Somebody is taking a lot of pains to know your whereabouts. There was some scuttlebutt around the office today about a New York meeting and that even drones had been assigned to it. They may be for surveillance only. But they could be armed. It blows me away that it is possible that they are tracking you."

We had been as close as two brothers could ever be. Dad called us "Frick and Frack." It was almost like a calling. Jonathan had always felt the need to take care of his younger brother who had come into the world a mere ten minutes after him. The day before our high school prom, he had lectured me for hours on the finer points of social etiquette, and made sure that I had enough money to buy my date a few Cokes and a couple of hot dogs at the Sonic afterward. He even taught me how to make a knot in my tie that night. And there were some other added benefits to being his brother. None of the high school bullies dared mess with me.

Jonathon slid his cell phone across the table and stood up. "Here, you might need this. It has a Maps App. I am sure New York City is on it. Maria, take care of him."

Then looking down as if he saw through the table top a scene unfolding before him, he said, "Remember what Mom always said to us, David?"

"I don't …."

"She would say, 'When you get to the other side, look for me just inside the Eastern Gate. I'll be waiting for you.'"

And then, he was gone.

It took me a second to digest what had just happened. Then it hit me. He was taking the bullet for me. He thought he was going to die. Instantly, I was on my feet. "No! No! No!" I screamed, as he walked through the door, "You are not going to do this! Come back here. Oh, my God, please… "

Frank and Emery were immediately by my side — one on each arm. Their grip indicated something more than a desire to comfort me. Frank took me by the lapels and began to shake me, "What's going on here?"

Maria spoke up, "It's a family thing. They just lost their mother, that's all! You all go back to your table. He'll be all right. I'll take care of him." They reluctantly retreated to the other end of the diner.

We fell into the booth, put our noses against the plate glass, cupped our hands to keep out reflections and peered into the dimly lit street. Maria was praying in the Spirit.

"There he is. Over there. Under the street light," she whispered.

Jonathan was walking toward his pickup about 25 yards away. Looking back on it, I don't know if I actually saw the source of the explosion or not. But it seemed that a dark object streaked toward him — a white flash — I don't remember the sound — just a bone numbing concussion and the shattering of the heavy plate glass window.

It was pitch black for a second or two and then the lights flickered in the diner and came back on. I could see that Maria had a small laceration inside her hairline.

"Thank the Lord, I'm alright," she said. "Are you okay?"

Frank and Emery were standing near the front entrance. Both were on their cell phones and were looking straight at us while they talked.

I took Maria's hand and announced, "I think it's time to leave."

Over the counter, through the kitchen, out the back door and around the corner of the diner we went. We found quick refuge, scrambling into the passenger side of a large gasoline tanker parked across the street at a Seven Eleven - its engine running. We climbed into the sleeping berth. The driver immediately opened the door and climbed up behind the wheel. He didn't see us. I could see Emery behind the diner still glued to his cell phone and Frank was running toward the tanker.

"Roll down the window."

"Yes sir."

Holding up his badge and identification, "My name is Frank Adkins. I am with the US Secret Service. I am securing the area. Do not move this truck."

"Officer, I never seen anything like it in my life. I was getting ready to fill up the gas tanks here at the store and started across the street to get a sandwich to go. I didn't have anything to do with it. Ask the station manager if you don't believe me. He saw it all."

"Get out of the truck."

"Yes sir."

"Did you see a man and a woman leave the Diner?"

"I didn't see no woman, no, sir. All I seen was that poor fellow getting inside his pick-up and... Kaboom! It knocked me down."

Frank immediately began running back toward the diner. He turned and shouted pointing at the driver, "Don't move the truck!"

By this time I was behind the wheel of the big tanker, trying to figure out the controls. I locked the doors as Maria slid out of the berth into the front seat.

"Hey!" the driver screamed.

"Hang on honey." The tractor was automatic but had low gear and I jerked it into first. I over accelerated and we quickly lurched into the street. I had driven an eighteen-wheeler when I worked for my uncle hauling coal in West Virginia in my early twenties. I knew that I had to make some big allowances for the length of the truck and trailer on the sharp turns.

Maria began quoting the Scriptures, "A thousand may fall at your side, and ten thousand at your right hand; but it shall not come near you... a thousand may fall at your side, and ten thousand at your right hand; but it shall not come near you."

"Maria, I'm concerned for you... are you sure...?"

"Don't be silly. It's too late, now. Besides, I love you, David Flink. Just keep on truckin'."

"Oh, David! Maps App to the rescue. I think I know the best way to get us there... Holy Spirit please guide us... Please guide us, Lord."

Her assurances did not convince me. One thing was certain. It was not planned that we would be driving an eighteen-wheeler full of high octane gasoline through downtown Manhattan on a Friday night.

"Maria, get Frank on the cell!"

"Turn left at the second light."

"Okay, Okay, just get Frank on the cell phone!"

The first light was green, but the next one was red. We were one car back from the intersection. Still in first gear at twenty mph, the big diesel was making a lot of noise. I laid on the air horn and didn't let up until the intersection cleared.

"David, you are scaring the people."

I swung wide and made the first turn successfully, barely missing a parked BMW.

We could hear what sounded like dozens of police cars and fire trucks and they were closing in.

Maria screamed, "It's Frank. He's on the line."

"Frank. Here's what I want you to do. Tell them not to try and stop me. I will bust through any roadblock they set up. I want clearance south on West Street to I-278 through Brooklyn across the Bay to I-95. Then I'll go until I run out of gas. That way nobody gets hurt."

Maria continued screaming, "Honey, you aren't abandoning the mission, are you? You aren't are you? Are you?"

"No, just creating some confusion."

Frank was on speaker. "You're crazy, David! I don't know what you are trying to do, but it won't work. You're dead meat."

"Did you hear what I said? Nobody gets hurt. Broker that deal, Frank, and you'll be a hero. Frank, do you hear me?"

Maria screamed, holding one hand over her mouth and pointing with the other. "There, right there."

Off to the front port side of the tractor, about 10 or 12 feet away, was a dark metallic object hovering at windshield height and moving with the truck in the same direction at no more than 15 mph. It was smaller than a brief case, but clearly visible as we neared a streetlight. I had seen pictures on the internet. It had a small blinking red light and a plastic bubble that housed a camera. Small antennae projected from it, which I assumed were triggers for the explosives inside.

"There's more! Look over there, David!"

"They're Kamikazes!"

"What?"

"I think they're Kamikaze Drones. They could be surveillance. But I don't think so. They're Kamikazes. They explode on impact with the target. They are bombs… that's all they are… remote control bombs."

I threw on the brakes and the big tanker came to a grinding halt. The sirens were closing in, but none were in sight. A crowd was gathering to observe the tanker with a drone hovering over its hood.

"Maria, praise God! Praise God! This is good! They made a mistake. They sent the wrong Drones. They won't dare blow up this tanker in downtown New York, and they sure don't want to bomb a crowd."

"What do we do now?" I thought to myself.

"David, I know where we are. The Starbucks is right up there. I have done runway at Sac's around the corner. I know where we are. There's a pedway up there that goes across to the parking garage that Jonathan told us about. I used to park there. I know where we are!

"See that alley over there just beyond the crowd? I'll bet we can get to the pedway through there."

"Okay, Maria, let's just meander through the crowd. Don't run or appear in a hurry!"

Maria and I slowly and calmly got out of the tanker on the driver's side and made our way through the crowd hand-in-hand. Except for a couple that tried to talk to us, nobody seemed to even notice that we had gotten out of the truck. They were too busy watching the drone. When we reached the edge of the crowd, we stopped and looked back. The drone had turned as if on an axis and seemed to be looking straight at us — as if it had life and intelligence of its own and had a score to settle.

We darted quickly into a long alley and ran as hard as we could. We came to a small alcove partially blocked by a dumpster. I leaned up against it.

"Whew! I'm out of breath," I rasped. "Just a minute, please."

"It's just a little farther, David."

We could see two Kamikazes circling above us. We backed slowly into the shadows behind the dumpster.

"They are like vultures!"

"These service alleys are too narrow for them to maneuver in. They won't come in after us."

It was a miracle how it all fell into place. Maria and I ran through a Starbucks and down a crowded street into a shopping mall. We took the elevator to the second floor and began running across the pedway leading to the parking garage.

We finally reached the heavy metal steel door that led into the garage. There, we hesitated and looked at each other.

"Here goes!" and I opened the door. Maria refused to budge.

"David, let's pray! 'Lord, we thank You ahead of time for bringing us to the studio. For the angels that watch over us. You shut doors that no man can open and You open doors that no man can shut. We are depending wholly on You. Please give us Your protection.'"

We took off running as hard as we could go. Maria pointed to an exit sign with an elevator nearby, "Over there!"

I reached it first and pushed the 'Up' button.

Maria was right behind me. Clapping her hands with a big smile on her face and wiping tears with the back of her hand, "We're here! We're here! Thank God, we're here. The taxi should be waiting upstairs!"

Stress levels mounted. We could hear the elevator coming to a halt. Finally, the door opened. There is no way we could have prepared for the surprise we got. Frank emerged with his gun drawn.

"Don't move! You're under arrest! Hands behind your heads!"

We froze! No sooner had Frank advanced three feet into the garage when "Whack!" his gun went cartwheeling through the air and sliding 20 or 30 feet across the pavement under a car.

"Ooomph!" Frank's feet flew off the pavement. He was slammed against the back of the elevator. The scene resembled a Three Stooges movie with an invisible Moe punching and poking at the eyes of Curly and Larry. Frank cupped his hands over his eyes, "Oooohhh," he yelled.

Emery somehow wiggled out of the elevator door past Frank's big frame and began running away, only to be jerked back by an unseen force apparently gripping his left wrist. Emery went in a full 360-degree circle, his feet leaving the ground, and like a rock from a slingshot was sent sprawling down the exit ramp. Recovering quickly, he jumped to his feet and disappeared, running in the opposite direction.

By this time Frank was recovering from his recent trauma. He took his hands off his eyes and was attempting to peer through layers of tears. We were standing only a few feet directly in front of him.

"No! No! Get away from me," he screamed, backing into the elevator door which had closed now. "No one will ever know I saw you tonight. You don't have to worry about me. I won't kill you. Just get away from me! Get away from me!" Then he slid down the door into a sitting position and began to cry.

Maria shoved me and pointed, "The stairs."

We scurried to the top of the steps leading to a metal door that opened onto the third level. And sure enough, waiting for us was a Yellow Cab with engine running, headlights on, and the driver graciously holding the door motioning for us to get inside.

"We are going to this address." I handed him the slip of paper. "Do you know where this is?"

"Yes sir, with my eyes closed. I have been doing this since high school."

"A fifty dollar bill if you can get us there in ten minutes," I yelled.

"I can do it in fifteen."

"It's a deal!"

I think I heard rubber peel. We were on the street in seconds. I closed my eyes and reached for Maria's hand. She was trembling. Fire trucks and police cruisers were racing past us with their sirens and horns screaming full blast. It all seemed so surreal — like watching a movie in slow motion and without sound. And then in my spirit I was someplace else. I was back at the Diner.

I don't know how Maria knew, but she began stroking my hand, "I am so sorry about Jonathon," she said. "There is nothing I can say that will make sense to you right now except maybe this, 'He's with the Lord, David. Your mother is with the Lord, too. They are waiting for us.'"

"Why are we doing this, Maria? I am angry and very lonely tonight. My only brother just gave his life to save a nation that is too tired and morally bankrupt to even care. Why are we risking our lives for America?"

"David! I believe Frank and Emery came to the Diner to kill you. It's too late. We have no other choice, except to go ahead. Besides, there are many good people in America who have not bowed the knee to Baal. Let's stand up for them and for their children. Somebody has to stand up. It looks like it will be you and me, tonight, David. I believe our mission is not in vain. Others will follow."

"Maria!"

"Yes, Sweetheart!"

"Can we get married as soon as we get back to Washington?"

"David? Are you serious?"

"We can quit our jobs and move to Israel. I know some people there. I will be able to find work. I know I will."

"David Flink! Of course, I will! You silly bird. We can get married on a boat on the Sea of Galilee. The same boat we were on last year."

"I want three kids, Maria."

"That sounds so good to me. If the Lord blesses us financially, we will have a home in the United States, too."

"Oh, Honey! That's a great idea. God showed me before I left Jerusalem that we would be coming back there soon to live. We will sit under our own vine and fig tree with kids screaming, laughing, and chasing each other around the house."

We held hands the rest of the way. A deep peace settled over me. Maria was relaxed. She must have felt it, too. It lasted until the taxi came to a stop.

"Oh, no! Maria, No! No!" I shouted.

"What?"

"Jonathan gave us the wrong address. This is not where we are supposed to be. He made a mistake. A big mistake! These people will never air our story."

Directly in front of us across the street from where the taxi had stopped was the TV studio — and the signage on the building left nothing to the imagination — I was sure we had come to the wrong place. It read, "NEW WORLD NEWS GROUP."

We stood and stared in disbelief. I screamed at the driver, "How could this happen? You brought us to the wrong place."

"David, we have to trust in God. We have no other choice. Don't you remember what the angel told you in Tel Aviv? That the one thing you would learn on this mission was that 'with God all things are possible.' Don't you remember what the angel did to Frank and Emery? He told you in Tel Aviv that he would see you in New York."

We looked at each other and said at the same time, "Let's go!"

I don't remember crossing the street, but we began banging on the big glass doors of NEW WORLD NEWS GROUP. It was no surprise when six uniformed security came running up to the other side of the glass, swiped an electronic key and opened the door.

I had prepared a speech. I was going to ask for the person in charge and tell him… but the minute I saw all the uniforms I forgot it. My only option was to depend on the Holy Spirit …

"I am fully aware of how outrageous my actions may appear, but I have been sent from God with a message to the nation. He led me here. Can you get me to a microphone?"

"Is your name, Flink?"

"Yeah." I glanced at Maria. Her eyes were big as saucers and her lower jaw was sagging.

"Identification please."

"Yeah, sure. Here it is," as I scrambled for my driver's license.

"And yours, Ma'am."

"Sure."

"Come with me."

Two of the security personnel went with us and the other four remained in the lobby. The spokesman for the group quizzed us as we got on the elevator, "What's all the hullabaloo about out there? Sirens have been going off for the last thirty minutes."

When neither Maria nor I responded, he attempted to answer his own question, "Ain't no telling. Could be anything. Must be something big. After twenty-five years on this job, I still get surprised sometimes with what goes on around here."

The elevator stopped on the sixth floor and the door opened inside the reception area of an elaborate suite of offices.

The minute we stepped out of the elevator a man with a big smile and a commanding presence appeared. His tie was loose and draped around his neck, and his sleeves were rolled up. He extended his right hand. "Welcome, Mr. Flink. My name is Ben Thomas. We have been waiting for you. And who is this, may I ask?"

"My name is Maria."

"Please step into my office."

It was a large office and, as you might expect, it had a view of downtown New York City.

I was trembling from head to foot. I was the one most surprised at the authority and boldness that came out when I opened my mouth.

"Sir, we want to thank you for the gracious reception we have received here tonight. You have been most kind. I am not trying to be rude, but I am here for one purpose and one purpose only. Let me repeat what I said when I first spoke to security downstairs. 'I am fully aware of how outrageous my actions may appear, but I have been sent from God with a message to the nation and the world. He led me here. Can you get me to a microphone?'"

"Well, since you are so quick to cut to the chase, Mr. Flink, may I be blunt and to the point, also?

"Your credentials are impeccable. We have checked you out through every intelligence source available to us. Everything from your childhood to your present internet habits — and you are squeaky clean. We have no reason to believe you are not telling the truth. But..."

"Thank you, sir."

"... but... but...the information that you bring to the table is unimaginable. It is earth shattering, to say the least. This kind of news story comes along once in a century... if that often... you just happen to be the hottest potato on the planet... you will make Snowden look like a choir boy. Do you have any documentation to support your claims?"

"Before we go any further, Mr. Thomas, I have a question to ask of you first."

"Go ahead. I will try to answer it if I can."

"How can I trust you? The people at NEW WORLD NEWS GROUP would have been the last people on earth that I would have thought would air this content."

"I understand your concerns, Mr. Flink, but ... even if I am the chief executive, I just work here. I do not make policy for this network. I do what I am told to do. Maybe, I can help you with that."

"I hope so."

"First and foremost we are reporters. Our job is to report the news. I admit that all of us spin it sometimes to serve the interests of those we work for — but you... I think you are about to rattle the foundations of Western Civilization. The stakes are too high not to tell it like it is. From the top down, we have decided to hear you out on this matter. I will tell you this. Leaks have come from two other sources in the past two days that lend almost absolute credibility to your story.

"And, too, I don't want to be too hypocritical. Ratings are probably playing a role. This one will take us to the top of the stack. And show the world that we are fair and impartial in our reporting.

"Let me say this. The Board of NEW WORLD NEWS GROUP is fully aware that you are here. Things have gone much too far. We will let the chips fall where they may. Do you trust me?"

"That's a tough question ... but I guess I'll have to, won't I?"

There was a pause in the conversation. Finally, Mr. Thomas broke the ice, "Ahem! We have a lot of work to do. Let's get started. Now, back to the documents you have. Do you..."

"I have some, yes, State Department papers and my diary of events. You will find it all on this flash drive." I reached in my jacket pocket and handed it to him. He in turn handed it to an aide that had just entered the room.

Then he said, "Follow me." We went into the main studio, which I instantly recognized from my habit of surfing the television news channels to see who covered what and, of course, to view the latest news.

A man was seated with his back to us in what I imagined was an extra studio chair that wasn't being used. He appeared to be asleep. When we walked in, he stood up and turned around. I instantly recognized him.

"Meet Ed Calipari."

"Mr. Calipari," I nodded.

"Please, just call me Ed. You must be David! Your brother is my best friend. He told me about your mission. Where is he tonight? I've been concerned about his safety. Is he okay?"

I knew I couldn't respond to the question. He asked again, "Is he okay?" He looked at Maria, and back at me.

"What happened?"

Tears began to well up. I was determined not to break down. Then I answered, "He's with the Lord. He went to be with the Lord, tonight."

"Wha...?" And then he caught a deep breath.

Trembling, I managed to answer, "He gave his life for his country. He said, 'I will be your decoy.'"

"David, I am so sorry. So very sorry. I can't believe it. I can't believe all this is happening." Then he broke. He began to weep. Maria grabbed some tissue from a box on a nearby counter and handed it to him.

"He was my very best friend. My mentor in the Lord. He led me to Christ."

Then, smiling through the tears he said, "You look just like him."

The room was silent... each of us privately reaching for the meaning of the terrible loss of Jonathan. I think that we all instantly realized that there was no time to grieve — the night held the fate, perhaps, of millions of Americans. They had a right to know what was about to happen.

I followed Mr. Calipari into a large conference room. He took notes on a legal pad as we talked and Maria slept on a sofa nearby. As far as I knew, nothing was recorded. Three hours later he announced, "I'm ready. The restrooms are down the hall if you need to freshen up." He laughed and added, "You really don't look so hot, you know."

"I'm tired, I guess. It's been a tough day."

Maria caught up with me on the way to the restroom, "You forgot all about me, didn't you?"

"No, sweetheart, I didn't."

"Don't you forget what the angel told you in Tel Aviv, 'Don't plan ahead what you are going to say. The Holy Spirit will tell you what to say.'"

"Thank you for reminding me."

I walked into the studio and Ed was already seated in one of two chairs that were placed for the interview. He motioned for me to join him.

"You know, Jonathan and I studied the Word together at least two or three days a week since my conversion six months ago. He loved the prophetic portions of the Bible that dealt with the last days."

"Oh, yeah, he came by it honestly. Our mother loved the study of prophecy."

"The topic of the Counterfeit Christ fascinated me. In fact, I have read several books on it. I believe he is already here and his identity is unknown."

"That's what our Mother said. And that he would be a mix of Muslim, Christian and Socialist. That he would rule from the eastern leg of the Roman Empire."

"Come down, David! Come down! Planet Earth calling David!"

"Oh, I'm sorry, Honey!"

Suddenly, Ed rotated his chair toward the control room and shouted, "Are we ready?"

He then swung around and faced me, "David, do you think we are doing the right thing?"

"If the people don't act now, it will soon be too late!"

He turned back, "Three minutes and counting!"

Maria asked, "Can we pray?"

Ed quickly replied by inviting Maria to the set and holding out his hands to form a human circle, "Sure, that's a great idea. Let's do it!"

"I just want to pray what God has laid on my heart."

We all bowed our heads. When she cleared her throat, I knew that she was going to sing her prayer. Her beautiful soft voice would need no accompaniment. She began,

"God bless America, land that we love
Stand beside her, and guide her through the night
With a light from above
From the mountains, to the prairies
To the oceans white with foam
God bless America our home sweet home
God bless America our home sweet home"

By the time she had gotten through the first stanza everyone in the studio had joined her. I stood up mid-song and raised my hands to God, pleading silently for His mercy upon our nation.

"Alright, let's go for it!" Ed shouted.

The cameramen were now in place. One of them held up ten fingers and then five... and then four... three... two... one...

"Ladies and gentlemen, we interrupt our regular programming this morning to bring you news of grave national and international concern..."

THE END

Curt Davis is the host of weekly TV broadcast *The Kingdom Dimension* as well as *Rebound America*, a streaming daily radio program. In his younger years, Davis was a full-time Christian minister and youth director, and for the last decade he has led citywide evangelistic meetings.

Davis began his law practice in 1981 and gained recognition as a criminal defense lawyer before shifting to a successful career as a personal injury attorney.

Davis was moved to write *The Chaos Strategy* when he returned to the United States after a 2013 crusade to Nicaragua where he saw events unfolding that could undermine the United States as a Christian nation.

Davis lives with his wife, Alma, in Somerset, Kentucky. They have three children and four grandchildren.

For more information contact:

Curt Davis
C/O Advantage Books
P.O. Box 160847
Altamonte Springs, FL 32716

info@advbooks.com

To purchase additional copies of this book visit our bookstore website at: www.advbookstore.com

Longwood, Florida, USA
"we bring dreams to life"™
www.advbookstore.com

CPSIA information can be obtained
at www.ICGtesting.com
Printed in the USA
FFOW03n0729110217
32127FF

9 781597 554114